# BAD VIBES

## JOYCE HOLMS

BLOODY BRITS PRESS
Ann Arbor and Alnmouth
2009

Bloody Brits Press
PO Box 3671
Ann Arbor MI 48106-3671

BLOODY BRITS PRESS FIRST EDITION
First Printing August 2009

First published in Great Britain in 1998 by Headline Book
Publishing, a division of Hodder Headline PLC, 338 Euston Road,
London NW1 3BH

Printed in the United States of America on acid-free paper

Cover designer: Bonnie Liss (Phoenix Graphics)

Bloody Brits Press is an imprint of Bywater Books

ISBN 978-1-932859-63-8

*For John*

# Chapter One

When the screaming started Fizz was reading Walker and Walker on the *Law of Evidence*. Reading, that is, in the sense of starting at the top of the page and running her eyes from word to word till she got to the bottom. Most of the words, taken individually, made perfect sense; it was only when she tried stringing them together that she got bogged down and, although she had read the page at least four times, it might have been written in Basque for all the intelligence it conveyed to her.

It had, however, been a long hard day and the hands on the clock above the reception desk were now edging toward midnight, so it was only will power that was keeping her going. That, and the thought that she'd be back at university in less than four weeks with at least a third of her holiday reading unscanned.

Nine evenings out of ten, she could count on having at least two hours, more or less, to herself, from the time the dining room closed till she went off duty at twelve o'clock. The Royal Park Hotel was not one of your open-all-hours, rocking-round-the-clock sort of establishments. The clientele was, for the most part, middle aged or elderly and, if they didn't retire early to their rooms, they usually slobbed-out in the TV room or the lounge, minding their own business and bothering nobody.

Tonight, however, there was a bus party in residence, a gaggle of Americans en route to the Highlands, and they had no sooner checked in than they sallied forth again to some pipes-and-drums concert in Holyrood Park. By eleven thirty they were back in again, queuing for their room keys, hanging around the reception area in convivial bunches, and destroying the atmosphere of quiet and comfort that was so necessary to Fizz's concentration.

1

Jenny May McGill was one of the last to call it a day. She was an enormous woman in her late forties with an enormous personality and an enormous voice and—possibly for that reason—she was something of an outsider in the group. A large part of Fizz's evening had already been taken up with attending to her multiple special requirements, which ranged from camomile tea to non-feather pillows, so it was Fizz whom she latched on to when her fellow bus-passengers froze her out.

"I tell you, honey, those pipes and drums are really *something*." She leaned over the counter so that her spicy perfume wafted ahead of her like a bow wave. "I cried like a baby, I have to tell you. Like a *baby!* You would not believe it!"

Fizz could believe it all too easily, if the state of Jenny May's mascara was anything to go by. "Very moving," she agreed. "Not that I've ever—"

"*Moving?* Poppet, when you have Scotch blood like I have it's not just moving, it's *overwhelming*. When I think about all the pain and suffering my own family went through when they were cleared off their land to make way for deer parks and sheep and everything it just breaks my heart."

"*Your* family?" Fizz's interest perked up. "Your forebears came from the Highlands?"

"My *clan* came from the Highlands," Jenny May asserted, as though it were the same thing. "Well, Clan Menzies country is in Perthshire and the McGills are a sept of Clan Menzies, so I guess they come from around there too. I checked it out in the Tartan Centre in Princes Street this afternoon. That's why I felt it—the pibrochs and all—so ... so *keenly*."

Fizz mimed sympathy and understanding, wondering meanwhile who she could get to sew this woman into a weighted sack and drop her off the Forth Bridge.

"And such *darling* men! So handsome in their plaids and their military jackets. Mister Krefeld—*Herr* Krefeld in the room along the corridor from mine—such a sweet man—he lent me his binoculars, so I felt—you know?—that I was right there in the center of *everything* with the sound of the pipes going straight through me like a chain saw! I swear, honey, I was *never* so

2

stirred up inside in all my life. I'll remember it until the day I die!"

Fizz's forefinger, keeping her place in *Walker and Walker*, was flat and bloodless by the time Jenny May shut up and took herself to bed. With only fifteen minutes or so before the night porter took over, it was barely worthwhile starting again, but she made the effort anyway in the hope that some small but important fact might lodge in the gray porridge inside her skull.

When the first scream split the silence apart like ripping calico, it plucked her clean out of her chair, every nerve jangling, and it took her a moment to register that it was Jenny May's coloratura soprano that was powering it. It seemed to go on forever, reverberating around the high, Edwardian cornices of the reception area, and swelling in volume as she raced up the stairs.

Zeroing in on the noise, her one thought was that the chances of a single guest sleeping through it were virtually nil. At that point, she was still working on the hypothesis that this was a spider-in-the-bath situation, but at each step the screaming kept getting louder and higher pitched and seemed to be interspersed with the sort of whoops and gasps that could be considered indicative of total hysteria.

She met Jenny May halfway down the second floor corridor, flattened against the wall and just getting into her second wind. Already there was a cluster of guests around her, begging her, with varying degrees of sympathy, to cool it.

Fizz went through the crowd like a poker through a sponge cake. "Stop that immediately!" she snapped, and completed Jenny May's neuro-linguistic programming with a slap that loosened her fillings.

This had a wonderfully therapeutic effect on both of them, cheering up Fizz considerably, cutting off the scream in mid-cadenza, and bringing on a flood of tears that put the finishing touches to Jenny May's makeup.

"Please try to pull yourself together, Miss McGill," Fizz said briskly, reaching up (Jenny May being some eight inches taller than she was) and gripping the howling woman by the shoulders. "You are disturbing the other guests."

The other guests—and by now there was quite a bunch of

them—looked on with avid interest, their eyes bright with anticipation, but Fizz had no intention of satisfying their curiosity. Judging from past experience, if Jenny May had a spider in her bath they'd all want one.

"Thank you for your prompt response," she said, smiling round the circle of faces. "I'm sorry you were disturbed, but you can leave Miss McGill in my hands now. I'm sure that, whatever upset her, it's something I can put right."

Some of them had already tired of hysterics as a spectator sport and were returning to their rooms, the others dragged their feet a bit, exchanging doubtful looks and eyeing Fizz with visible distrust. That slap round the head had evidently given them cause to wonder about the Royal Park Hotel's human rights policy, but Fizz gave them her basilisk stare and they decided quite quickly that Jenny May wasn't worth the hassle.

When they had passed out of earshot, Fizz swung back to the vision of Jenny May's ruined face. The areas of wrinkled cheek that were not streaked with mascara were now smeared with tomato-red lipstick, and tears had worn channels in her pancake makeup down either side of her nose.

It wasn't a sight to arouse a lot of sympathy, but Fizz did her best.

"Miss McGill, *please!* Do try to stop crying and tell me what has upset you."

There was no reply to this other than a prolonged and totally incomprehensible burble, punctuated by hiccups and an occasional sound like a wellie being withdrawn from a peat bog.

"I'm sorry...?" Fizz said, hanging on to her patience and wondering if she could get away with another slap. "I didn't quite catch that."

The sound of a footfall behind her made her look over her shoulder and she discovered the courier of the bus party hurrying toward her. Seeing her spot him, he stopped where he was and beckoned her urgently down the corridor. He didn't say anything, but the look on his face put Jenny May out of Fizz's mind immediately.

"What's the matter?" she asked quietly and he gestured toward a half-open door a few paces away.

4

"It's not very pleasant, miss. Not a sight for a young person like you to be faced with, if you know what I mean. The best thing to do would be to get the manager."

Fizz was accustomed, not to say sick to death, with being taken for a teenager. Sometimes it came in handy; other times, like now, it was a complete piss-off. "I'll just take a look for myself before I go to red alert, Mr. ... Mr. Hustley, isn't it? I'm supposed to be in charge till the night porter clocks on at midnight and my bosses, Mr. and Mrs. Renton, don't like to be disturbed unnecessarily."

"No, no. You don't understand, miss." Mr. Hustley grabbed her arm as she stepped round him and dropped his voice to a murmur. "There's a man dead in there."

Fizz hesitated. "Dead? You're sure he's dead?"

"No question. You don't want to see it, miss. Take my word for it. I'm sure Mr. Renton wouldn't expect a young lass like you to have to deal with this sort of thing."

"Yes, well, you may be right, Mr. Hustley, but I'll just make sure we're not going off half-cocked before I do anything else."

Jenny May's wellie-boot noises rose in volume behind them as they approached the open door. The sound of running water was audible from the corridor and a scarf of steam drifted out as Fizz leaned through the opening into the short passageway beyond.

The entrance to the en suite shower room was immediately inside the doorway and she could see straight into it from where she stood. The shower, as she had already realized, was running full blast, and the shower curtain had been torn from its rings. It lay partly across the ankles of the old man who was sprawled face up, half in and half out of the shower cubicle.

It was Herr Krefeld, and he was quite unmistakably dead. His eyes were wide open, staring up at the ceiling, and his false teeth had slipped down over his lower lip with a sort of Bugs Bunny effect that was anything but amusing. There seemed to be a great deal of blood around, pooling under his arm and trickling slowly across the wet tiles toward the drainage outlet in the middle of the floor.

Black and white shower curtain, white tiles, silver fittings, pallid, grey-haired corpse: the picture was completely monochromatic

5

except for the shocking brilliance of the arterial blood. The upper part of the room was shrouded in a thick pall of steam through which the light above the mirror shimmered like the sun trying to break through on a cloudy day.

One glance was enough to tell Fizz all she needed to know. She was shocked—more than she had expected to be—by the sight of Herr Krefeld lying there like that, but she was far from traumatized and, in point of fact, her only coherent thought was that there might not be enough hot water left for the rest of the guests.

"I'll switch off the shower for you if you like," offered the courier, watching her face with fatherly concern.

Fizz reached round him and pulled the door shut. "No, I don't think so, Mr. Hustley. It looks to me like we'll have to call the police about this, so we should leave things as they are, just in case. Did Jenny May go inside, do you know?"

"No, she just pushed the door and started screaming." He held out an old-fashioned pair of binoculars in a leather carrying case. "I was coming along the corridor from the staircase when I saw her standing with these in her hand, tapping at the door."

Fizz glanced down the corridor to where Jenny May was slowly sliding down the wall. "Well, Mr. Hustley …"

"Andy," he said.

"Well, Andy, at least it's not one of your bunch, eh? Thank goodness you were discreet about this, otherwise we'd have had everybody up all night."

"I'm just glad I saved you from walking in on it unprepared." Andy looked a little disappointed that mouth-to-mouth resuscitation was not going to be required of him. "I must say you're taking all of this very calmly for a young lass."

"Yes, well, I'm not all that young, Andy. I'm twenty-six and I've seen a dead body before. And in a worse state than this one, I can tell you."

"Really," Andy said with obvious disbelief. "Still … all that blood. It's not right that you should have to deal with this sort of thing and I'll be telling Mrs. Renton that when I see her."

Fizz started to say she'd give him open-heart surgery if he said a word, and then rephrased it: "I wish you wouldn't, Andy. I'm trying

6

to live on a student's grant and this job makes the difference between eating and not eating, so it's not going to be too helpful if Mrs. Renton replaces me with somebody older. Anyway, we haven't had many suicides since I've been here—this is the first, actually—and most evenings I get a fair bit of studying done. So you see, I'd quite like to keep my job if I can."

"Well, I wouldn't like to see my daughter having to do—"

"Andy … another time, OK? Right now I have to let Mr. and Mrs. Renton know what's happened. Could I ask you to take care of Miss McGill till I get back, and stop her from broadcasting this any farther? Perhaps you could take her back to her room and make her a cup of tea or something?"

Andy looked at Jenny May without enthusiasm, but Fizz didn't hang around to hear his objections. She ran up the stairs to the top floor, where the Rentons and some of the senior members of staff had their quarters, and hammered on the door of the owners' suite.

It was Mrs. Renton who opened the door, which didn't surprise Fizz one whit since Mr. Renton was a committed supporter of the Scottish malt whisky industry and probably slept like the dead. It wasn't the best time of day for Mrs. Renton, either physically or emotionally, and there was very little charm in her voice as she said, "What the blazes …?"

"Herr Krefeld has popped his clogs," Fizz said, breaking it to her gently. "Could be suicide—at least, there's a hell of a lot of blood around, as if he'd slashed his wrists. He's lying in his bathroom and Jenny May McGill is having hysterics all over the second floor."

"Oh, my God! *Frazer!*" Mrs. Renton dizzied away from the door and disappeared for a minute, yelling at her comatose husband to wake the hell up. Then she came back, clutching her dressing gown together across her enthusiastic bosom.

"Great!" she said bitterly. "That's all we need. We've already experienced every other disaster out of *Fawlty Towers.* I suppose the 'Body in the Laundry Basket' scenario had to happen eventually. Do any of the other guests know about this?"

"Only Andy Hustley, the driver of the coach party. He's keeping Jenny May quiet as we speak. At least, I hope he is."

Mrs. Renton drew in a deep breath. "Thank God for that anyway.

OK, you'd better take charge of Miss McGill, Fizz. Try and keep things quiet and I'll be down in a minute."

"Roger."

Fizz made for the stairs, but before she got there a door opened and the chef leaned out. Fizz was unprepared for the spectacle of his bald head, since she had never before encountered him without his tall hat and, indeed, in the dim light of the fire-safety fixtures she would scarcely have recognized him but for his uniquely virulent acne.

"Whassup?" He evidently hadn't expected to come face to face with Fizz and was just too late to prevent her seeing the well-thumbed copy of *Weightlifting Monthly*, which he hastily shoved behind the door.

Fizz slowed but didn't break her stride. "Guest died."

Johnnyboy gasped and laid a delicate hand to his cheek. "But, sweetie! You don't intrude on La Renton for a little thing like that. She hates to be disturbed when she's shedding her skin. Who was it?"

Fizz was already too far away to answer without raising her voice, so she didn't bother. It wouldn't have made much difference to Johnnyboy anyway since he rarely came into direct contact with the punters. Even on reception, one didn't get past the "Good evening, sir," level with most of them and certainly Herr Krefeld had not been one to push a casual acquaintance. He had only been resident for a couple of days and in that time Fizz had had no contact with him to speak of beyond giving him his room key.

She found Andy Hustley and Jenny May drinking tea in the latter's room. The hysterics were, thankfully, a thing of the past and Jenny May had progressed to talking through her experience in a mean-ingful and therapeutic way, of which Andy had clearly had enough.

"I'll just get back to bed, then," he said, as soon as he could get a word in, "and leave you ladies to it."

"Well, I'm not sure that would be a good idea, Andy," Fizz told him, trying to recall what she had learned about medical jurispru-dence. "Accidental death outside the home. You have to report it, and the police will almost certainly want to talk to you. And to Miss McGill."

"Not tonight! Not after what I've been through! I'm in no fit state to talk about it," Jenny May announced, ignoring the fact that she had been doing nothing else since she'd stopped screaming. "I'm going to take one of my pills and try to get some sleep."

"Well, I think Mrs. Renton would appreciate a word with you first," Fizz stalled. "She'll be here any minute and she'll probably want to know how you came to discover Herr Krefeld's body."

"Why, I took his binoculars back, of course, that's how I discovered him! You can tell your boss that as well as I can, honey. When he didn't come to the door, I thought he couldn't hear me knocking because of the noise of his shower—I could hear it from the corridor—so I opened the door to call to him and … there he was, poor man … dead at my feet! I declare, my heart jumped straight out of my body! I *never* had such a shock in my entire life! I nearly died!"

Maybe next time, thought Fizz, nodding with profound sympathy and understanding.

The arrival of Mrs. Renton at that point cut short what looked set to become an extended monologue, and Fizz was conscious of a distinct sense of relief at being able to hand over responsibility to someone else. Diplomacy had never been her strong suit, she'd have been the first to admit it, and it wasn't always easy to find the right balance between authority and deference. Mrs. Renton, however, was in a bad mood and didn't give a bugger about all that.

"I'll hear your side of the story in a moment, Miss McGill," she said crisply, her fat fingers checking that she had remembered to fasten the zip of her skirt. "I'll just take a look in Herr Krefeld's room first. Fizz, come with me."

When they were outside in the corridor, an undercurrent of agitation began to show through her calm efficiency. "No point in asking that silly woman to keep this from the other guests. She'll have told everyone in the breakfast room before she's finished her cornflakes and you know what *that* means—half of them checking out and the other half wanting to capture the scene of death on their holiday video. God, I think I'm getting too old for this business!"

She pushed open the door of Herr Krefeld's room, but halted on the threshold as though the full impact of the picture had rocked her a bit. "Oh, dear!"

The cloud cover was now considerably thicker and there was rather less blood on the floor than previously, owing to water condensing on the floor tiles and starting to drain down the center drainage hole, but it still wasn't a sight to cheer the heart. Fizz found herself taking in things that she hadn't noticed at first glance: the clothes flung carelessly on the floor, the broken glass beside the old man's hand, the way the shower curtain draped across his feet.

Mrs. Renton stepped carefully across the body and turned off the shower. Her expression showed acute distaste as she did so, but considerations of economy clearly overcame any delicacy of feeling.

"Where *is* that man?" she was muttering as she emerged, and as she glared along the corridor Frazer hove into view looking as though he had been hastily assembled from a collection of spare parts. His eyes, behind strongly magnifying lenses, always looked as though they belonged to a creature of much larger proportions, but now his bulky torso looked too big for the thin white legs that stuck out beneath his dressing gown and his hair might have been harvested from someone else's plughole.

"There you are," exclaimed his loving wife in a tone that suggested she would have more to say on the matter of his tardiness when occasion permitted. "Just look at this, will you! As if we didn't have enough on our plate without this sort of publicity! What do you think? Do we have to call the police?"

Frazer opened his mouth to answer, but Mrs. Renton swept clean over him like a tidal wave. "Fizz. Go and phone the police. The phone number is written on the list inside the door of the key cupboard. Tell them I don't want any sirens or flashing lights at this time of night and tell them that if I have the newspapers round here first thing in the morning I'll be on the phone to the Chief Inspector before they can cough. What time is it? Half past twelve. Hollis should be on duty by now. Go down with Fizz, Frazer, and wait with Hollis till the police arrive." Her eyes appeared to register Frazer's relaxed dress code for the first time. "And for God's sake,

Frazer, go and put some proper clothes on as soon as you can! Let's at least try to maintain the fiction that we can function adequately in an emergency!"

Frazer still appeared to be in the process of waking up and said nothing till they were at the ground floor, when he suddenly gave Fizz an unexpected pat on the shoulder.

"Can't have been nice for you, Fizz, having to deal with that. You handled it very well. There will be a little extra in your pay packet this week to make up for it."

That was what Fizz liked about Frazer. He said it with money. "That's very kind of you, Mr. Renton. I don't think any of the other guests know precisely what Miss McGill was screaming about. Not yet. In fact, I'm sure even she thought it was just a case of sudden death, so maybe it won't cause too much of an upset."

"You think it was suicide?" Frazer whipped off his specs and polished them agitatedly with a fold of his dressing gown. "God! No wonder Gloria was so distraught! I thought she was just afraid that we might be done for compensation—for having no handrail in the shower or some such rubbish. I hope to God you're wrong, Fizz. The last thing we need is for this to get into the papers."

Fizz thought he was probably on a losing wicket there since foreigners didn't top themselves every day in Edinburgh, and if that turned out to be what had happened tonight the papers were sure to get hold of it.

"Well," she said, "if you need a good lawyer, remember I have friends in the business."

Frazer's eyes twinkled at her like friendly headlamps. "The people you work for in the afternoon?"

"Not every afternoon, just two days a week. But, yes. Buchanan and Stewart. They're excellent solicitors, and Tam Buchanan's an easy guy to talk to."

She was rather looking forward to talking to Tam Buchanan herself in the near future. There were one or two small but interesting discrepancies in the matter of Herr Krefeld's demise about which she'd value his opinion.

11

# Chapter Two

Buchanan was already beginning to wonder if he had made his first serious mistake as senior partner.

It wasn't as if he hadn't thought hard and long before employing Dennis Whittaker, and it wasn't as if he hadn't consulted both his father and their third partner, Alan Stewart, before making his choice, but maybe he had been swayed too much by a brilliant CV. Now, within a couple of days of taking up employment, Dennis was already beginning to expose facets of his personality that gave Buchanan serious cause for concern. His attitude to women, for one thing.

It had been clear from the outset, i.e., Monday morning, that Margaret, who had been secretary to Buchanan's newly retired father for seventeen years, was not the sort of secretary that Dennis was used to and he had not hidden from either Alan or Buchanan that oomph would get his vote over a good typing speed any day of the week. Alan found this amusing; Buchanan smelled trouble, especially as Margaret was being boot-faced about working for the new partner. She had, she informed Buchanan, been the senior partner's secretary up till now and it was painful to her *amour propre* to be asked to skivvy to a junior partner at this stage in her career. Her solution to the problem was that The Wonderful Beatrice, Buchanan's own guardian angel, should be demoted to Dennis's office while she herself should assume the mantle of helping hand to the new head honcho, namely Buchanan himself.

This, as far as Buchanan was concerned, was never going to be an option, but adjustments would have to be made somewhere along the line, and soon. It was only Wednesday afternoon and already Dennis was beginning to suss out the other typists with a clear view to upgrading to a more desirable model than the one he had been issued. Worse, his tactics were likely to cause offense to the ladies of the outer office, who were used to Alan's olde worlde charm and Buchanan's rigid politeness.

What Buchanan hadn't foreseen—and should have—was Dennis's reaction to Fizz. Fizz only worked two afternoons a week, Wednesdays and Fridays, so she had escaped Dennis's preliminary surveys and it was the middle of Wednesday afternoon before she swam into his consciousness.

"Who," he demanded, sashaying into Buchanan's office in a glow of anticipation, "is that delightful little number with the dimples?"

Buchanan was up to his ears in a complicated transfer of ownership and took a minute to surface. "Number with what?"

"The blonde in the filing room. Dimples. Cute little pixie face. Masses of golden curls. Seventeen or thereabouts." Dennis's eyes glittered with impatience. "Why haven't I seen her before?"

"Because she's just a part-timer," Buchanan said unwillingly. "She's studying Law at the university and she comes in twice a week to help with the filing. If I were you, I wouldn't—"

"Law student, eh?" Dennis looked into space with an expression that suggested he was seeing a *Playboy* centerfold, and absently straightened his Paisley patterned bow tie. "All alone in the big city, is she? First time away from Mummy and Daddy? Breathless to grab life by the throat and start experiencing the realities of existence? Ah, I remember the feeling. Not so long ago either, eh Tam?"

Since he and Dennis were much of an age, Buchanan reckoned that it must be at least twelve years since either of them had been a freshman, which was long enough for Dennis to have learned some sense. He said, "Actually, Fizz is not as immature as she looks. She'll be starting her second year in October and she's nobody's—"

"Fizz?" Dennis focused on what interested him and turned a deaf ear to the words he would have done well to heed.

"Short for Fitzpatrick. But listen, Dennis, she's—"

"Fizz. I like it. Makes you think of champagne, doesn't it?"

It made Buchanan think of the sound of a lit fuse, but then he knew Fizz and Dennis didn't.

"If you're thinking ..." he started to say, and then stopped as the

13

door opened and the object of their discussion came in with a pile of folders. She looked, to Buchanan's eyes, even more cherubic and defenseless than was her wont, and she was wearing one of her Oxfam bargains (he knew because she had once used it as a production in an argument about his prodigality), which was navy blue and skimpy and reminded him of a gymslip. All in all, a sight to set Dennis's teeth watering.

"Well, hello," murmured the new junior partner, in tones several octaves deeper than when he had last spoken.

Fizz's expression, as she lifted limpid blue eyes to his, was that of a startled fawn.

Buchanan experienced a wholly reprehensible frisson of anticipation at the prospect of the carnage to come. It should have been beneath him to enjoy the sight of a virtually defenseless creature being destroyed by a vastly superior adversary, but he found this one-sided contest particularly piquant. If anyone could teach Dennis a lesson he wouldn't forget, he was looking at her right now.

He leaned back in his chair. "This is our new partner, Fizz. Dennis Whittaker."

"How do you do, Mr. Whittaker. Welcome to the firm." Fizz essayed a small smile and held out a hand, which was enfolded by Dennis in both of his.

"Dennis, *please*," he crooned. "I hope Buchanan and Stewart is not the sort of firm to insist on formality. We're all cogs in the same machine, after all, and there's no reason why we shouldn't be friends as well. I'm sure you and I are going to be good friends, Fizz."

Buchanan held his breath and pretended to scribble a note on his pad.

Fizz appeared, for a second, to be lost for words, then she gave a tiny giggle, and said rather breathlessly, "I ... I hope we will, Mr. ... er, Dennis."

Dennis was in no hurry to release her hand but she withdrew it, gently and with downcast eyes, as he said, "And you are ... in the filing room, I think? Do you like it there?"

"It's all right."

"Just 'all right'?" Dennis looked sympathetic. His voice was like audible molasses, dark brown and sickly sweet. "I dare say someone of your intelligence might find it a little boring. Don't you type?"

Perceiving the direction the conversation was taking, Buchanan hid a smile. If Dennis thought he had a chance of netting Fizz as a secretary, he was wasting his time. Fizz, for all she had wormed her way into Buchanan's employment by claiming otherwise, couldn't type any better than he could himself, and besides, she was due back at university the first week in October.

Dennis's questioning appeared to be causing her a little embarrassment. "I don't mind working in the filing room, not really," she muttered, flicking a covert glance in Buchanan's direction as though to intimate that she could hardly say anything else within his hearing. "It's only a couple of afternoons a week, so I don't have time to be bored."

"Well, we'll have to see if we can find some way of brightening your day, won't we?" Dennis's lips curled in what was quite unequivocally a leer.

Buchanan saw Fizz's lip twitch and knew that Dennis had gone too far. Fizz had shown remarkable and quite uncharacteristic restraint thus far, but now there would be blood on the sand.

But no. It was not to be. Her face may have stiffened a fraction in response, but all she said was, "Well, meantime I have work to do."

She turned away and fixed Buchanan with a blank look, exhibiting neither pain nor pleasure at Dennis's crassness. "Here are the files you asked for. Beatrice is still working on the Carrington folder, but you're not in a hurry for it, are you?"

"No, but let me have it as soon as you can."

Buchanan was disorientated and deeply disappointed. He was in no doubt whatsoever that Fizz could, if she had so desired, have dealt with Dennis in a manner guaranteed to leave him with a deep-seated neurosis and a lifelong fear of women, and he'd have put good money on the chance of her so desiring. He noted the shy smile she sent the new partner as she left the room and it pierced him like a stiletto. Surely to God she didn't find him attractive?

Dennis ran a hand over his sleek, seal-like skull and drew a long breath. "Now there's an employee who's ripe for promotion, surely,

Tam? You can tell how bright she is just by looking at her. Two afternoons a week—that isn't making full use of her potential. Not by a long chalk. Don't you feel able to offer her something that would make more use of her potential?"

"If you're thinking of a secretarial position, Dennis, forget it. She doesn't have the time to devote to anything but her studies and I don't happen to think that offering her longer hours would be doing her any favors. She's already working six evenings out of seven in a hotel, and when that job folds she'll be back at the uni. Two afternoons a week is as much as she can afford to take off her studies."

Buchanan could have added that he had already sacked Fizz twice in the past year and that the fact that he hadn't changed the locks on the office doors to keep her out was due solely to the interventions of his father, who thought the sun shone out of her left ear.

"Fizz is a one-off," he said carefully. "Just bear that in mind when you try making any judgments about her. She doesn't conform to any known criteria and, believe me, she could eat you for breakfast."

Dennis was quite incapable of treating this advice other than as a joke. "She can have me for breakfast any time she likes," he paused in the doorway to remark, with a ribaldry that failed to amuse his boss, "as long as I can come round the night before."

Buchanan rubbed a hand hard over his face and tried to focus his thoughts on the transfer of ownership, but a part of his brain went on worrying about Fizz's uncharacteristic reaction to Dennis. It was the first time he'd seen her pass up a chance to deflate a rampant ego, and that included his own. Not that he had ever tried to chat her up—he had no suicidal tendencies and, besides, she wasn't his type.

His type, he mused, still staring blindly at his papers, was someone tall and slender and sophisticated, a lady he'd be proud to be seen with around town, intelligent, educated, and sensitive to the mores of polite society. Someone like Janine, to whom he had been virtually engaged till Fizz galloped into his life like a fifth horseman of the Apocalypse and rocked it to its foundations.

16

Fizz herself, on the other hand, was small and girlish. She laughed in the face of propriety. She had her own brand of intelligence, but it was a warped intelligence that clashed with Buchanan's at every turn and questioned all the precepts which he held to be sacred. Education was something she had, until recently, had no use for. She had checked out of Edinburgh School of Art after one year and spent the next eight years bumming her way around the world. Money was a commodity you worked for if and when you needed to buy something, but she managed, otherwise, to do without. Things like microwaves, video-recorders, and Caribbean cruises were for misguided people like Buchanan, and things like white weddings, cosmetic surgery, and designer jeans were simply a big joke. OK, she had a pretty little face and there was nothing wrong with her body—except that it was attached to her head.

Dennis Whittaker, to a rampant feminist like Fizz, should have been like a red rag to a bull. Faced with that cheesy grin, bow tie, and sleek round head, Fizz's lip should have been curling before he even opened his mouth, and after the barrage of unctuous flattery with which he had greeted her she should have been, to use her own phrase, strumming his giblets like a banjo.

Buchanan was, to say the least, curious.

Fizz, when she returned a little later with the Carrington folder, made no reference to her encounter with the new partner which, in itself, was odd because she had no qualms about discussing people behind their backs, and with anybody who would pay attention.

"Listen," she said, parking herself on the corner of Buchanan's desk with a familiarity born of long contempt. "A funny thing happened at work last night."

"Funny ha-ha?"

"No. Funny peculiar. One of the guests, an old German guy, died in the shower." She picked up Buchanan's propelling pencil and twirled it in her fingers. "At least, it looked like he died in the shower and fell out on to the bathroom floor."

Buchanan wondered why she felt it necessary to share this with him, particularly as she appeared to expect the announcement to

17

set a longish conversation in motion. "Mm-hmm," he said, noncommittally. "Are condolences in order?"

"Not really. I hardly knew the poor old thing, but he seemed fairly harmless. Just an ordinary guest, really. A little older than the average, a bit shaky on his pins, walked with a stick. They're saying it was probably a heart attack."

"Who're saying? The police?"

"Mr. and Mrs. Renton. I don't know what the police concluded. It was after midnight when they arrived, so I just told them what I knew and left them to it. We'd thought the guy had slashed his wrists, but the policemen said right away that there wasn't enough blood for that."

"Right," Buchanan nodded, awaiting the punch line. Presumably there had to be more than this.

"The thing is …"

Fizz had extended the lead of the pencil to such a length that when she started to doodle on Buchanan's scrap pad it broke. He removed it from her fingers and put it in his drawer (he had lost pencils to Fizz before) and said, "Uh-huh?"

"The thing is, I don't see how it could have been a heart attack."

Buchanan glanced back at the work on his desk. It was nearly four thirty and he had made very little progress since lunchtime, what with one thing and another. "Heart attack, seizure, brain hemorrhage, stroke. At that age it could have been anything. Does it really make a lot of difference which it was?"

"It could have been suicide, for that matter," Fizz said, with the sort of sour expression she put on when she thought Buchanan was being particularly obtuse. "But I don't get the feeling it was that, either. I think there's something fishy about the setup."

It didn't occur to Buchanan for an instant that he should take this remark at face value. It was quite clear that Fizz who, like himself, had been involved with violent death twice in the past twelve months, was now beginning to see a murder in every fatality. It was hardly surprising. He had felt quite traumatized himself for a time, particularly after the last occurrence when he had, at one point, fully expected the next fatality to be his own.

"Fizz," he said, "after that business in the spring with old Bessie Anderson, it's very easy to imag—"

"Don't start, Buchanan," she said, cutting him off in mid-word. "Just give it a miss, OK? I'm not losing my marbles and I'm not leaping to conclusions just because I know what a murder victim looks like. I'm telling you, there was something odd about the way that old man was stretched out."

Buchanan composed himself to listen. There didn't appear to be much alternative. "Something odd? I imagine you mean to tell me what, precisely."

Fizz gave him her sweetest smile. She got down off the desk and held wide her arms in a theatrical gesture. "OK. I'm the old German guy—Herr Krefeld—and I'm taking a shower, right?"

She soaped her arms vigorously. None of the voluptuous gratification of the TV ads: when Fizz showered it was evidently in, scrub, and out in very short order.

"Now the heart attack kicks in. Ah … ooyah … ah … I fall out of the shower … I make a grab at the shower curtain, but it rips loose … I fall to the floor and expire."

She evidently felt that she could safely leave the actual death throes to his imagination, merely stepping into the role of spectator and indicating an imaginary body at her feet.

"So, how come no part of the shower curtain was under the body?" she demanded. "All of it was beside him on the floor as if it had been ripped off its rings and flung down after he had fallen there. Well, to be accurate, one small fold was across his shins, but I've tried falling several different ways and I'm sure that curtain had to end up at least partly under the body."

"Oh, my God …" Buchanan said, with the intention of continuing along the lines of: it's a far cry from that to suspecting the old guy was murdered. But Fizz was not one to take kindly to having her flights of fancy slapped down out of hand, so he changed the remainder of the sentence to: "I hope you're not expecting me to get involved in more detective work, Fizz. We did have an agreement—remember?—that if I helped you find out what happened to Bessie Anderson there would be no more of this sort of thing."

Fizz straightened her gymslip and wasted another smile on him.

"Relax, my dear Watson, I'm not asking you to get involved, I'm just letting you in on it in case it should prove interesting later."

"Fine." Buchanan shuffled his papers in a pointed manner. "I'll be interested to hear if there are other developments."

"Actually," Fizz remarked, ignoring the hint, "it was more than the bad vibes. There was something else that might turn out to be significant. There was a broken glass beside Herr Krefeld's hand, as if he had been carrying it when he fell. He had cut his arm on it and bled a bit, which was what made us think, originally, that he had slashed his wrists."

Buchanan nodded with assumed interest. "Uh-huh? And what did you deduce from that?"

Fizz shrugged, propped one hip against the desk, and started fiddling absently with the automatic address book. "Nothing concrete, I suppose. I just thought, what was he doing with a glass in the shower?"

"Maybe he wasn't in the shower. He might have been walking past it and simply grabbed the shower curtain as he fell."

Fizz shook her Shirley Temple curls. "He was bollock naked."

"OK," Buchanan conceded, wincing only slightly. Fizz's habitually picturesque speech could still appall him, but he had learned not to encourage her by appearing shocked. "Maybe he had just come out of the shower and got himself a drink and …"

"It's possible, but I don't think so. The shower was still running. He'd have turned it off before he got out, wouldn't he? Or, at least before he did anything else. And surely he'd have got himself a towel first?"

She jabbed a finger at the address pad and the H's popped up showing Janine's phone number in red at the top of the page. It gave Buchanan a bit of a jolt, since he hadn't phoned Janine since she broke off their almost-engagement and took off for a new life in Aberdeen, but it also reminded him that any close association with Fizz was liable to end in trouble.

"Yes, well," he said firmly, getting his propelling pencil out of the desk and drawing his papers purposefully toward him. "I dare say the police will be looking into the incident pretty carefully. Since he didn't die in his own home, there will have to be an inquest, so you can be sure that if there's anything not quite kosher it will show up."

"You think so?" Fizz made another stab at the address book, but Buchanan covered it with a hand before it popped open. "I bet there are ways of killing someone so that it doesn't show up in a post mortem. An icicle pushed into the ear is supposed to melt and leave no trace, isn't it?"

"Fizz," Buchanan said, his patience hanging by a thread, "will you get out of here and let me get on with my work, please? I want to clear this lot up tonight while there's still enough light for a game of golf. Now, scoot!"

She got off the desk, just to show willing, and leaned on it with both fists. "You know people in the CID, Buchanan. How about ..."

"*No*, Fizz! No, no, and again no. Watch my lips: *No!*" Buchanan leaned across the desk till his eyes were six inches from hers. "I am not getting involved. Not even on the fringes. I am a solicitor, not a private investigator, and I have enough on my plate without this."

She raised her eyebrows in mock surprise. "Oh pooh! You always say that, but you know you love pitting your brains against—"

"This is not about pitting my brains, Fizz." Buchanan was amazed that he could sound so calm and matter of fact. "This is about getting involved in something like that debacle at your Grampa's place last spring when I was not only staring death in the face for hours but came within an inch of being arrested as an accessory to your criminal act and saw my career teetering on the edge of annihilation."

"My God, you're a worse pain in the neck than Dracula, y'know that, Buchanan? You don't half exaggerate. And, anyway, it wasn't all my fault."

"No," Buchanan admitted, not without chagrin. "It was all my fault. I should have said to you last time what I'm saying to you now: count me out. God knows, I should have learned my lesson by that time, after going through what I did with Murray Kingston. It was sheer stupidity to let you involve me a second time and there sure as hell isn't going to be a third!"

Fizz tipped back her head and laughed with real amusement. "Oh God, you're funny, Buchanan, you really are! Your responses are so conditioned that you don't know when you're enjoying yourself and when you're not."

She sat down in the clients' armchair and folded her arms on the desk. Because the chair was too low, and because she was so short, she was able to rest her chin on her forearms, which forced her to look up at him through her lashes. The effect was so cute that Buchanan had to remind himself not to smile.

"The thing is," she told him, "you are too fixed on the idea that the things that make you happy have to cost money—a good golf club, a night at the opera, a seafood dinner at Poseidon's. You don't remember how happy you felt when you discovered that you weren't going to die, after all, or when the police decided not to press charges against us. *Living* is what makes people happy, sonny boy, living and struggling and walking toward a goal; not watching other people doing things or drifting with the current or actually *achieving* one's ambition and having nothing left to strive for."

"Oh, yes?" Buchanan leaned back in his chair. "And where did you read that?"

Fizz smiled, but not pleasantly, and Buchanan knew he had sounded snide. "Well, you know, I'm just a silly little woman, boss," she said sweetly. "I don't read none too good. I just had to think it up myself."

"I didn't mean—"

"Sure." She cut him off with a gesture, standing up and flexing her shoulders. "I'll leave you to your exciting life then, *mein Führer*."

Buchanan ground his teeth. "Keep me posted anyway, Fizz," he said as she reached the door, and added in a pathetic attempt to make amends, "Maybe I can at least give you the benefit of my opinion, if you should need it."

She glanced at him over her shoulder and nodded, saying nothing, but he had the feeling, as the door closed softly behind her, that she had got what she came for.

He reached for his pencil and tried to pump up a new length of lead, but the spring was knackered.

# Chapter Three

Having successfully withstood her first inspection of the new partner without submitting to projectile vomiting, Fizz withdrew to the filing room to await their second encounter.

She suspected that she would not have long to wait because the filing room was not overlooked by any of the other offices and thus provided an excellent venue for dalliance, which appeared to be the item at the head of Dennis Whittaker's agenda.

It was a pity he was obnoxious, but that was OK. She could handle obnoxious, especially when it was teamed with puerile. Had Buchanan chosen someone as uptight and dogmatic as himself, things would have looked considerably blacker, because nobody with Buchanan's savvy was going to be quite so easy to manipulate as was Dennis.

Contrary to what Buchanan believed, and frequently reiterated, Fizz did not enjoy manipulating people. She particularly disliked allowing people like Dennis to take her at face value, i.e., as a mindless bimbo, but she had learned long ago that survival frequently meant using whatever horseshoe you could slip in your glove. She didn't have a rich daddy or a family business or a degree to fall back on like Buchanan did, and sometimes absolute honesty was a luxury she couldn't afford. Like now.

Existing on a student's grant in Edinburgh was like trying to read a newspaper in a howling gale. No sooner did you get a job that put a little gravy on the lentils than the soles fell off your Docs, the cooker blew up, or some bastard nicked your only waterproof from the cloakroom.

The hotel job was great, not only because it gave her time to study but because she got a free evening meal and also saved on heating bills. Unfortunately, it was tourist oriented and the tourists would stop coming, to a large extent, by the end of September. After that, she would be dependent on the few pounds she earned from Buchanan & Stewart, and there was small chance of getting more work from that source now that her friend and mentor, old Mr. Buchanan, had retired.

Buchanan junior had, Fizz knew, never been one of her biggest fans, not since the string of disasters that had resulted from their first sortie into the realms of crime investigation. He tolerated her—actually, he did more than tolerate her, he got along with her rather well, only he didn't know it. And although he himself was virtually impossible to live with and got up Fizz's nose something rotten, for the most part they jogged along together pretty well.

Actually, if Fizz hadn't gone a little over the score during their last collaboration, she might have expected to feel more established with Buchanan & Stewart by this time. As it was, two afternoons a week were as much as Buchanan was likely to allow her into the office, and that was simply not going to bring in enough money to see her through next term.

The final few months of last session had been pretty scary, living on carrots and lentils and getting deeper into debt day by day. She needed more paid work, and she needed it from Buchanan & Stewart because in a couple of years' time she'd be looking for a two-year period of training in a legal firm to complete her Law degree and, in a city stuffed full of law students, such placements were like gold. By that time, she'd have to have her foot firmly in the door of Buchanan & Stewart. Thus far, she had managed to survive Buchanan's attempts to sack her, but it now behooved her to get the new partner very firmly in her camp.

It was almost five before Dennis tilted his round head through the doorway.

"Still here?" he said, opening his eyes in quasi-surprise.

Fizz glanced at the clock. "Not long now. I've only got this bundle to sort out and then I'm finished for the day."

Dennis smoothed across to the bank of cabinets and laid an arm along the top. "And what then?" he asked. "Out for a pint with some of your university chums?"

Fizz's university chums were, on average, eight years her junior and she found their half-digested opinions, ephemeral enthusiasms, and painful self-centeredness a complete turn-off. "Nope. I don't socialize much with my classmates. Don't have the time."

He moved a little closer, leaning his head to the side as though he were addressing a toddler. Fizz could smell his aftershave and wondered if he had replenished it before moving in on her.

"That's too bad," he said, putting on a concerned look. "All work and no play, etc. You have to make time for relaxation: a proper meal, a few glasses of wine, maybe a good film."

Fizz found no difficulty in producing a smile. The difficulty lay in not bursting out laughing. This guy was something *else!* "Unfortunately, student grants don't stretch to nights out," she said with a sigh, "and I have to tell you, Buchanan and Stewart don't pay that sort of money either, not for two afternoons per week."

"Well, we'll have to see about that," Dennis said in an avuncular manner. "We can't have our employees subsisting on a starvation budget, not even part-timers. I think we could afford a small incentive now and then."

Just the two of them, no doubt, and if they happened to get swept away by the ambience of a delightful evening and end up in the sack, that was just the way the cookie crumbled.

Highly entertained, Fizz got on with her filing. "Unfortunately, I have to work evenings as well to make ends meet. I fill in for the receptionist in a hotel from six till midnight, which doesn't leave me any time to myself."

"Not every night, surely?"

That was an awkward question, but Fizz was adept at appearing to say "yes" when she was actually saying nothing. "It's only temporary, so I have to make as much money as I can while it lasts. Of course, it would be better if there were more filing for me to do here, but ... well, there isn't, so that's that."

Dennis looked seriously put out at this but not, Fizz assumed, because he was concerned for her well-being. She could see him re-thinking his campaign and was ahead of him when he said, "That can't be good for you, Fizz. We'll have to see if we can't find a few more hours' work for you here in the office so that you can

25

afford to stop moonlighting every evening. How are you on matters secretarial?"

Fizz communed with her conscience. Her attempt at flannelling her way into Buchanan's employ by claiming she could type had not been a lasting success and it was unlikely that she'd get away with it a second time, even if she pretended to have been taking lessons in the interim.

"Not great," she admitted reluctantly. "But, I do think I have other skills that could be of real benefit to the firm."

"Such as?"

Fizz hesitated, chewing her lip. One could look too pushy and Dennis was the type to back off if he suspected he was the manipulatee, rather than the manipulator. "Somebody said you were taking over the conveyancing side of the practice and … and, I just wondered …"

Dennis smiled encouragingly. "Go on. You just wondered …? Don't be afraid to ask, Fizz."

"Well, it's awfully cheeky but … but I know I'd be really good at showing houses to prospective clients."

"Really? You fancy that, do you?"

The suggestion seemed to strike Dennis as a particularly attractive one and his thought processes were writ large on his face for all to see. He was stuck with a middle-aged secretary, but there was still the prospect of occasional drives out into the surrounding countryside with a nubile assistant, the necessity of shared lunches—and possibly the odd glass of wine—and afternoons in empty houses, some of them with bedrooms that were still furnished. Such duties might not normally form part of the workload of the junior partner, but what the hell?

"Strange that you should say that, Fizz. I've actually been thinking that I could do with some help along those lines," he said seriously. "The property market is starting to boom again in this area and I can see we're going to need someone to take over the responsibility for showing property, rather than just leaving it to whoever can spare the time. Do you drive?"

Shite, Fizz thought. That was something she didn't dare fake. "I'm afraid I don't. But I've driven a tractor often enough on my grampa's farm, so I reckon it wouldn't take me long to get a license."

Dennis swept that minor difficulty aside with a robust gesture. "I'm sure it wouldn't. I could give you a few lessons myself, for that matter. And I'm quite sure you would be extremely well suited to the job: good appearance, articulate, pleasant manner. Why don't we give it a try and see how you get on?"

Fizz put on an excited face. "Really? You'll let me try?"

"Why not? We don't do a lot of real estate business, but there ought to be the occasional hour's work for you from time to time. I'll have a look and see what's being advertised at the moment."

Fizz knew exactly what properties were likely to be shown in the near future because she had just finished filing the brochures. Most of them were within the city boundary and therefore within easy reach of her flat.

"Gosh, that's super," she stuttered, batting her eyelashes like mad. "I don't know how to thank you, Mr. ... I mean Dennis."

Dennis dropped his eyelids a fraction to indicate that he'd think of something, but didn't push his luck. "Not at all, Fizz, I'm sure the firm will benefit as much as you." He patted her gently on the shoulder (getting her used to being handled, Fizz surmised) and oozed toward the door. "Well, I'd better let you get finished up."

Fizz didn't reply. She was distracted by the thought that her guardian angel was still grafting away on her behalf. Dennis Whittaker might not look like manna from heaven (whatever that looked like), but if it had been Buchanan's intention to employ a partner that Fizz could work with he could not have chosen better.

The atmosphere at the hotel that evening was noticeably subdued. According to the chef, all Mr. and Mrs. Renton's attempts to keep Herr Krefeld's demise from the rest of the guests had been to no avail, thanks not only to Jenny May's big mouth, but also to the fact that the mortuary van had arrived to collect the body right in the middle of breakfast.

"The boss-lady was popping Prozac pills like Smarties," Johnnyboy reported as he gave Fizz her dinner in a corner of the kitchen. "She made them drive round to the back door and smuggle the body out through the cold store. *Not* very hygienic, Mrs.

27

Renton, I told her, I don't know what the Health Inspector would say to it!"

"She'd love that," Fizz said, wishing she'd been there to witness the exchange. The running battle between Johnnyboy and Mrs. Renton had been keeping the staff entertained for a long time, but Fizz invariably missed the best bits because she was sequestered at the reception desk.

"I won't repeat what she said to me, Fizz, but I can tell you it did her no credit. No credit at all. Is that pastry all right? Here, you may as well have a splash of this sherry and mushroom sauce, it's wasted on those philistines out there anyway."

"Johnnyboy, you spoil me."

"Just hide it from the boss-lady if she should walk in, won't you sweetie, I don't want to hear any more of her coarse language. She has been taking this business very badly, you know." He went back to slicing tomatoes, his knife moving faster than the eye could follow. "Frazer said this morning that she would be having a bit of a lie-in, but she turned up as usual to supervise breakfast, eyes like pissholes in the snow."

"That's the trouble with being your own boss," Fizz mumbled around a mouthful of parsnip and walnut puff, "when you phone in sick, you know you're lying."

"Yes, well you know what darling Gloria's like: nothing is ever done properly unless she's there to nag. If she had stayed in bed, the body wagon would have come and gone before she knew about it and there'd have been less hassle for everybody."

"I dare say she knew it would be arriving sometime this morning and didn't trust Frazer to deal with it on his own." Fizz concentrated on her food for a minute or two while Johnnyboy dotted in and out of the storeroom, preparing for the first of the guests' orders to come in and shouting instructions to the commis chef. He regarded himself as something of an artist and felt he had to work himself into a frenzy every evening to give of his best.

Finally he came back and got on with whatever it was he was composing with the tomatoes and Fizz said, "Gloria *is* making rather a drama out of it, isn't she? After all, the police didn't seem to think there were any suspicious circumstances—at least, not up till the time I left. If it's just a heart attack, I don't see that it's going to cause a drop in bookings or anything like that, even if it gets into the *Scotsman*."

"Sweetie, who knows how her mind works? Gloria doesn't confide in me, I can tell you that." He gave a brittle trill of laughter at the very idea. "We haven't been on speaking terms since she bought that trashy pile of gadgetry in Jenners sale."

"The salad shredder?" Fizz had noticed it on the shelf but had never seen it out of its box. "It does all that fancy stuff, doesn't it? All those spirals of cucumber and frilly bits of carrot."

Johnnyboy made meaningful eye contact. "That's not all it does, my love. It can make a nicely presented meal look like a dog's break-fast in twenty seconds. I told her: it's not coming in *my* kitchen, I said, not while I have my strength! You should have heard her! Oh, we had a right ding-dong and no mistake! *She* said it was reduced to nine pounds fifty: *I* said it should have been reduced to ashes! *She* said she was the boss around here: *I* said not in my kitchen, she wasn't. *She* said, well who pays the wages? *I* said—"

Just as things were getting interesting, the door burst open and Mrs. Renton appeared in her Margaret Thatcher suit and her three-inch heels, one arm outstretched toward Fizz in an attitude of supplication. It was only when she was a few paces away that Fizz realized that she was proffering a mobile phone.

"Fizz, you speak German, don't you? Will you take this call for me? I cannot make out a word the woman is saying, but it's some-thing to do with Herr Krefeld. She's phoning from Germany. Talk to her, will you?"

Fizz threw her paper napkin on top of her illicit pastry and took the phone. It was five years since she had lived in Germany and she expected her vocabulary to be a bit rusty, but within a few words she had forgotten she was speaking in a foreign language.

"This is Mrs. Renton's assistant speaking," she said, promoting herself, for the moment, in the cause of clarity. "Is there something I can do for you?"

"Thank God," muttered the voice at the other end of the line. "Your German is much better than my English. Maybe now we can get somewhere."

29

"I'm sorry you've had trouble making yourself understood," Fizz said. "I believe you are phoning about Herr Krefeld?"

"Yes. I am his sister. Someone from your police station telephoned me this morning to say that my brother had died in your hotel last night."

"Yes, I'm afraid that's true. It appears he had a heart attack, or perhaps a shock of some kind. I'm sure it was very quick."

There was a short pause as the caller absorbed this information, so Fizz put her hand over the mouthpiece and gave Mrs. Renton a brief résumé, which seemed to have a calming effect.

"There has to be a post mortem examination, I understand. Can you tell me when this will be?"

"I can't say for sure," Fizz temporized, "but I'd imagine it will be done today or tomorrow."

"And then I can bring my brother home?"

"I'd imagine so, yes."

"Good. Then I will take a flight to Edinburgh tomorrow morning. Can you book me a room at your hotel for two or three nights? Perhaps longer, since we don't know how long it will take to complete the formalities."

"Yes, certainly. That's no problem."

"Thank you. You have been most helpful, miss. I hope you will be available to translate for me when I arrive?"

"I come on duty at six p.m., but I'm sure Mrs. Renton will be able to look after you till then."

"Ah, well. We shall see. Till tomorrow, then."

The phone went dead before Fizz could reply. She handed the receiver back to her boss.

"She's arriving tomorrow to collect the body from the morgue. I told her I didn't know when the post mortem would be completed, but she's apparently planning to wait for a couple of days at least. I said we could give her a room."

Mrs. Renton looked as if she didn't quite know how to take this but feared the worst. "Well, I suppose she'll be moping around the place and depressing all the other guests, but it can't be helped. At least her English is practically nonexistent, so she'll have to keep her sorrows to herself to some extent. Thank God Jenny May McGill

30

leaves tomorrow. The last thing we want is for her to be giving *her* Technicolor version to a grieving relative!"

"She's been going on about it, has she?" Fizz asked.

Mrs. Renton paused to roll her eyes, giving Johnnyboy the chance to put in his ten pence worth.

"According to the waiters, she put everyone off their breakfast by broadcasting the gory details all over the dining room. We had kedgeree this morning too! I could have killed her!"

"Which reminds me," quoth his employer, turning on him like a terrier. "Next time you make kedgeree, John, please try to remember you're not feeding the five thousand. It may look good on the menu but hardly anybody ever orders it and there's damn all we can do with the leftovers."

Johnnyboy, chagrin mantling his alabaster cheek with flushes, muttered something about mayonnaise and curry paste, but Gloria ignored him, striding to the door and turning there to fix them both with a stare. She was no more than an inch taller than Fizz but she held herself like Sylvester Stallone and she could pack as much intimidation into a single look as Fizz had ever seen. She was reminded of a certain sheepdog belonging to her grampa, but Shep had never achieved quite that level of malevolence.

"I've told the rest of the staff, Fizz, and now I'm telling you. I don't want a word of this sudden death to leave these doors. I can do nothing about Jenny May, but I can warn my employees that if the newspapers get hold of the story I'll want to know who let it out. Understand?"

Fizz gave her a chirpy smile to show how cowed she was. "It's not exactly headline material anyway. I can't imagine anyone being much interested."

"You're probably right," Mrs. Renton nodded. "Still, I don't want any bad publicity. God knows," she added with a lowering glance at Johnnyboy, "I've got enough to put up with as it is!"

"Bitch," Johnnyboy said when the door had closed behind her. "I wonder if I should have a rabies shot?"

"She's just upset," Fizz said soothingly.

"She's just making a big drama out of nothing," Johnnyboy returned sullenly and went back to pulverizing garlic cloves. After

31

a minute, he said, "You're right, though, Fizz. That's just what you were saying, isn't it? She does seem to be getting her panty girdle in a twist. It's not like her."

That was the odd thing. Gloria had never looked like the type to let things get on top of her. The persona she presented to the world was that of a hard-boiled businesswoman, and one would have expected her to regard a little thing like the death of a resident as nothing worse than a minor irritation. Fizz could see no reason for her concern.

Not unless Mrs. Renton, like herself, had found something to worry her about the scene in Herr Krefeld's bathroom.

# Chapter Four

For the remainder of the evening, and for much of the following morning, Buchanan could not quite rid his mind of the memory of Fizz's reaction to Dennis Whittaker.

The fact that she might have been hiding her natural revulsion for reasons of her own had, of course, occurred to him, but had been almost immediately discarded. He had seen Fizz dissemble on more than one occasion, and with a facility that spoke of long practice, but he had never once seen her use sex as a tool. She was too much of a feminist for that. Yet, although she must have noted at first glance that sex was what Dennis had in mind, she had done nothing to slap him down and, indeed, had almost seemed to be receptive to his blandishments.

The obvious conclusion was that she was attracted by the new partner, and though Buchanan could see nothing that might be deemed appealing in Dennis's saccharine approach, it had to be admitted that he was not a bad-looking bloke. Women went for that type: big and beefy, with heavy shoulders and grins that promised tantalizingly dangerous liaisons.

He, himself, could never be like that. He would never be beefy, not without the help of drugs, and he would never have Dennis's preoccupation with the opposite sex. He didn't know, really, whether he'd want to be another Dennis, given the chance, but he had to admit it would be nice to have a more modern, more easy-going attitude to personal relationships.

As to Fizz, her sexual habits were, like a lot of things about her, *terra incognita*. Given her enfranchised attitudes and her liberal lifestyle, which till last year had been that of an itinerant opportunist, one could assume that sexual freedom might be quite in character. Buchanan had not, till now, given the matter much thought, since their own relationship had always been, at best, platonic, but now that he considered the matter it didn't seem like Fizz to be free with her favors. He, himself, would have serious reservations about making a pass at her, but that could be due to his own hang-ups as much as to a fear of instant retribution.

Yet Dennis had suffered no retribution. Why was that? Fizz had to have enough savvy to appreciate that he was bad news. It just couldn't be possible that she was one of those women who were habitually drawn to men who were guaranteed to leave them emotionally scarred. Or could it?

It was none of his business, of course. He kept telling himself that every time he forced the subject out of his mind, but that didn't stop it returning to irritate him every time he clapped eyes on Dennis. He knew he should have been happy that it was Fizz who had drawn the junior partner's attention. It took the heat off the other female members of staff and she was certainly not one to turn to her boss for help in dealing with sexual harassment.

All the same, Dennis's plans for her future redeployment fell on stony ground.

"Oh, I don't think so," was Buchanan's immediate reaction. "I don't think I'd be happy to see Fizz showing house purchasers round our real estate. Not unsupervised."

"No, no, of course not," Dennis said hurriedly. "Not unsupervised. At least, not right away. I thought I might go along with her for the first few times. Give her a few pointers. Make sure she doesn't drop any serious clangers."

Buchanan was horrified at the prospect of allowing Fizz anywhere near his clientele. "I really don't think she's cut out for that sort of thing, Dennis. You don't know Fizz but, take my word for it, you never know from one minute to the next what she'll get up to. She's … what I'm trying to say … she's unpredictable. She doesn't think about consequences. I don't really think she *means* to cause trouble, but trouble follows at her heels like a dog. Believe me, I've seen it happen."

Dennis brushed an imaginary fleck of dust from his trouser leg and sent Buchanan a speculative glance. "I'm told there's a special relationship between you and Fizz … or, is that just office gossip?"

Buchanan refused to admit to himself that he was embarrassed. He supposed that there was bound to be talk around the office, especially after he had spent a fortnight's R&R on Fizz's home patch after his gall bladder operation earlier in the year. Women would always put two and two together and, if the truth was disappointingly prosaic, they'd make five, or even six if they possibly could. He gave a short laugh.

"Any relationship with Fizz is 'special', Dennis. She doesn't conform to any conventional behavior patterns that don't appeal to her. She'll treat her employer exactly as she would treat any other colleague, in terms of familiarity or respect. She's liable to invite you to meet her family or tell you off for eating too much saturated fat, or drop by your home if she happens to be passing. And the same goes for clients. They're just people like everybody else. Here in the office she's under some kind of restraint but, honestly, I—"

"Give her a try, Tam," Dennis said stubbornly. "She can't be all that much worse than the typist who usually does the job. I mean, look at her …" Dennis waved an arm as though Fizz were standing between him and Buchanan's desk. "She's clever, she's imaginative, she's creative, she's a trier. And, Tam, she needs the money quite badly. I don't like to think of her not being able to eat properly."

Buchanan suffered a sudden pang. "She said that? What about her evening job?"

Dennis shrugged. "I don't think she expects it to last much longer. Surely we can find her an extra couple of hours a week?"

That was the sucker punch. Buchanan might be running a business, not a charity, but he knew that if Fizz was forced, through poverty, to give up her course at the university, he'd have to live with the thought that he was, in part, responsible.

"OK, Dennis," he said, smiling in the face of adversity. "On your head be it. But, for a trial period only. Say, six weeks. After that, we'll review the situation. And listen, she's Miss Fitzpatrick in front of clients, OK? If she wants the job, she's going to have to drop this 'Fizz' business."

That, at least, would be a small victory. Fizz had always refused, in the past, to be addressed either as 'Miss' or by her given name, but if *he* could make a concession, so could she.

Dennis had a hard job dimming his delight to a semblance of detached satisfaction. "Thanks, Tam. I think you'll find you've made the right decision."

Buchanan felt himself unable to agree with that. If there had been any other job that Fizz could have turned her hand to, he would have felt much happier, but she had no job skills whatsoever, other than her considerable nous, so there was no point in blaming himself

When Dennis had taken himself off, the picture of Fizz toiling into the night refused to go away. Six till midnight. That meant she'd be walking home alone—she never used public transport unless she had to—just when the pubs were coming out, along streets that were probably ill lit and teeming with itinerant beggars, druggies, and all manner of miscreants. Buchanan was ashamed of himself for not thinking of that before.

And, as if that were not enough danger to put herself in the way of, now she was starting to poke her nose into a sudden death that might, after all, turn out to have serious connotations. Worse—she had invited his support and he had refused. He had left her to her own devices without even considering what danger she'd be in if it turned out that the old man had been murdered after all.

"Damn the girl," he growled, not by any means for the first time, and reached for his phone index. The spring had packed in, but he prized it open and found the number of St. Leonard's police station.

"This is Tam Buchanan here," he said to the switchboard operator. "Is it possible to speak to Detective Inspector Fleming?"

"One moment, please."

It was two or three minutes before Fleming finally came on the line. "Tam? How're you doing?"

"Can't complain. How about you, Ian? Getting in any golf these days?"

"Not as much as I'd like. Rushed off my feet as usual."

"I won't take up too much of your time then, Ian. Just something I wanted to check."

"Sure. What can I help you with?"

Buchanan hesitated. "There was a sudden death on your patch a couple of nights ago. An elderly German tourist called Krefeld. I just want to check when the body will be released for burial."

"Yeah, right. The Royal Park Hotel. Hang on a minute, Tam." Fleming's voice, muffled by his fingers across the mouthpiece, could be heard speaking to someone close by. After a minute, he came back on the line but still talking to his informant. "Who did it? Kimball? Aye, well we could wait all day for the paperwork ... You there, Tam ...? Right. It looks like tomorrow morning at the earliest. The PM's been done, but the dockets aren't through yet."

"Right," Buchanan said, carefully saying nothing to confirm what he knew Fleming would assume: that he was asking on behalf of a client. "Did you hear what the cause of death was?"

"Not specifically, no. Ken ... what was it? Heart attack? You didn't hear?"

"It's not important," Buchanan said quickly. "Just idle curiosity."

"Heart attack, yes," Fleming was still talking to his colleague but returned to say, "Yes, the usual: senile myocardial degeneration. Just what I'd expect."

"Thought as much," Buchanan muttered. "Anyway, thanks for your time, Ian. Talk to you again soon."

He got off the phone before the DI made any remarks that would necessitate Buchanan's specifying his connection to the case. Fleming knew Fizz and, although he would probably not have quibbled about divulging the information, Buchanan didn't want to be caught out acting like a neurotic parent.

It was a comfort, however, to have his own opinions on the death of Herr Krefeld so unequivocally confirmed. Had any anomalies shown up during the autopsy, DI Fleming would already know about it, so as far as Buchanan was concerned, Fizz could amuse herself by playing detective as much as she liked.

It might serve to keep her out of some other mischief.

The same piece of information, when she heard it from Johnnyboy, came as rather a disappointment to Fizz.

"Heart attack? You sure?"

"That's what I heard." Johnnyboy slipped a haddock fillet onto

37

a plate, hid a couple of scallops in wine sauce under a lettuce leaf, and added a tomato and cucumber garnish. "Here you are, sweetie. Get yourself outside those scallops before the boss-lady spots them."

"Gawd luv yer, guv'ner. Yer a gent!" Fizz ate the scallops first, while her taste buds were raring to go, and only then descended to the level of the haddock.

"So, Herr Krefeld's sister has arrived?" she asked when she could spare a moment. "What's she like?"

"No Mother Teresa, according to eyewitnesses," Johnnyboy said, returning to checking the pots that were simmering on the range of gas burners. "My spies tell me that she's been giving Frazer and Gloria hell: wanting to know every little detail of what happened as if she were hoping to sue them for damages. Gloria hasn't been fit to live with all afternoon."

"I don't see how any blame can attach to the hotel," Fizz said. "It's not the Rentons' fault that he chose that particular night to have a heart attack."

Johnnyboy went to the door of the main kitchen and shouted through to the commis chef that he could get on with Vandyking the tomatoes. "According to Jason, who happened to be just out-side the door," he said when he came back, "your name came up in the conversation once or twice."

Fizz's mouth was open to receive a slice of cucumber, but she lowered her fork and stared at him. "*My* name? What the hell have I got to do with anything?"

"Well, you found him, sweetie. And completely *au naturelle*, according to what Jason overheard. I don't think the sister was too pleased about that."

Fizz gave a short laugh. "Tough. But if she thinks I was ogling the old soul, she's batty. He looked like he had pajamas on at first—I just thought they needed a damn good press, frankly."

"Well, apparently the sister thinks someone older should have been in charge. I kept you a nice rum baba from last night. Want some ice cream to cheer it up a bit? Also," Johnnyboy added, en route to the refrigerator, "she was at the police station this after-noon and came back in a raging temper. Gloria was doing it in her support tights, I can tell you, sweetie. Something missing from Herr Krefeld's gear, so it appears."

Fizz didn't like the sound of that. Any suspicion of thievery was always bound to reflect on the staff. Fortunately, she herself had the tour bus driver to confirm that she had not entered the room, but it was also true that she had omitted to lock the door while she went to alert the Rentons. Anyone could have entered between that time and some ten minutes later when she had returned with Gloria.

"What's missing?" she asked.

"Search me, ducky. Something important, Jason says, judging by the way the voices were being raised."

Fizz scraped the last of her rum baba off her plate and left Johnnyboy to it at that point because the orders were starting to come in and she couldn't stand the frenetic atmosphere that immediately started to build up. She had worked in a kitchen only once, on a kibbutz, and she had promised herself when she moved on that she'd starve before she'd do it again.

Rosemary in reception was ready to make a sharp exit as soon as Fizz arrived, and for a while there was plenty to do, with guests returning from their day's sightseeing and others turning up to book in. By about seven o'clock, the usual evening hiatus had set in. Most of the residents were either in the dining room or getting dressed for dinner, so Fizz was able to do a quick tour of inspection around the lounge and cloakrooms.

She was returning to the reception desk with a bunch of discarded newspapers and looking forward to doing the crosswords before she dumped them in the waste-paper sack, when she saw Gloria coming downstairs with a gaunt-looking woman in her middle seventies. Herr Krefeld's sister, no doubt, and clearly Johnnyboy's informant had not lied when he'd said she was no Mother Teresa. You didn't get a face like that in your old age by being sweetness and light all your life.

"Fizz." Mrs. Renton's expression betrayed nothing of the angst that was probably boiling in her matronly bosom, but her voice had a strangled quality that gave the game away. "A moment please." She turned to the stony visage at her shoulder and cracked a smile.

"This is the young lady I spoke of earlier, Frau Richter. Miss Fitzpatrick. Fizz, I'd like you to have a word with Frau Richter for me. She has a few problems and I'm not perfectly sure that I understand exactly what she is trying to tell me. Perhaps you would see if you can straighten things out for her?"

"Sure," said Fizz and switched to German. "Please allow me to offer my condolences on the death of your brother, Frau Richter. We are all very sorry."

"Thank you. I think we spoke already—"

"Forgive me," Gloria lifted the counter flap and edged around the desk. "Why don't you sit in the TV lounge, Fizz. It's empty just now. You can tell me later what transpires."

She looked to Fizz as though she was desperate to get as far away from Frau Richter as possible.

Fizz nodded. "Would you like to come through to the TV lounge, Frau Richter? We'll be more comfortable there. Can I order you a cup of coffee? Some tea?"

Frau Richter shook her iron-gray head. "Tea I have been drinking all day. Here, the police station, the undertakers, everyone gives me tea. But I will be glad to sit quietly and talk in my own language. I do *speak* a little English, but I do not *hear* it very well, especially when it is spoken as quickly as Mrs. Renton speaks it. I think she is an excitable woman."

Fizz chose corner seats, well away from the TV set. The only sounds were the subdued clink of crockery from the dining room and the faint drone of piped music from the main lounge. "Mrs. Renton is still upset and distressed by the death of your brother. As we all are."

Frau Richter settled herself into an armchair, crossed wrinkled hands over the handbag on her lap, and viewed Fizz with steely eyes. "But it was you, I think, who found Bernd?"

"Yes. Well, no actually. It was a guest who found him. An American lady who had borrowed his binoculars."

It suddenly occurred to Fizz that it might be the binoculars that were missing. She couldn't remember seeing them after Mrs. Renton took the helm. Oh God, she thought, please don't let Andy Hustley have gone off with them!

"But you were in my brother's room the night he died?"

"No." Fizz shook her head firmly. "I didn't go in. A tour bus driver who was with the American party had drawn my attention to the open door and we both looked in, but neither of us entered the room."

Frau Richter nodded, her cold eyes never leaving Fizz's face. "So. And now I wish to ask you: when you were looking in at the door, did you see—in the passageway, in the bedroom, perhaps—a picture, or even a parcel that might have been a picture wrapped in paper?"

Fizz didn't even have to think about it. "I'm sorry. I saw nothing but the bathroom. The lower half of the bathroom, actually, because the top half was full of steam. I didn't look along the passage toward the bedroom."

"I see." Frau Richter didn't bother to hide her dissatisfaction with this reply and her rattrap mouth barely moved as she muttered, "That is a great pity."

"May I ask why?" Fizz asked, conscious that she was pushing somebody who looked like she could have distinguished service medals from the SS.

Frau Richter's eyebrows twitched angrily. "Because an oil painting that should have been among my brother's effects is missing."

An oil painting seemed to Fizz a strange choice of object to take on holiday abroad, but she had seen stranger things in her life. "What size of picture was it? Perhaps the chambermaid will have noticed it."

"I am not sure of the size, nor of the subject matter." A small chink appeared in Frau Richter's iron self-confidence. Her eyes flickered away from Fizz's for a moment and an expression of pain softened her thin lips. "All I know is that Bernd bought an oil painting the day he died. That evening he telephoned me, very excited, to say he had bought me a present that I would be sure to love. An oil painting."

She paused, stroking the rough moquette of the chair arm and clearly holding back tears. Fizz looked away for a moment to give her time to compose herself and, in the ensuing silence, the memory of the scene in Herr Krefeld's bathroom returned like an

41

action replay. Maybe she had been right in her suspicions regarding the old man's death. Maybe, in spite of what the autopsy had revealed, somebody had wanted that picture enough to kill him for it.

"He wouldn't tell me what the subject of the painting was," Frau Richter went on after a moment, "just that it would bring back happy memories. He admitted that he had spent too much on it, but he was sure it would give us both great pleasure." Her voice quavered as she added, "But there was no painting among the luggage returned to me by the police this afternoon. They say they know nothing about it."

Her shoulders sagged and for a second she was no longer a grim-faced harridan but a sad, lonely old woman dealing with bureaucracy and indifference in an unfamiliar tongue and among unfamiliar people. Without thinking, Fizz reached across and laid a hand on her arm.

"How upsetting for you. But please don't worry, Frau Richter. I'm sure there is some explanation for this. Leave it with me and I'll get to the bottom of it for you."

Frau Richter blinked at her in surprise and seemed momentarily touched by the solicitude, then she straightened and lifted her chin. "I would be, of course, grateful for anything you can do. The police have taken note of the theft and say they will look into it, but I can see that they do not necessarily believe that such a painting ever existed, and I cannot prove it."

"Well, let's not jump to the conclusion that we're talking about theft," Fizz suggested. "There are other possibilities. Your brother may, for instance, have taken the painting to be framed or cleaned. He may have decided to return it for some reason."

Frau Richter pursed her lips as though she were suffering from acid indigestion. "No, that is clearly not the case. Bernd was pleased with his purchase, and if anything needed to be done to improve it he would have waited till he got home. He was only here in Edinburgh for one more night, you know. His tour was due to leave for Loch Lomond and the Trossachs the following morning." She tugged her mohair shawl across a bosom that seemed to Fizz to heave with suppressed fury. "No, no. The painting has been stolen

42

and I will get it back. If the police force will do nothing, I will go to my embassy. I will give the story to the newspapers, yes, and show how foreign tourists are treated in your capital city."

"I'm quite sure that won't be necessary," Fizz said quickly, but Frau Richter gave an angry shake of the head, slung her bag over one forearm, and stood up.

"Then my picture must be found and returned to me immediately. The day after tomorrow, I return to Germany with my brother's remains and I will have my picture with me."

There was little Fizz could reply to that. It was quite clear that Frau Richter believed not only that the picture had been stolen by a member of the hotel staff, but also that the management could, if sufficiently hectored, put the finger on the thief. And Fizz could not accept either of those hypotheses. She started to say, "I quite understand your concern, Frau Richter—"

"I hope you do," the old lady interrupted, laying a hand on the back of her chair and nailing Fizz with a hard stare. All trace of tiredness was now banished from a face that might have fallen off Notre Dame. "Quite apart from the fact that it was my brother's last gift to me, the painting was an expensive work of art. It probably cost several hundred pounds, so I will expect every effort to be made to have it traced and returned to me."

Fizz trailed her, murmuring assurances, as Frau Richter stalked straight past Mrs. Renton at the reception counter and made for her room. Her back, as she climbed the stairs, was like a ramrod and, even from behind, you could tell she was a force to be reckoned with. She might be a bit of a shite, Fizz thought, watching her exit, but she was nobody's victim. You couldn't help but like her.

# Chapter Five

Around the same time that Fizz was having her parley with Frau Richter, Buchanan was setting to work on painting his living-room wall.

Once he got started, he felt rather good about it, since he'd been putting it off for over a year, ever since the day of Janine's departure, when she had thrown an avocado at him and missed. The resultant skull-shaped blotch had resisted several optimistic attacks with stain removers and nothing but overpainting was going to hide it. Luckily, he still had half a can of the original off-white emulsion, so there was no excuse for procrastinating any longer.

Selena thought at first that he was doing it for her amusement. From her favorite perch on the ledge of the fanlight above the hall door, she observed his preparations with evident anticipation, urging him on with soft meows. But after a short tussle with a paintbrush she appeared to consider that she had exhausted the possibilities of the apparatus and fell asleep on the couch.

The paint, unfortunately, went everywhere, spraying off the back of the roller and getting as much on Buchanan as on the wall. He lashed a plastic bin bag around his middle and donned a pair of yellow kitchen gloves, but the bottom half of his old jeans acquired a haze of pale droplets.

By nine o'clock, he had applied one coat to the stained wall and it looked pretty good. There was still plenty of paint left and, for a while, he debated with himself whether to use it to freshen up the other three walls while he was at it. Lethargy won, however, so he was starting to get cleared up when the doorbell rang.

"It's me," said Fizz, on the entry phone. "Beam me up, Scottie."

Buchanan had given up being surprised by her not-infrequent and always unannounced appearances. One could deprecate the habit, but even Canute would not have considered it worthwhile trying to break her of it.

"Don't tell me," she said, pointing a finger at his attire. "Vivienne Westwood, right? And, what's the smell? You haven't—! I don't believe it!" She stood staring at the still-wet wall with her hands on her hips. "You've done it at last! Congratulations, I knew you had it in you." She leaned forward for a closer look. "You can still see the mark."

"Rubbish!"

"You bloody can. It'll be quite obvious by the time it's dry. You'll have to give it another coat."

Buchanan followed her pointing finger and thought she was probably right. Par for the course, he thought bitterly. She's only been in the place for a matter of seconds and already she's trod on my *joie de vivre*.

"To what do I owe this unexpected honor?" he asked politely.

Fizz did her usual pratfall on to the couch, bouncing Selena to a rude awakening. "I have a job for you, muchacho."

"No thanks."

"You'll love it."

"No, I won't."

"You will. Honest."

"Forget it."

"God, Buchanan, you're such a misery guts. Oh, sharper than a serpent's tooth it is to have a thankless boss!"

Selena, having tried to stare Fizz into an early departure, threw in the towel, clawed her way up the curtains, and exited by way of the two-inch gap at the top of the window. Buchanan walked over to watch her disappear down the ivy to the cobbled yard below and then turned back to Fizz.

"I hope you're not going to tell me there have been developments in the case of the German tourist?" he said severely. "If so, I don't want to know about it."

"'Course you do." Fizz smiled at him with quite spurious affection. "Before you sit down—have you any of that apple tea left?"

Buchanan scowled at her but went through to the kitchen and

put the kettle on. It was the quickest way to get rid of her. Probably the only way. Even if he refused to open the door to her, she would only shout through the letterbox and disturb the neighbors.

When he returned with the tea and a plate of biscuits, she was stretched out on the couch, twirling Selena's catnip mouse by the tail.

"OK. So what brings you here, Fizz?" he said, stirring his own instant coffee. "Couldn't it have waited till tomorrow?"

Fizz lifted her shoulders and let them fall. "Time is of the essence," she said, continuing her Shakespearean theme. "I have Herr Krefeld's sister threatening to raze the Royal Park Hotel to its foundations and curse the entire staff even unto the tenth generation, I have Mrs. Renton planning to end it all while she still has the strength to raise a gun to her head, and I have Johnnyboy having a fit of the vapors because somebody said he was as much a suspect as anybody else."

Buchanan felt his heart sink. "A suspect? Of what? Not of murdering the old guy. That's—"

"No. It turns out I was wrong about that—according to the police pathologist, anyway. Apparently he had a heart attack." Fizz examined the plate of biscuits and chose two. "However, his sister—Frau Richter—arrived today, claiming that he had phoned her the night he died to tell her he'd bought her a painting. An expensive painting—probably several hundred pounds' worth. Unfortunately, it's not among the luggage the police took from his room and Frau Richter is going bananas. She's threatening to cause a hell of a stink unless she gets it back, and PDQ."

"She's on a bit of a sticky wicket," Buchanan said, relaxing somewhat. "If she can't even prove that such a painting ever existed, she's not going to get a lot of police time allotted to the search."

"Mmm," Fizz agreed with a full mouth, and swallowed impatiently. "A teenage constable came round this evening and talked to Gloria and Frazer, but I reckon that's as much of an investigation as we're likely to see."

Buchanan watched her sample another biscuit and wondered why she was here. There didn't seem to be much meat on the mystery as it stood, even for someone as insatiably nosey as Fizz.

There was no murder involved and even the picture was probably imaginary, so it was difficult to see why Fizz should be interested, far less himself.

"You realize, of course, that the painting could be purely fictional, don't you?" he said.

"Oh, sure, but I get the feeling it's not. When you speak to Frau Richter, you'll see what I mean."

Buchanan smiled. "I'll take your word for it, since the chance of my speaking to Frau Richter is extremely small. I really don't have time to start looking for missing property, Fizz, you ought to know that."

Fizz waved a biscuit in denial while she chewed and swallowed. "Nobody's asking you to look for the picture. I just want you to talk to Gloria for a minute and tell her that it's not going to ruin her business even if it turns out there *was* a picture and it *was* nicked by a member of staff. She's been on the loo all evening and Frazer has been hitting the Famous Grouse like prohibition was coming in tomorrow."

"Overreacting a bit, aren't they?" Buchanan remarked. "From what you've told me of Gloria, I hadn't pictured her as the neurotic type. Quite the opposite, in fact."

Fizz glanced at the empty biscuit plate as though she had designs on the crumbs. "No. Well, neither had I, but this business appears to have thrown her a bit. Seeing Herr Krefeld like that … worrying about the effect on the other guests if it turned out to be suicide or even murder …" She drank some of her tea. "I told her there was no chance of her being sued—either for Herr Krefeld's fall or for not taking care of his property—but she's in too much of a state to listen to me."

Buchanan sighed. "If she wants legal advice, she can pop into the office tomorrow and I'll put her mind at rest."

"Well … yes, I think she'd be happy to do that, but right now she's got Frau Richter stalking the corridors like Ghengis Khan and I felt sorry for her. I said I'd get you to phone her."

"What? Tonight? You're not serious! For a simple matter like suspected theft …" He looked closely at Fizz for signs of perfidy. Feeling sorry for people was not something Fizz made a habit of and

Gloria Renton, by all reports, seemed an unlikely candidate for her sympathy. "You are telling me everything, aren't you, Fizz?"

Fizz's already guileless face took on the expression of angelic innocence she used only when under suspicion. "Of course I am," she smiled, dimples dancing around her curved lips. "I don't mind admitting that I did think it a wee bittie odd that Gloria should be *quite* so devastated by this business. There may be more in it than meets the eye, but that doesn't affect you. All that's required of you is to spell out her legal position in case she's done for damages. That's all. Honest."

"Tonight? She's that worried?" Buchanan shook his head. "Sorry, Fizz …"

"Buchanan, I swear to God I'm not trying to work a flanker. The woman is jittering like something in aspic. Even Frazer is taking it all very seriously. It was he who gave me the time off to come and talk to you." She swung her legs down off the couch and put her cup on the coffee table. "You've got to give them a ring, Buchanan, at the very least."

"Why? Because you told them you'd make me?"

"No. Because I told them you were a nice guy and wouldn't turn your back on them."

That made Buchanan pause, but only momentarily. Then he concluded (a) that it wouldn't have been the first time that Fizz had said something she didn't necessarily believe, and (b) that she had probably couched her assurances in somewhat different terms when addressing Gloria, and if the word "mug" had not been used it had doubtless been implied.

Fizz had been right about one thing, of course, however she had phrased it: he couldn't grudge someone in distress a five-minute phone call, even at half past nine in the evening.

He raised a forefinger. "Just let me say this, Fizz. If you are putting one over on me again …"

"Pooh!"

Shirley Temple couldn't have delivered that line with more cuteness.

Buchanan wondered at himself as he reached for the phone.

48

Precisely how that five-minute phone call developed into a personal visit to the hotel the following morning was something of a mystery to Buchanan.

Possibly the realization that Gloria Renton sounded like a woman on the edge of a nervous breakdown had something to do with it, or he may have been swayed by the fact that, unlike Fizz's previous lame dogs, this one was willing to pay the going rate for his services.

Curiosity also played a part, that was certain. He had been subjected on a regular basis to Fizz's anecdotes about her other job and he had to admit to a certain morbid curiosity to discover if she had been exaggerating the eccentricities of her colleagues at the hotel. Furthermore—and if he were honest, probably more to the point—if she was ferreting into something that might prove dangerous, he wanted to know about it now, not when she was in over her head.

When he got there, at eleven thirty, the place looked deserted. There were no cars or tour buses in the parking lot at the rear of the building and the reception counter was unattended. He could hear a vacuum cleaner wailing somewhere on the upper floors, and beyond a pair of swing doors at the rear of the entrance hall Judy Garland was bewailing the Man that Got Away.

Choosing the nearest of the two leads, Buchanan pushed through the swing doors and found himself in a white-tiled anteroom to the kitchen. Crockery was stacked on open shelves around the walls and stainless-steel dishwashers were ranged under long counters equipped with toasters, microwave ovens, and coffee percolators.

A thin chap with terrible acne and a chef's hat was sitting at a counter on a high stool, scribbling on a jotter and singing along to the Judy Garland tape.

"Excuse me ..."

"Oh my gawd!" The chef—who could be no other than the notorious Johnnyboy—drew a swift and unintentional lightning flash on his jotter and stood up. "Where the blue blazes did you pop up from, dear?"

"I'm sorry. I ... I heard the music and as there doesn't appear to be anyone around I thought—"

"Oh, there never is at this time in the morning, no, just the

49

chambermaids, but they're all upstairs doing the rooms. You gave me a right old turn there, I can tell you. Gawd! Now I know what colonic irrigation feels like! Who was it you were looking for, love?"

"Mr. and Mrs. Renton. I have an appointment to see them at half past eleven."

The chef fingered a large purple swelling at the angle of his jaw. "Poor Gloria isn't at her most effervescent this morning, to be perfectly honest with you, dear. She disappeared as soon as breakfast was over and I dare say she's lying somewhere in a darkened room with a cold compress and a handful of Prozac pills."

Buchanan tried to look sympathetic. "And Mr. Renton?" he asked with saintly patience. "Is he likely to be available?"

"Tell you what," Johnnyboy said, leaning one hip gracefully against the counter. "I'll send my commis chef to look for him and make you a nice cup of coffee while you're waiting. Would that be nice? I don't think I'd be lying if I said there's some chocolate gateau in the cake tin."

Buchanan tried to cover up his sudden lunge backward by coughing a little too heartily. "I don't want to put you to any trouble. I'm sure I can find—"

"It's no trouble at all, dear," sang Johnnyboy, waltzing toward the kitchen doorway and yelling, "Jason! Jace, pet, see if you can track down Frazer for me, would you? He could be down the vegetable garden looking at his sprouts. Tell him there's someone here to see him; a Mr. ...?" He sent Buchanan a questioning look over his shoulder.

"Buchanan."

"Buchanan. *Buchanan?*" He did a perfect double take and returned to his counter. "Tam Buchanan, as I live and breathe! Why, Fizz has told me all about you, Tam. I feel like we're old friends!"

"Really?" Buchanan said, this being the most tactful of several replies that occurred to him.

The chef regarded him with judiciously angled head. "You're not at all what I imagined."

That figured. Buchanan wasn't too sure what sort of a picture Fizz would paint of her daytime boss, but he was fairly sure it wouldn't be flattering.

"You don't want to believe everything you hear from Fizz," he said smiling, but not too bewitchingly, and then firmly changed the subject. "I imagine everyone has been upset by Herr Krefeld's death, not just Mr. and Mrs. Renton."

Johnnyboy swirled hot water in a teapot, testing its warmth with his cupped hands. "I tell you, Tam, it's been like Bedlam in here ever since that sister of his arrived yesterday. That dreadful woman doesn't care *who* she upsets! All this fuss over a silly little picture that nobody remembers seeing." He spooned tea into the pot, drawing down the corners of his mouth in indignation. "She had two of the chambermaids in tears, you know—yelling at them in German—and poor old Gloria ...! I never thought I'd feel sorry for that woman but, whatever it was that hideous old Valkyrie said to her, it really got her scanties in a bunch, *I* can tell you! Honestly, dear, I've never seen poor Gloria so prostrated in all the years I've worked here. I won't be one bit surprised if she ends up in a psychiatric ward, the way she's going. Frazer is positively worried to death about her ..."

The swing doors suddenly burst open, clattering against the wall, and a square, middle-aged woman in a power suit and vertiginous heels stood in the opening, legs astride, arms outstretched to hold the doors apart, and radiating ruthlessness and vigor from every pore.

Johnnyboy shriveled visibly. "Cancel the wreath," he muttered.

"Mr. Buchanan? I do apologize for keeping you waiting. Someone should have been looking out for you at reception, but we are all at sixes and sevens this morning." She advanced on Buchanan and shook hands, her eyes registering Johnnyboy's half-prepared tea tray as Buchanan politely dismissed her apologies. "Have that sent through to the TV lounge, John. Do come this way, Mr. Buchanan. Jason has gone to get my husband and he'll join us in a few minutes."

Buchanan followed her back through the entrance hall and into a small lounge, which smelled of an air spray that clashed unfortunately with the tobacco smoke it was intended to overwhelm. There were deep armchairs covered in pleasantly faded chintz and a large ewer filled with bronze chrysanthemums.

51

The vision of a strong, confident woman that had impressed Buchanan at her entrance through the swing doors had deserted Mrs. Renton by the time they got themselves seated. Clearly, she was trying to put on a good face in front of the paid help, but once out of their sight she didn't have the energy to maintain it.

Buchanan crossed his legs and regarded her with an encouraging smile. "This is my sort of hotel," he said, giving her time to relax. "There's a really tranquil, homey atmosphere. It makes a difference from the big hotel chains where everything is arranged for the convenience of the staff, not of the customer."

Gloria managed a small smile. "We do make comfort our first priority," she said, tugging her skirt over her sturdy knees. "We've just completed our first full year here and we had only recently started to feel that we were beginning to get it right—and then this has to happen."

"Well, you know, it's not the end of the world," Buchanan started to say, but Gloria shook her head.

"This sister of Herr Krefeld, she's such a forceful woman and she is bent on making trouble. That's why I am so grateful to you for coming here today instead of seeing me at your office. I'm sure, if you could just speak to Frau Richter ... if she could see that we are doing everything possible to investigate the matter."

"I'm not sure that's a good idea," Buchanan told her. "If there is any question of litigation between you and Frau Richter—not that there will be, I'm sure—but if there is, it would be better if I communicated with her through her lawyer and not in person. You see ..."

Gloria's eyes slid past him to something beyond with an expression that made him turn to look behind him. A red-faced chap whom he had no difficulty in identifying as Frazer Renton was holding the door for an elderly woman who could only be Frau Richter.

Gloria performed the introductions and no sooner had everyone settled down than a girl arrived with the tea tray, which caused further delay. Finally Buchanan was able to say to Frau Richter, "I understand the police have agreed to look into the matter of your missing painting?"

"They say this, yes, but all they are doing is asking questions to

Mr. and Mrs. Renton." Her accent was so thick that Buchanan had to supply most of the words by guesswork and it was clear that the Rentons were finding it just as difficult to understand her. "No one believes there ever was a painting, so why should they waste time to look? They think they are dealing with a helpless old woman, but I will show them that I am not so helpless! I will not be stolen from like this."

"But, Frau Richter, we are doing all we can … aren't we, Frazer?" Gloria insisted, and pressed on before her husband could open his mouth. "I have questioned all the staff very closely indeed and I am totally convinced that none of them would have dreamed of taking the picture."

"*Some*one took it," Frau Richter returned with a glare. "A member of staff, a guest, a sneak thief, I do not know. But no one does anything to find out. It is outrageous."

"It would be impossible to trace all the other guests. Wouldn't it, Frazer? I don't know all their home addresses and they could be scattered all over Europe by now anyway. Even the police would have a hard job tracking them all down."

Frazer showed no sign of being able to force his way into the conversation nor, apparently, did his wife expect him to do so, notwithstanding her routine appeals for his opinion. There was little doubt in Buchanan's mind regarding which of them was the driving force in their relationship, but Frazer appeared detached rather than browbeaten. No doubt the whisky that Buchanan, fore-warned by Fizz, could detect on his breath, had something to do with that.

Seeing his reluctance to speak, Buchanan took the opportunity to forge ahead. "The first thing we have to do is to find some proof that Herr Krefeld actually purchased a picture. Once you have proof of purchase, the police are bound to treat the matter seriously." This positive approach having secured the attention of all the combatants, he said to Frau Richter, "If the picture was as expensive as you suspect, there would surely have to be a receipt among Herr Krefeld's papers. Have you looked for one?"

Frau Richter had to have this repeated twice before she caught the meaning, at which point she shook her head firmly. "No receipt.

Nothing. No check stub, no letterhead, no notes in his address book."

"Then I'm afraid the only thing you can do is to trek round every art shop in Edinburgh till you find which one sold your brother a picture," Buchanan told her, rephrasing the remark several times before he hit on the words that were in her limited vocabulary. It was a wan piece of advice to someone as physically and linguistically unfit as Frau Richter, but it was obviously the only thing she could do.

"But I fly home on Saturday morning," Frau Richter returned, jerking her head angrily. "I must take my brother to be buried in Germany. How am I to do this when it could take weeks?" Her eyes came to rest on Buchanan's face. "Will you do this for me?"

"Regrettably, Frau Richter, I am a solicitor with a business to attend to, but I'm sure I could recommend a firm of private investigators who would be happy to be of help to you."

"This will be expensive?" Frau Richter wanted to know.

"It might—" Frazer began, but Gloria laid a restraining hand on his arm and leaned forward.

"For the sake of my hotel's reputation I would be happy—more than happy—to share the expense."

"Really, that shouldn't be necessary," Buchanan said, assessing Gloria's insistence on going over the score as clear evidence of a mind at bay. "Probably one of your own staff could do it just as successfully as a professional investigator. It's just a matter of foot-slogging, after all."

"That's right," Gloria said, her face brightening. "No reason why one of the waiters shouldn't earn a bit of overtime. That's a wonderful idea, Mr. Buchanan. Fizz told us you and she had done a bit of detective work together from time to time. I knew you'd be able to put us on the right lines."

"Fizz," said Frau Richter, evidently grasping the one familiar word in Gloria's observations. "Yes. She is a clever girl. I will pay her to do this for me. You will arrange this, Mrs. Renton?"

"Fizz?" Gloria spread her hands. "Certainly. If you'd prefer her to do it, then by all means. I'm sure she'd be quite willing."

Buchanan felt tempted to interfere at this point, but couldn't really justify it. Fizz certainly needed the money and there seemed little harm in letting her earn it in this way if she so chose. No violent crime was involved and there were unlikely to be any unfortunate repercussions. And, give her her due, she had proven more than once that she had a certain talent for not just asking questions but for listening to answers.

Frau Richter raised her head and rested her hooded eyes on each of them in turn. It would have been an overstatement to say that her expression softened, but perhaps there was a slight crack in her implacability.

"Good," she said, making the concession with visible reluctance. "We progress."

Gloria's relief was pitiful to witness.

# Chapter Six

It came as a pleasant surprise to Fizz to hear that Frau Richter was willing to pay her to do what she had intended to do anyway, namely poke her nose into something that was none of her business.

She had been fairly sure that Buchanan's visit to the hotel would succeed in alleviating matters for all concerned. Say what you like about Buchanan, he did have an aura of calm competence that worked like magic on fraught females of Mrs. Renton's kidney, and while Frau Richter was a somewhat tougher nut to crack, it appeared that she had also succumbed, to some extent at least.

Buchanan himself could have shown a little more pleasure at this unexpected boost to a colleague's finances, but that was par for the course. Fizz had long ago given up expecting him to show emotion about anything.

She had just come out of his office after debriefing him about his visit to the Rentons when Dennis appeared with a prosperous looking couple in their late forties. The man was a couple of inches shorter than his wife but both of them had designer hairdos and a similar taste in gold jewelry.

"Ah, Miss Fitzpatrick ..." Dennis gave Fizz a discreet wink, his back to the other two.

Fizz winced. She had reluctantly agreed to being addressed as "Miss" not only because "Ms." was for plonkers, but because it was irritatingly unpronounceable. She did see that a slightly more formal mode of address was going to become necessary sooner or later, as she progressed in her legal career, but still, at this point in time it represented a come down, maybe even a change in values that she didn't like to think about too closely.

"This is Miss Fitzpatrick, my assistant," Dennis was telling his clients. "Miss Fitzpatrick, Mr. and Mrs. Wainwright are interested in seeing Greydykes, out at Ravelston, and I'd like you to come along." He turned back to Mrs. Wainwright, ushering her along the passage with a hand on her elbow. "I find it's an advantage, sometimes, to have an educated opinion from a woman, don't you? I can give you the benefit of my professional opinion, but I think you'll find Miss Fitzpatrick has a more creative approach and picks up on details that a man might not notice."

Fizz had no time to bone up on the schedule, but she had a vague idea of what Greydykes looked like because it was part of her job to file the particulars of properties for sale and this one had been on the market for months. It was a massive Victorian mausoleum, situated in a pleasant enough though not particularly upmarket suburb, and whoever bought it would be coughing up on a regular basis for its upkeep.

She grabbed her jacket off the back of her chair and smiled at Mr. Wainwright as he held the door for her.

"Are you relocating to Edinburgh, Mr. Wainwright, or do you already live in the area?"

"No, we're from down south."

Not far south, though, Fizz guessed. His accent was unmistakably Scottish, and the border was only an hour's drive away.

"We've moved around quite a bit, in our time," he said, "but this will be our first time in Edinburgh."

"A change of job, is it?"

He seemed discomfited and took a moment to answer, closing the office door behind them as though it were a task that needed all his concentration. Fizz didn't need Dennis's warning glance to know she'd made a *faux pas* but couldn't think how to cover it up without making it worse.

"No," said Mr. Wainwright finally, meeting his wife's eyes in a fleeting glance that nobody else was supposed to notice. "Just a change of scene. My wife has a fancy for a more rural setting."

Their little group had now reached Dennis's car and although Fizz would have liked to know why Mr. Wainwright couldn't have found a more rural setting than Ravelston, she found herself firmly separated from the husband and shunted into the back seat with the wife.

Mrs. Wainwright was wearing a lot of cash. Clothes, by and large, were just clothes to Fizz, but she could tell cashmere when she saw it and she could identify Versace sunglasses because the name was blazoned on them so you couldn't miss it. Nor did she have any doubt that the perfume which now filled the car with enough pungency to make your eyes water had cost upward of a hundred pounds an ounce.

These were people who could buy Greydykes out of the petty cash, but the trouble was, they could easily afford something much better.

It wasn't all that easy to instigate a discussion without asking questions, Fizz found, and since Dennis's eyes in the rearview mirror took on a wary look every time she opened her mouth the conversation in the back seat was somewhat stilted for much of the twenty-minute journey.

Mrs. Wainwright wanted to talk about shops and restaurants, which left Fizz totally out on a limb, Oxfam and economy self-catering being more her area of expertise. Dennis, however, was able to fill that gap and on arrival at the moldering pile, on a hill overlooking Murrayfield golf course, he took complete charge, exhibiting a degree of knowledge and competence of which Fizz had not, hitherto, suspected he was capable.

The Wainwrights seemed less than enthusiastic, but Fizz loved the house. OK, it smelled of damp in places and it certainly needed a lot of work, but it had real character and it was sad to see it going downhill. After the guided tour, while Mr. Wainwright and Dennis were exploring the garden, Fizz was left alone with Mrs. Wainwright in the kitchen.

"It's not what I'm used to," Mrs. Wainwright said apologetically, curling a plum red lip at the old-fashioned decor. "My present kitchen is top of the range. Navy blue and stainless steel with halogen lighting, complete air conditioning, garbage disposal unit, gas and electric cooker, and, of course, every electronic gadget you can think of."

"Do you do a lot of cooking?"

Mrs. Wainwright smiled, conceding a point. "Well, not a lot, but I do like a pretty kitchen and I like it to be in situ when I buy the house. The thought of workmen tramping around ripping out cupboards and creating havoc ... I couldn't face that."

"No, nor could I," Fizz agreed. "The only thing you could do would be to have the work done before you move in. It's usually much quicker that way—probably only a couple of weeks—and at least you'd have everything exactly the way you yourself want it down to the last electric socket."

"Well, I suppose you have a point there."

Fizz looked around the square, high-ceilinged room. "That old range in the alcove would be worth keeping for a feature. Imagine the wall behind it done in white tiles. And, if you were to take this wall down to incorporate the pantry area, you'd have not only a massive amount of space to play with but a view of the golf course and the hills beyond. I bet you haven't got a view like that in your old kitchen."

Mrs. Wainwright looked thoughtful. "No. My kitchen in Hawick looks out on to my neighbor's garden. It's very nice but ... yes, I see what you mean. Being on a hill makes quite a difference."

She opened the window and stuck her head out, waving to her husband and Dennis on the lawn below. "How far are we from the shops?"

"Walking ... maybe ten, fifteen minutes. Five by car."

"Oh dear. Just too far to walk, isn't it? And I hate having to take the car out every time I want to pop out for a magazine."

Fifteen minutes' walk, to Fizz, was hardly worth putting one's shoes on for. "Living here, you'd find you had a completely different outlook," she said, hanging on in there. "You'd probably want to get a bike."

"A bike?" Mrs. Wainwright seemed appalled at the thought. "I don't think that's quite me. Besides, dear, *I'm* not seventeen any more."

"Neither am I, not by a long chalk," Fizz assured her. It was obvious that Mrs. Wainwright took that with a pinch of salt, but it was all one to Fizz. She said, "There's nothing like a bike, particularly in a place like this. Look how flat it is. And you'd be tooling along that beautiful little lane with the wild fuchsia hedges on both sides, smelling the grass, listening to the birds, and keeping your figure at the same time. You'd never want to be in a car again."

"Oh, I don't know ... I like to be handy for the shops."

This scarcely tied in with her desire for a more rural setting. Either Mr. Wainwright had been stretching the truth when he claimed his wife was responsible for the impending change of abode or she had a very odd idea of what rural living entailed.

"Well, you can't have this degree of privacy and be close to the shops as well," Fizz told her flatly, her patience totally expired. "What you're looking at here is a complete change of lifestyle. This is the sort of house that imposes its own protocol. It wants dogs running around. It wants barbecues on the lawn. It wants owners who can learn to love gardening on a grand scale and enjoy hunting down the sort of furniture and fittings that fit, instead of a job lot from Habitat. This isn't just a home, it's a way of life."

That should have been the end of it but, perversely, Mrs. Wainwright looked almost inspired. She looked around her as though she could see through the walls. "It would make a change," she said uncertainly. "Sometimes I wonder what to do with my time, back home in Hawick, with my husband out all day at the plant. The garden is all lawns and mulched shrubberies and the house ... well, we arranged it to be as labor saving as possible and now that there's just the two of us there's very little to do." She wandered back into the hallway and looked through the open doorway at the hills. "I'd love a dog," she said, half to herself.

Her husband came up the steps from the garden, Dennis tagging along behind with his clipboard under his arm.

"Well, dear, I think we've seen enough and I'm sure Mr. Whittaker and Miss Fitzpatrick have other things to do."

"Yes, I'm coming, Harry." Mrs. Wainwright stared back into the hallway as though she were imprinting it on her mind, but, as Dennis moved up to lock the door, her husband was already back in the car.

It was fairly obvious on the journey back that Mr. Wainwright was not wonderfully impressed. He didn't say much either way, but Fizz could detect no sign of enthusiasm, and although Mrs. Wainwright still appeared interested in the local amenities as they passed through the town center, even she said nothing positive.

"Well, at least you tried," was Dennis's adjudication as they dropped the Wainwrights off at their car. "Whether you managed to say the right thing is anybody's guess, but that's something you'll learn with time. One tiny suggestion, though."

"I know," said Fizz. "Don't give them the third degree."

"Right. It was quite obvious that they didn't want to discuss their private business. Some people don't. So, in future try to keep your questions focused on discovering your clients' requirements."

"Yeah. But it was curious how shifty they were. I'm damn sure he was lying when he said it was her idea to live out of town. And she said he was out all day, which means he has a job. Yet he claimed it wasn't a change of job. He can't be intending to commute to Hawick."

Dennis bent close to grin at her and flicked her cheek with his finger. "Listen, my angel, that's none of our business. Just concentrate on getting rid of Greydykes. If you can get that white elephant off our list, there'll be a slap-up dinner at Chez Julien for you."

Which, of course, would have been considerably more of an incentive if Dennis hadn't been part of the package.

It was about five thirty when Fizz arrived at the hotel, salivating happily in anticipation of her dinner, but a big bus party was just checking in, so she had to pile in with Rosemary and Frazer till they had the passengers all filed away in their correct rooms.

"You'd better grab a bite to eat right away, Fizz," Frazer said, as the last one was shunted into the elevator. "Rosemary's going off now, but I can man the fort for half an hour. You know Frau Richter wants a word with you?"

"Uh-huh. Buchanan told me. Some cookie, huh? I bet you won't be closing the hotel for the afternoon in mourning when she leaves."

Frazer cast a wary eye over his shoulder in case they were overheard and rolled a conspiratorial eye. "I can't say I'll be sorry to see the back of her. Thank God she flies out tomorrow morning. For God's sake, Fizz," he added in a murmur, "do your best to get to the bottom of this, won't you? There'll be a nice little bonus in it

61

for you if you manage to get that old harridan off our backs. And as quick as possible."

Fizz couldn't ever remember a period in her life when so many people were willing to give her money. Until now, the idea of starting the new session with enough money to see her comfortably fed and housed till next summer had seemed an impossible dream, but suddenly there was at least an even chance of achieving it.

Finding out where old man Krefeld bought his picture—if, indeed, he ever had one—would be simply a matter of time, and Fizz doubted if it would take her more than a couple of days at the worst. The day of Herr Krefeld's death had been a "free" day for his coach party: a day when the passengers could make their own plans. Few of them would have chosen to roam far from the hotel, which was situated just off the Royal Mile and within easy walking distance of just about all the Edinburgh landmarks.

Herr Krefeld certainly wouldn't have gone far. He wasn't all that energetic, but people on bus tours usually liked to have a chance to stretch their legs a little, which meant that he had probably just done some very local window shopping or visited some of the galleries and museums in the High Street, of which the Royal Mile formed a section.

Admittedly, there were dozens of art/antique shops in the High Street and in Princes Street, which was barely five minutes' walk away, but it would be highly unlikely that the old man would have walked any farther than that. Two or three days ought to be ample time to check out the likely places.

"Money for old rope, ducky," was Johnnyboy's opinion. "I wish someone would offer *me* money to do it, I can tell you. With a bit of luck, you'll have traced the dealer in the first couple of hours. Is anyone talking in real figures, or is it just the 'I'll-see-you-all-right-mate' kind of set-up?"

"Nothing you could get a loan on, not so far," Fizz admitted, submitting a sprig of stir-fried ginger broccoli to a long luxurious chew. "But, to tell you the truth, I fancy doing it anyway."

"Well, hold out for an hourly rate, in case it takes longer than expected." Johnnyboy's pointed look was indication that, if he were the one to be paid to trace the picture's provenance, it would take as long as he could possibly swing it.

Fizz didn't work that way. If she contracted to do a job for an agreed remuneration, she did it to the best of her ability. There had been plenty of times during her travels, and occasionally since she had become a student, when she'd had to exaggerate her capabilities a little to get a job, but once she had nailed that job she earned her wages. She had never once been late for work or taken a day off without good cause, and if she sat around doing nothing, as she did frequently in the hotel, it was only when there was nothing to do.

"I think Frazer wants to get it cleared up quickly and put Gloria's mind at rest," she said.

"Everyone's whipping themselves into a frenzy over this missing painting. It's sheer lunacy, that's what it is, and if Gloria says another word to me about all of us being equally under suspicion I'll lose the place, sweetie, I really will." Johnnyboy slurped red wine angrily into a fragrant mixture in a saucepan and yelled over his shoulder, "Pop out to the storeroom and get me a can of black cherries, Jace. And don't take the tourist route, pet, OK?"

He whisked vigorously and pulled the pan to the side of the cooker. "It's all a big production over nothing, that's what *I* say. I told your nice Mr. Buchanan yesterday, I said ..."

"He's not *my* Mr. Buchanan," Fizz pointed out.

"Well, sweetie, I'd do something about that if I were you. That man is *scandalously* attractive and not short of pocket money either, if I'm any judge of a business suit."

"Yeah, well, looks and money aren't everything, old chum. Shut me in the same room as that guy for twelve hours and I'd be at his throat with a serrated bread knife. Besides, there isn't room in my life for a man right now." Fizz leaned back in her chair as the chef presented her with an apricot mousse surrounded by raspberry coulis. "Not unless it's a man like you, Johnnyboy. I reckon you could make me very happy."

"Enjoy," said Johnnyboy, watching her taste the first nibble with a "look-on-my-works-ye-mighty-and-despair" expression on his spotty face.

It was a crime to bolt haute cuisine but, with the thought of Frazer waiting to be relieved from reception duty, Fizz could do little else. She was, in any case, impatient to have another talk to Frau Richter, because it had occurred to her as she ate that finding the shop which sold the alleged picture to Herr Krefeld would be only the start of the trail. Frau Richter would then want to know what happened to the picture and how she could get it back, and it might be not too difficult to convince her that a private investigation, as opposed to a police inquiry, would yield faster results. Of course, if it turned out to be something more than just a common-or-garden robbery—i.e., if Herr Krefeld's death proved to have been assisted by a person or persons unknown—the police would have to be allowed to take over. Which would be a bit of a bummer.

It was after nine before Frau Richter appeared at the reception counter, as ramrod straight and po-faced as ever. "I believe Mr. Buchanan has spoken to you about the inquiries I wish you to make for me?"

"Yes, he did mention it," Fizz said, "and, of course, I'd be happy to do anything I can to help you find your painting." She came round the end of the counter and led the way to a couple of armchairs beside the fireplace, from where she could keep an eye on the reception desk.

"Good. I am happy to hear that." Frau Richter looked anything but happy, but Fizz was willing to take her word for it. "You are very young, yes, but I can see you are an intelligent girl. No, no. I was a teacher for almost forty years and I know intelligence when I see it. And you are a perfectionist. You see? I know that because of the way you speak German. You take trouble to use the correct intonations, not like the English who care only about making themselves understood."

"Well, I did live in Augsburg for six months, which helped a bit," Fizz admitted. "But, in any case, you can be sure I'll do my best to trace the dealer who sold your brother the picture. I take it Herr Krefeld didn't give you any clues as to what part of Edinburgh he visited that day?"

"No, nothing like that. We did not speak for more than a few minutes." Frau Richter studied the burning logs beside her for a moment, thinking. "He was so excited about finding the picture. All he told me was that it was to be a surprise and that it would bring back happy memories."

"Perhaps of your childhood together?" Fizz wondered.

"Perhaps. Yes, I wondered if it might be a Black Forest landscape. We lived near Karlsruhe till the beginning of the war and then our parents moved to Stuttgart. Or it might have been a view of the Schluchsee where we went on holiday." She gave her head a brisk shake. "But, it may not have been a landscape at all. Bernd would not say. It could have been a house, a still life, even a portrait of an old friend that ended up in someone's attic."

"Well, I don't suppose it will make a lot of difference to my chances of identifying where it was bought," Fizz said. "It was only purchased last week, after all, so even if it was a biggish studio they would probably remember selling it, and to whom."

"I will give you, first of all, some money for expenses and, of course for your time." Frau Richter opened her ancient alligator handbag and produced a wad of notes that did Fizz's heart good just looking at it. "One hundred pounds. This is enough?"

Fizz said, yes, that was fine, which was the understatement of the year. "Judging by similar investigative work I've done for Mr. Buchanan, I doubt very much if I'll take more than a few days to get a result."

"You have done this sort of thing before, then?" said Frau Richter, rising to the fly.

"Twice," Fizz said with becoming modesty. There was no need to go into details like who had asked her to carry out the investigations and whether she had been paid to do so. "They were more serious crimes, in both cases, but essentially just a matter of asking the right questions and chasing up leads. This inquiry, by comparison, should be fairly straightforward. Of course," she added, as though the thought had just occurred to her, "finding the art dealer is just the beginning of the search for your brother's picture. If I turn up any more leads, do you want me to follow them up or pass on the information to the police? I'd be happy to do either, but if I ask the police to conduct an inquiry they won't allow me to get involved as well. On the other hand, how much police time are they

65

likely to spare for the case and, more importantly, *when?* Personally, I like to follow up clues when they're fresh, not after witnesses have forgotten the details."

Frau Richter's eyes glittered. "You are saying that you would be willing to take the inquiry farther? You would try to establish who took the picture and endeavor to have it returned to me?" She took her time thinking about that and then nodded, almost cracking a smile. "You are quite right, of course. If I want my painting back, I must strike while the iron is hot."

"I have to say, Frau Richter, that I believe that to be your best chance of success."

Frau Richter studied her fingers as they smoothed the surface of her handbag. "Very well. We will see how things go. I will continue to pay you as long as you have viable leads to follow, and if you are able to have my property returned to me I will pay you five hundred pounds. Is that arrangement satisfactory to you?"

Fizz managed a cool affirmative, but the inner woman was dancing on her tippy toes. The five hundred pounds was probably pie in the sky, but her expenses were unlikely to be more than a few pounds per week, so the remainder could go straight into the bank.

"Then that is agreed. If you should uncover any further information, I would be obliged if you would telephone me. Here I have a label with my address and telephone number, which you can stick on to your notebook. So. I will hope to hear from you in the near future."

"Yes, certainly. I'll make sure I keep you posted. Tomorrow's Saturday, so I can make a start right away."

Fizz was filled with an enthusiasm that was only partly fired by the thought of the extra money. Already the specter of lentil and carrot rissoles was beginning to fade and tomorrow was bursting with all manner of exciting possibilities. She couldn't wait to tell Buchanan.

# Chapter Seven

Buchanan really cherished his Saturday mornings. From about eight o'clock, when Selena habitually sat on his chest and patted him gently awake with her paw, till at least lunchtime, he did little except enjoy an extended breakfast and conduct an in-depth study of the *Scotsman* and the *Financial Times*.

Selena preferred the windows to be open so that she could either sunbathe on the windowsill or glissade down the ivy to visit her other friends and suppliers. She had always been what Fizz called a peripatetic cat and she still preserved a wide circle of acquaintances, both human and feline, with whom she networked on a daily basis. Buchanan's only objection to this was that maintaining an open-door policy admitted not only more fresh air than one actually wanted but also a good deal of not-too-distant traffic noise. There might be little through traffic in the mews where Buchanan lived, but there was a constant rumble from the main road.

But at weekends that rumble was reduced to a sporadic hum, allowing Buchanan to fancy himself in some leafy suburb instead of a scant five-minute walk from Princes Street. The flat was immaculately tidy, because Dolores, the cleaning lady, came on Fridays, and there was the thought of his regular Saturday foursome at the golf course to look forward to in the afternoon.

He was on his fourth cup of coffee and page five of the *Weekend Scotsman* when the doorbell rang. Selena made a rush for the ledge of the fanlight in the hallway, not because she could spot the caller from there but because she liked to drop on to the shoulder of anyone who came through the door. This little habit had won her few friends, even among those who had learned to anticipate her,

67

and Buchanan kept forgetting to chase her down before opening the door.

"Hello," he said into the entry phone.

"Open sesame," said Fizz's voice.

"Bloody hell!"

Buchanan relieved his feelings by dropkicking the paper into the corner before opening the door.

"Hi," said Fizz, stepping over the threshold and doing a fast side-step, which allowed Selena to plummet to the floor, missing her shoulder by a claw-width. "I hope I'm not interrupting anything? No Friday night orgies still in progress? No yogurt-coated sex goddesses still languishing between your black satin sheets?"

"You just missed them," Buchanan growled, retrieving his tattered *Scotsman* and following her into the lounge in time to see her throwing off her jacket in evident preparation for a long stay. "Don't bother taking your Docs off," he said. "You're not stopping."

"Oh great," she said, putting on her orphan-of-the-storm expression. "That's real Scottish hospitality for you."

"It's my day off, dammit! I'm not running a teashop here, you know. All I'm asking for is a couple of hours' peace and quiet to read my paper and bone up on the financial scene. Is that too much to ask?"

Selena stalked in from the hallway with her tail like an exclamation mark and, passing them both without a glance, exited in a pointed way via the window. She and Fizz were never going to make a go of it. Brought up in a farming community, where animals were raised for a purpose—either to work or to be slaughtered—Fizz saw the cat merely as an animated mousetrap, and the fact that she and Selena had both started life on her grampa's farm meant nothing to her. Selena, for her part, had sensed early in the relationship that she was wasting her sweetness on the desert air, as far as Fizz was concerned, and kept her distance.

Fizz laid an arm along the back of the couch and gave Buchanan a sparkly smile. "You know, muchacho, if I didn't know you were just joshing, I'd think you weren't glad to see me. Any coffee left in that pot?"

Buchanan gave up and went into the kitchen to put on some

more coffee. You couldn't argue with Fizz. As long as you were more use to her alive than dead, you could say what you liked to her and she'd laugh it off. When he got back, she was reading the financial section of the *Scotsman* with what appeared to be unnatural avidity. Her face was fixed in the expression of someone watching the last ten minutes of *The Guns of Navarone*, and her eyes looked like they were virtually snatching the words off the page.

"What are you finding so interesting in the *Scotsman*?" Buchanan asked, pouring her a mug of coffee and topping up his own.

"Hm? Nothing."

"You looked quite absorbed."

"Nope. Just passing the time."

"You were frowning."

"Was I? God, I hope I don't need glasses." She threw the paper on the couch beside her. "I see that mark has appeared on the wall again. What did I tell you?"

Buchanan had tried to avoid any close examination of the offending stain but was now forced to admit to himself that another coat of emulsion was going to be necessary. He sighed. "Fizz. What are you doing here?"

She held her coffee to her lips and blew on it while, with her free hand, she raked through her shoulder bag and dragged out her notebook.

"No," Buchanan said instantly. "No, no, no, Fizz. Do your bit of detective work for Frau Richter if you so choose, but don't involve me in it. Particularly not on a Saturday morning."

"Don't you want to hear the amazing stuff I uncovered already this morning?"

"No. It can wait till Monday."

"Ah, but *can* it?"

"What's that supposed to mean?"

"Well, who knows whether it will wait or not?" She tapped her notebook with one fingertip. "I have leads in here that will have to be followed up and if I leave them till next week they may cool off."

Buchanan shrugged and looked out of the window. "So, follow

them up. You don't need my permission. As far as I'm concerned, you're doing this job on your own time. You're a freelance. I never even recommended you."

"I bet you didn't," muttered Fizz darkly and then put her notebook back into her bag. "I thought you'd be fascinated, that's all. I thought you mentioned something about keeping you posted."

"But not bloody twenty-four hours a day!" Buchanan made a grab for his disappearing patience and rubbed a steadying hand across his face. The gesture reminded him that he hadn't shaved and that his hair was probably still standing on end from being toweled dry after his shower. "OK, dammit!" he snarled. "You can have five minutes, then you're out of here. Talk fast."

She shook her head at him with affectionate reproach like a mother reproving a fractious toddler. "OK. You're just dying to know, aren't you? And, *don't* grind your teeth, Buchanan, God knows what you're doing to the enamel!" She opened her notebook with a flourish. "Well, then … I was damn sure that old man Krefeld wouldn't have walked very far from the hotel, so I started in the Royal Mile and hit the bull's-eye within an hour. A tiny little art/antique/curio shoppe just round the corner in Blackfriars Street. Chap called Phillip Ure."

She paused to gulp some coffee, giving Buchanan the opportunity to say, "He sold the painting to Herr Krefeld? Well done. Mission accomplished."

"Well, we'll see about that," Fizz murmured and then went on, "We had a very interesting conversation, actually. He told me the picture was quite small—about sixteen inches by twenty-two. It was an oil painting of a lake in the Black Forest. Probably close to where Frau Richter says she and her brother lived as kids. But what I found intriguing was that when Phillip bought the picture—at a small auction in Comrie—it had been painted over with another oil painting, probably by an amateur."

"Mm-hm." Buchanan looked at the clock on the mantelpiece. "Very interesting."

"You don't think so?" Fizz queried, interpreting his tone of voice correctly. "Well, it was interesting for Phillip, I can tell you. He bought the picture for sixty pounds, cleaned off the crappy garden scene that had been slapped on top of the original, and sold the landscape to Herr Krefeld for five hundred and fifty. I'm telling you, Buchanan, we're in the wrong game."

"Yes, well ..."

"Another thing he told me ... sorry, is my time up?" She knew exactly when she was safe enough to say that.

"Yes, but you can tell me what else he told you if it's all that interesting."

"Well, Phillip said that, after the deal had been completed, Herr Krefeld said he fancied getting the picture valued. It looked to Phillip as though the old boy suspected the painting might be worth even more than he'd paid for it."

"Bit of a sickener for your friend Phillip, then."

Fizz waggled her head uncertainly. "We-ell, I don't think so, not really. He'd already made a killing on it and he thought Herr Krefeld was being a trifle optimistic, but he gave him the name of a dealer in George Street who would take a look at it. Pettifer and Williams."

"Right." Buchanan had been to several showings at the Pettifer and Williams gallery during his Janine period, she being very heavily into that sort of thing.

"OK, so I go zapping round there straightaway to find out what the picture was actually worth—which could be *vitally* important. I mean, what if it was an old master?"

Buchanan nodded with angelic patience. "Right."

"Right. But the bastards won't talk to me." Her denim blue eyes blazed with frustration and the wispy curls that had sprung loose from the elastic band at her neck danced in front of her ears like golden springs. "Arrogant sods, the lot of them. At first the assistant claimed to remember Herr Krefeld, but when she went for her boss he said he could not give out confidential information and anyway he had no record of anyone of that name."

"Mm-hm. Well, it's not very surprising. They presumably charged Herr Krefeld for giving him a valuation of the painting, so why should they give you the same information for nothing? Besides, you have no real standing in this matter. No credentials, no authority to be asking questions."

"I told them the background," Fizz returned impatiently. "I told them I was acting for Herr Krefeld's sister, but it was obvious that they didn't believe me. They said it was a police matter."

"Well, so it is," Buchanan pointed out.

Fizz glared at him. "Frau Richter said I could continue the investigation if my original inquiries led anywhere promising. I'm damned if I'll pass this on to the police just because those arty-farty tossers won't talk to me. I'd rather be fired from a cannon. You'll have to lean on them."

Buchanan sat up hurriedly and pointed at his chest. "Me?"

"Sure, you. You know them, don't you? You used to get asked along to those wine-and-canapés nosh-ups of theirs when you and that praying mantis with the blonde hair were an item. They'll listen to you."

"Fizz, they don't know me from Adam. It was Janine who was part of that scene. And anyway, even if they recognize my name, they won't give out that information over the phone. Not when they've just had a similar query from a louche character like you. They're bound to think it's just you again, getting someone to front for you."

"Right. That's just what I was about to say," Fizz nodded, draining her mug.

"Good." Thank God they agreed about something, Buchanan was beginning to think, when she added, "That's why I came round to get you. There's nothing else for it: you'll have to go in to the saleroom in person."

Like hell, Buchanan thought.

Had the supercilious young lady in black hipsters who approached them—very much at her leisure—as they waited in the showroom been a mind reader, she would not have used quite the tone she did when she drawled, "*Was* there something?"

That, to Buchanan, was the last straw. He had *had* pushy females up to here this morning. One was too many; two were simply not on.

"Yes," he said, through clenched teeth. "There *was*, surprisingly enough. If you can spare a moment in your obviously full schedule, I would be obliged if you would tell Mr. Williams that Mr. Buchanan would appreciate a word with him. Tam Buchanan."

The air of languid boredom evaporated and a dull flush crept from her high black collar to her plum-tinted hair. She took the business card from Buchanan's fingers and, without looking at it, indicated a pair of high-backed Charles Rennie Mackintosh chairs. "If you'll have a seat, I'll see if I can find him."

She hurried away into the gallery, her hips thrashing about like two wildcats in a sack, and Buchanan lifted a finger to silence Fizz before she spoke.

"I can see you enjoyed being a witness to that brief encounter, Fizz, but don't crow just yet. One wrong word out of you, and yours will be the next head to roll."

She looked at the ceiling. "Who got out of the wrong side of the bed this morning, then?"

Buchanan walked away from her and pretended to study a waste of good gouache in an ornate frame till the urge to strangle her had passed. It wasn't really Fizz he was angry with, at rock bottom, it was himself, Muggins. Fizz's unfailing patsy. The softest touch in the northern hemisphere. Rent-a-Mug.

God had created people like Buchanan specifically as fodder for people like Fizz, just like He had created plankton for whales or rabbits for foxes. Buchanan might be bitterly ashamed of his kind heart, but that didn't mean that he could say "no" to someone who had no one else to turn to.

Fizz needed the money: it was as simple as that. There was no rich daddy in the background to see her through a financial crisis. There was her grampa, up north in Am Bealach, but what Buchanan had seen of their relationship had not been reassuring and he was sure that she got little support from that source. All she had going for her was her own wits and her own determination and, when it came to the crunch, Buchanan didn't have it in him to condemn her methods.

She looked so innocent, so baby-faced, so trusting, and so heart-wrenchingly vulnerable that no matter how often she shafted him, no matter how often he told himself that this time was positively the *last*, Buchanan ended up feeling sorry for her again and again. Which was exactly what she intended.

"How do places get away with flogging crap like this," she

demanded, stepping a few paces back from an all-black canvas and staring at it with her head poked forward. "You wouldn't get me parting with a fiver for any of it. I don't know much about art, but I sure as hell know bollocks when I see it."

Before Buchanan could tell her to put a sock in it, he heard footsteps approaching and found Barry Williams advancing on him with outstretched hand.

"Tam! Long time no see. How've you been?"

"Pretty good, Barry. And you?"

"Can't complain. It must be over a year since you've dropped by. Last summer, I seem to remember. The Michael Davies perspective, wasn't it? You and Janine—oh, of course ..." he hesitated, fingering the collar of his acid green shirt. Bulbous eyes flicked to Fizz and back. "I heard that you and she ... yes, I was sorry to hear that."

Buchanan edged him toward Fizz. "Fizz, this is Barry Williams— Barry, meet Miss Fitzpatrick who works for me. You may have met her already this morning?"

Barry shook hands urbanely, his eyes shifty. "I think I did see you in the showroom this morning. Was there something I could have helped you with?"

Buchanan took a breath to begin explaining matters, but Fizz beat him to it. "Actually, yes. I am conducting a private inquiry for one of Tam's clients, a Frau Richter, whose brother brought a painting in here to be valued last week. It was an oil painting of a Black Forest landscape. However, the owner has since died, the painting has disappeared, and Frau Richter is employing me to trace it."

"Of course," Buchanan pushed in, "we realize that the valuation might be considered a confidential matter, but since we are acting for the sole beneficiary under the owner's will I would hope—"

"Of course, of course Tam," Williams raised a restraining hand. "Not the least problem, I assure you. I'm sorry you've had to call twice, Miss Fitzpatrick. I just wish someone had thought to speak to me about it when you were here earlier. Why don't we go through to my office and have some coffee while I call the details to mind?"

He led the way through the main part of the gallery into a

sunshiny room beyond. Most of the free space was taken up by an outsize desk, which stood with its back to a pair of French windows that opened onto a small courtyard beyond. There were pictures and folders everywhere: stacked on the desk, hung on the old-fashioned picture rail, and propped against the walls.

When they were seated, both Fizz and Buchanan having refused the offer of coffee, Williams propped an elbow on the arm of his chair and pressed the knuckle of his forefinger against his lips.

"I didn't speak to the owner personally," he said, with a show of deep concentration, "but I do remember the painting. Our Mr. Trickett—who is, unfortunately, out of town today—dealt with the inquiry and he did, in passing, ask my opinion on whether the work might be that of Konrad Schlegel."

Fizz narrowed her eyes. "Konrad Schlegel? A German artist? I don't know the name."

"German, yes. Some of his early work was done in the Black Forest area and, certainly, the landscape Mr. Trickett showed me was not dissimilar to his later style." He leaned forward, toying with the papers on his desktop. "To be honest, Konrad Schlegel is not as well known in this country as, perhaps, he deserves. We see very little of his work and neither Mr. Trickett nor myself were one hundred per cent confident about this particular piece. We had to refer the owner to the local expert."

"This Konrad Schlegel," Buchanan asked, after a moment's thought, "is he a widely respected artist? If the painting were genuine, would it be worth a lot of money?"

Williams pursed his lips. "Not an enormous amount. If genuine … I would value it at about a thousand pounds, but I have to say that it would probably be a reasonable investment at that price. Schlegel has, as I said, always been underrated outwith his own country—actually, I don't think he received the acclaim he deserved in Germany either but, since his death, his work has gained in popularity and is still going up in price."

"A thousand," Fizz murmured, pensively. "And you thought it *was* probably genuine?"

"*Possibly*," Williams substituted, waggling a hand palm down to stress the uncertainty. "It was unsigned, undated, and the style—I'm not sure how to put it. Let's say it was very similar to the few later Schlegels I've seen, but it could—just possibly—have been a copy—*but*," he tagged on, raising a finger, "I will say that, if it was a copy it was done well—and by an equally good draftsman."

"Mm-hm. So, you were unable to give Herr Krefeld a firm estimate of the painting's worth, as it stood?" Buchanan said. "You passed him on to someone else? The local expert, I think you said."

Williams nodded and flicked open a fancy blue leather address book. "The few, the very few Schlegels we see in this part of the world are invariably sent to auction by Teddy and Marcia Marriner. Teddy Marriner was at one time Schlegel's agent and, at his death—some fifteen or twenty years ago—he and his wife inherited all Schlegel's work. I believe the greater part of the bequest is still intact, but one sees the occasional painting at auction." He copied an address and telephone number onto a scrap of paper and handed it to Buchanan, who passed it to Fizz. "Marriner and his wife run a sort of artists' retreat out at Lamancha, I'm told."

"Thank you," Fizz said, reading the address. "I'll have a word with them."

"Well, I wish you luck, Miss Fitzpatrick, although I can't guarantee that the gentleman in question actually contacted Marriner." Williams pushed his chair back from the desk, commencing the winding-down process. "He did, I believe, have very little time at his disposal. I think he was on a bus tour."

"That's right," Fizz nodded and stood up and Buchanan, smitten by a sudden pessimism, followed suit.

"You'll contact this Teddy Marriner by phone, of course?" he said when they got outside. "No point in trailing away out to Lamancha on the off chance that Herr Krefeld showed him the picture."

Fizz looked away into the distance and smiled a small smile. "What is it you're always telling me, Buchanan? When you're asking questions, you have to watch the guy's face, read his body language."

"Yes, but this guy is only peripherally involved. It's not as if—"

"How do you know that? Apart from the shopkeeper and your friend Williams, Marriner might be the only other person who knew

Herr Krefeld had that picture. Maybe it was more valuable than it appeared to be. Maybe Marriner wanted it for his collection and Krefeld refused to sell it at any price, because it had sentimental value." She shifted her bag from one shoulder to the other. "Anyway, I want to do the job properly. Where is Lamancha, anyway? Somewhere in the Moorfoot Hills?"

"Out in that direction, yes," said Buchanan, knowing that she knew as well as he did that public transport to that stretch of sparsely inhabited countryside was virtually nil. He sighed. "And, before you ask, I have a golf date this afternoon."

Fizz shone one of her prettiest smiles at him. "It's very sweet of you to offer, Buchanan. Tomorrow will be just fine."

# Chapter Eight

Fizz rather fancied herself as a map reader. She had, after all, navigated her way around three continents without any serious mishaps, so she had no qualms about finding the correct route to Lamancha, as, indeed, she did. It was only the last part of the trip which went seriously agley and that, as she informed Buchanan several times, was not her fault.

The Lochmore Foundation, which was the name given by Teddy Marriner to his artists' retreat, was not marked on any map and even those residents of Lamancha that she stopped in the street had never heard of it. In the end, because she refused to phone the place and ask for directions, they were forced to explore every meandering lane and rutted track till they found it at last, behind a high sandstone wall some distance from where they had expected it to be and miles from the nearest outpost of civilization.

Buchanan's smile, by that time, was wearing a little thin, but he was being angelically patient, no doubt because he regretted being such an old grouch yesterday. That, Fizz reflected, was par for the course. He might act the pig at being forced into a situation, but once he accepted it as inevitable he usually bit the bullet and did what was required of him with a good grace.

It was evident that most of the buildings that comprised the Lochmore Foundation had once belonged to a farm. There were two semi-detached cottages on each side of the cart track that led to the main building, which was an unattractive two-storied farmhouse. In addition, a massive wood-and-glass garden room stood apart, surrounded by mowed grass and linked to the cart track by a rough path. There were hens pecking around the gravel parking

78

lot and a family of white goats, Mum, Dad, and two kids, were visible by a row of wooden sheds beyond.

Fizz got out of the car and stood stretching her legs and looking about her while her driver put his jacket on. A movement at the doorway of the farmhouse attracted her eye and she spotted an elderly woman coming toward them, leaning on a narrow ebony cane. She was tall and bony with a thatch of straight, gray hair sticking out in all directions and a jaw line that was sharp as the prow of a Nantucket clipper. The gabardine coat she was wearing over a flowing, ankle-length skirt was too tight for her and had probably lived through the last war.

"Looking for one of the inmates?" she asked in a loud and harsh voice as soon as she was within earshot.

"Yes. We're looking for Mr. Marriner," Fizz said. "Is he around?"

"Oh, God, don't ask me. I haven't lifted my head since six o'clock this morning, not even to look out the window." She scanned the environs with a hawklike glare. "I know he's not in the house, but you may find him in the garden room. If not, he'll turn up there soon. It's coffee time. Shall we take a look-see?"

She indicated the wood-and-glass structure with a wave of her cane and turned to lead the way.

Buchanan said, "Please don't let us inconvenience you. I'm sure we could find—"

"You're not inconveniencing me in the slightest, young man," brayed their guide, her voice still pitched as if she were fifty yards away. "I'm on my way to the garden room anyway. There's always good coffee on the go there around this time of day. A little bribe to make the inmates socialize, otherwise we'd stagnate, each in our own little cell."

Beneath the flowing hem of her skirt, Fizz could see a pair of large, clay-spattered trainers. "You're a potter?" she asked.

"I am." She looked at her hands as if she suspected that these were what had given Fizz the clue. "The name's Kat Houston. I do decorative ceramics."

Buchanan introduced himself and Fizz and went on to ask, "Do you find that you can work better here than you do at home?"

"This *is* my home, dear." When she laughed, her skin, which, even in repose, looked like Anaglypta, contracted into a mass of wrinkles. Deep parallel grooves radiated from the corners of her eyes to curve across her cheekbones, meeting up with a mesh of finer lines scribbling up from the corners of her mouth. "I'm one of the Foundation Stones, as Teddy calls us. Bremner McGrath, the flower painter, and I have been here twenty-one years. Ever since Teddy and Marcia started the Lochmore Foundation."

"But most people just come and go, I suppose?" Buchanan said, cupping her elbow for a second as she staggered on the rough path.

"Oh, yes, people are coming and going all the time. They come for a week or a fortnight or, if they have some particular project that they want to work on, they may stay for months." She raised her eyes from the path ahead of her and directed a somewhat bleak look toward the windows of the garden room. "We have Dodie Galbraith with us at present. He's a regular visitor."

"Dodie Galbraith," Fizz said, riffling through her mental files. "I should know that name."

Buchanan knew it. "The painter who graduated from Barlinnie Prison's Special Unit. He was doing a life sentence for attempted murder—wasn't he?—but earned himself an early release a couple of years ago. I've seen some of his work. He has an unusual style." He looked at Kat Houston inquiringly. "I don't know what category one would class it in …?"

"Primitive, I suppose," Kat smiled faintly while still giving the impression that this was the kindest description she could think of. "I'm not sure what sort of label *he* would apply to it, but you can ask him yourself. That's him there."

The garden room being now only a dozen or so paces away, they could see through the mostly glass walls to the four people standing around within, among a medley of chintz-covered couches and rattan tables. As soon as she saw Dodie Gaibraith, Fizz remembered seeing his photograph in the *Scotsman*, remembered the exhibition of his dark and tortured paintings, remembered also the terrible violence that, according to the *Scotsman* article, had fueled his entire career. He was one of the Special Unit's claimed successes—a degenerate beast saved by the humanizing power of Art. So they said.

The overalls he was wearing were stippled with streaks and splashes of paint and hung from his squat body as though he had inherited them from someone twice his height. The legs were rolled up around his ankles and the crotch hung down almost to his knees, making him look like a refugee from the Planet of the Apes. Completing the simian theme, a dark shadow of beard wrapped his cheeks and throat, burgeoning into tufts of black hair that showed all the way down the unbuttoned front of his overalls. He was probably not much over forty, but his battered face and thinning hair made him look ten years older.

"Hullaw therr, gorgeous," he said to Fizz, she being the first through the door. "You lookin' fur me?"

"Dream on," said Fizz and forgot him as Kat overtook her and started trumpeting introductions.

"Andrew and Jean Samuel." She waved an arm at a middle-aged couple who were dispensing coffee from a Cona machine. "Andrew illustrates children's books and Jean is working on a commemorative tapestry for Ely cathedral."

Compared to either Dodie or Kat, the Samuels looked disappointingly middle class. Andrew's tweed jacket and slacks were B-movie boring and Jean's hairstyle had clearly not changed since beehives were in fashion thirty years ago. Andrew, however, was still very good-looking. He made Fizz think of Harrison Ford with a Jewish nose. Which wasn't easy.

"And Bremner," said Kat, grabbing another middle-aged man by the sleeve of his cardigan and dragging him forward. "Bremner and I have been together for so long it's time he made an honest woman of me!"

Bremner, who was at least ten years her junior, seemed embarrassed by this jest and couldn't think of anything to say in reply. He had floppy beige hair that fell over his forehead and his eyes were hooded by heavy brows so that, as soon as you looked away, you forgot what he looked like. He seemed painfully shy, but Kat led the conversation away from him almost immediately by saying to Buchanan, "And are you both artists, or just one of you?"

Buchanan, accepting a cup of coffee from Jean Samuel, looked round at her in surprise. "Oh ... I'm sorry, did you think we were planning on staying here? No, no. Miss Fitzpatrick and I called just for a chat with Mr. Marriner."

"We're trying to trace a Konrad Schlegel painting that was stolen last week," Fizz said, ignoring the warning twitch of Buchanan's brows. He might want to keep the matter low-key, but Fizz had to hear what, if anything, the "inmates" knew about it. "Tam here is a solicitor and I work in his office. It seems that the elderly German gentleman who owned the missing painting may have brought it to Mr. Marriner to have it valued."

The five of them exchanged nonverbal comments in a variety of modes: pursed lips, raised eyebrows, shaken heads, etc., but no one had anything constructive to offer.

"Teddy would have mentioned that sort of thing," Kat asserted. "We don't see many visitors as a general rule and I think at least one of us would have noticed if someone had visited Teddy. There haven't been any outsiders around."

"No' in the past week," Dodie Galbraith said, sticking a skinny roll-up between his lips and lighting it. "No' in the past few months, fer that matter. Fer all the contact wi' the outside world we get, there coulda been a fkn nuclear war goin' on out there and nane o' us any the fkn wiser."

Jean looked out of the window with a pained expression, her nostrils curling as though she were experiencing a bad smell. She wore the uniform of the middle-age-spread brigade: long shirt over comfy trousers, but a silk scarf tucked into the open neckline added a touch of genteel chic.

Her husband glanced at her and then offered Fizz a wan smile. "It's not the sort of place where people drop in very often. That's why we tend to assume that any strangers—and particularly those turning up at weekends—are likely to be coming to work here. There certainly have been no elderly German gentlemen around since Jean and I moved in at the beginning of last month. A French couple stayed for a week and did some watercolors, but otherwise no foreigners at all."

"There's no chance he might have come and gone without any of you noticing?" Fizz tried not to sound too wistful. "In the evening, perhaps?"

"It's not likely," Kat said. She had discarded her dingy coat to reveal a bizarre outfit made up of the flowing black skirt, a black cheesecloth blouse, and a multicolored waistcoat constructed like a rag rug, but with ribbons instead of rags hooked through a wide-meshed linen base. It was an outfit that, on her gaunt frame, would have looked less out of place had she had a turnip for a head. "Teddy and Marcia will be turning up soon for their coffee, so you may as well wait and ask them. Perhaps the German gentleman phoned instead of calling in person."

"Even Teddy can't value a painting by fkn telephone," Dodie told her, but Kat flashed him an indignant glare and returned, "That depends on the circumstances, surely? If the picture were one that he himself had just sold, he could probably confirm that it was genuine. That may have been all that was required of him."

"Does Mr. Marriner have a large collection of Konrad Schlegel's paintings?" Fizz asked.

Jean turned back from the window and took Fizz's cup to refill it, very much the gracious hostess. "He owns probably ninety percent or more of everything Schlegel produced." Her accent was pure Home Counties, whereas Andrew's had a vaguely Scottish—or possibly South African—inflection. "Teddy wasn't only Konrad's agent, you know. They went to art college together, I believe, and they were very close friends. Teddy was the only person in the world that Konrad trusted to be the custodian of his life's output."

Which might be quite interesting as far as it went, Fizz thought, but it didn't answer her question. She wanted to know if Konrad's bequest was worth millions or just thousands. She said, "And does that ninety percent constitute a vast body of work?"

"There must be quite a bit, but no one knows for sure," Jean smiled and turned to her husband. "He never lets anyone rummage through it, does he?"

"Not often," Andrew agreed. "I've seen the odd one or two pieces—the ones Teddy thinks are the best—but he's very careful to show only those that he thinks will enhance Schlegel's reputation."

"Even Bremner and I have seen only part of the collection," Kat put in, and yelled across the room at her fellow Foundation Stone,

83

who was reading a newspaper, "You haven't seen it all, have you, Bremner?"

Bremner lowered his paper and peeked out from beneath his bushy brows like a schnauzer dog. "The collection?" he said, in a thin and very precise voice. "I've seen some of it. Most of it, probably. I wouldn't dream of pressing Teddy to display the pieces about which he has reservations."

Kat nodded vigorously. "Nobody's criticizing Teddy, Bremner. I just hope someone will be so careful of *my* reputation when *I* fall off my perch."

"Well, of course, as Andrew says, they were very close," Jean agreed, "and it must have been a terrible blow to Teddy to lose his friend in that tragic way. I'm sure he must feel all the more compelled to keep Konrad's memory alive and unsullied."

Dodie Galbraith propped his behind on the windowsill and raised an eyebrow at Buchanan. The smoke from the roll-up crawled up his cheek and made him hold his eyes half closed. "You didn't know the guy committed suicide?"

"Konrad Schlegel?" Buchanan said with a quick frown.

"Aye. Topped himsel'. Went in aff the fkn rocks on some West Coast beach or ither and just kept walkin' till his bunnet floated."

His fellow inmates regarded him with unanimous revulsion.

"Why?" Fizz asked, this being the most curious aspect of the story. "Successful artists don't commit suicide; just the unsuccessful ones."

"The guy wiz a fkn loser," Dodie said, dragging on his cigarette. "Ye hiv tae fkn *die* in this business before yir stuff's worth the price of the fkn canvas it's painted on. Far as I can make out, old Schlegel never sold enough tae keep him in brushes till he walked the plank. His stock went up then, awright, but up tae that time Teddy and Marcia were—" he sniggered, glancing mischievously sideways at Jean—"they were what ye might call 'keepin' his heid above watter.' That no' right, Jean?"

Jean refused to respond to this sally. She turned and walked across the room to the coffee maker, all but holding aside the skirts of her raiment as she passed Dodie by, her stiff shoulders eloquent of disapproval. Kat and Andrew also looked pained at this disclosure, but neither of them denied it and Bremner just went on hiding behind the paper as though he were uninterested in the conversation. In the silence that followed, Fizz could hear a dog barking in the distance. She looked through the window and saw a couple approaching from the row of wooden sheds beyond the car park.

They were walking arm in arm and talking animatedly, and around their feet surged a pack of small dogs, which appeared at a distance to be longhaired dachshunds. Teddy—it had to be Teddy—was a tall man, big boned and carrying a lot of spare flesh. His meaty face had a high, unhealthy color and his silvery mustache was stained yellow with tobacco smoke. He looked to Fizz like the perfect candidate for a heart attack.

Marcia was head and shoulders shorter than her husband and trim-figured apart from a little thickening around the waist, which was, Fizz supposed, excusable in someone who wouldn't see fifty again. Twenty years ago she must have been seriously good-looking and even now her heart-shaped face and dark, intelligent eyes marked her as something special.

Kat met them at the door and brought them up to date with recent developments, news that appeared to be received with interest by both of them.

"Delighted to meet you," Teddy said warmly, when Kat had completed the introductions and taken herself and the others discreetly away to join Bremner at the far side of the room. "Do let's sit down and be comfortable. Marcia and I have been walking the dogs and, I'll be honest with you, the old legs aren't what they used to be."

Fizz wished briefly that she could introduce Teddy to her grampa, who was still climbing hills virtually every day at the age of eighty-two.

"You'd think miniature dachshunds wouldn't take much exercising—the size of their legs," Marcia laughed, "but they can run us off our feet!"

The dogs had come in with them and were now greeting each of the inmates in turn, a small tornado of wagging tails, sniffing noses, and lolling tongues.

"I see you like dogs," Teddy said to Fizz as she stooped to allow them to sniff her hand. "This one is called Link … here's Banger …"

Fizz saw him watching her face with a sort of amused anticipation as though waiting for her to twig something. "… and these two are Frank and Chip, short for Frankfurter and Chipolata."

Sausage dogs, of course, Fizz concluded. How twee! As she was about to compliment Teddy on his cleverness and originality, it occurred to her that it never paid to look too smart, so she kept her mouth shut and tried to look astonished when he went on, "All of them sausages, you see!"

He must have been telling that frightfully amusing story for years, but he was still much more entertained by it than Fizz was. She couldn't help but wonder what terribly clever names he had for his goats. Brandy, maybe. Peanut, for sure. And, of course, Parsley and Salted. *All of them "butters," you see!* He wasn't the stereotype of a high-powered agent, in fact he seemed even a little simple, but perhaps that was too hasty a judgment.

Buchanan had escaped their little exchange, being tête-à-tête with Marcia, who was telling him about the extent of their garden, but now Teddy leaned toward him and said, "So, tell me what I can do for you, Mr. Buchanan." He took a cup of coffee from the tray Jean was passing around and helped himself to enough sugar to give his pancreas an anxiety attack. "You're looking for a stolen painting, is that right?"

"Yes," said Fizz, drawing Teddy's eyes firmly to herself "I'm acting for a German lady, a Frau Richter, whose brother, a gentleman by the name of Krefeld, bought an oil painting in Edinburgh last week. We believe Herr Krefeld may have suspected that the painting could be an original Konrad Schlegel. We know he wanted to have it authenticated, and we wondered if he had asked for your opinion."

Teddy lifted one corner of his mouth in a sort of grimace and shook his head. "No, my dear, I'm sorry but I haven't heard from him yet. If he should contact me, I'll be happy to let you know but—"

"No, he won't be contacting you," Fizz said. "You see, he died almost a week ago, the same day as he purchased the painting.

Before he died, he phoned his sister to tell her he'd bought a picture as a present for her, only when she arrived to collect his body and his effects there was no painting among his luggage."

"Dear me, how distressing for the poor woman." Marcia, at close quarters, was still attractive. She had a delightful face: sweet natured and, right now, deeply sympathetic. "I imagine the picture would mean a great deal to her. I do hope you manage to locate it."

"You said you thought it was a Konrad Schlegel," Teddy said, clasping his hands and leaning forward in his chair. "Do you know what it looked like? I might be able to identify it."

"It was a landscape—somewhere in the Black Forest, I understand."

Teddy's heavy jaw sagged with sudden amazement. His eyes moved to his wife and then came back to Fizz as he muttered, "But that's surely impossible? I thought that all the paintings Konrad did on that holiday were in my possession."

"So, Schlegel did paint in that area?" Buchanan asked.

Marcia was looking at Teddy with concern, but she turned to Buchanan and tried to lighten her expression. "Konrad painted a lot in Germany in the early days, yes, but he only stayed in the Black Forest for three weeks, in 1977. It was the last real holiday we had together before he died. No, no, don't apologize. It's a long time ago now and we have been back for a holiday since then, so that ghost is laid and all our memories are happy ones."

"I wish your German friend *had* brought it to me," Teddy muttered. "I would have liked very much to see it. Was it a finished work, do you know, or …?"

"We don't know," Fizz told him. "All we know is that a comparatively rubbishy cottage garden scene had been painted on top of it. It was bought at an auction by an art dealer who cleaned it up and made a killing on it."

"Of course, we are rather jumping to the conclusion that it was genuine," Marcia put in, directing the remark at her husband, who was still looking somewhat aghast. "And, even if it were, darling, it might have been just a spoiled canvas that Konrad left behind in our chalet—probably picked up and re-used by some hard-up art student or some subsequent guest who wanted to pass the time.

Who can tell how these things disappear from one place and re-appear in another?"

Teddy gestured away an offer of more coffee from Jean, who was still circulating with the tea tray. "A botched canvas! God forbid! That's the last thing we want doing the rounds under Konrad's name. Forgeries are bad enough but sub-standard work won't do his stock any good."

"Well, as far as we know, the supposed Schlegel painting hasn't been seen publicly so far," Buchanan said, in his soothing trust-me-I'm-a-doctor voice. "I'll see that the police are kept informed so, if it should resurface at auction somewhere, it will be reported."

Fizz could see Marcia succumb to Buchanan's vocal massage, like better women before her, but Teddy was seriously upset and wouldn't let the matter drop.

"I don't like this sort of chicanery," he said, getting his cigarettes out and lighting up, his big clumsy hands moving with noticeable agitation. "It doesn't do an artist's reputation any good when there's a suspicion that someone is forging his work. It makes buyers nervous. Can't blame them, can you? I do hope you can get this matter cleared up quickly."

"We certainly mean to do our best," Fizz assured him. It was funny how many unconnected people were getting wasps in their pants over this business and agitating for an early completion.

Catching Buchanan's eye, she put her cup and saucer on the nearest table and stood up.

"Well, do please keep us in the picture, won't you?" Marcia said. "Drop by again sometime and we'll show you round. There's some really interesting work going on at the moment and we have our own little art gallery over in the house."

Both she and Teddy came with them to the car and stood, arm in arm, waving goodbye as Buchanan took the dirt track at a sedate pace.

"Well, that was nice," he said placidly, turning on to the main road and accelerating away as though he couldn't wait to get home. "Not particularly illuminating, but nice. It seems to be the end of the trail as far as Frau Richter's painting is concerned, though. Pity about that."

Fizz was inclined to agree, up to a point, but there were one or two small matters that could be worth looking into before she admitted defeat. It might be worthwhile spending some time among the newspaper back numbers in the Central Library, which, when she thought about it, would be quite convenient because she had planned to be there first thing on Monday morning anyway. She still hadn't got around to checking out the interesting item that had caught her eye yesterday in Buchanan's *Scotsman*.

# Chapter Nine

When Buchanan dropped Fizz off at her flat on Sunday night, he expected not to see her again till Wednesday afternoon, when she was due at the office. He was, therefore, considerably surprised to hear her voice at lunchtime on Monday, issuing from the office of his new junior partner. His immediate reaction was one of such profound shock that he paused by the half-open door and only just stopped himself from barging in and extracting an explanation.

It was none of his business, of course. Even if, as it seemed, Fizz and Dennis were becoming friendlier than, perhaps, was conducive to good staff/management relations, he most assuredly had no business interfering at this stage. It was just as ludicrous to pretend that he had Fizz's emotional well-being at heart, Dennis being considerably more at risk than she, but the discovery of their deepening relationship left him profoundly depressed.

He had no appetite for lunch, so he was still at his desk at one thirty when the door bounced open and there she was, cute as an Andrex puppy and shimmering with an unspecified excitement that must be the aftermath of her meeting with Dennis.

"Hello," Buchanan said. "What are you doing in the office this morning?"

She gestured airily with one hand and dumped a shopping bag full of fruit on the floor before throwing herself into the spare chair. Buchanan had never seen her sit down like a lady. She always dropped from her full height, to the detriment of any springs or rubber webbing involved in the upholstery beneath her. The couch in his own lounge had already developed a phantom pregnancy and the chair in the filing room had two wheels missing.

"I had to see Dennis about something and I wanted to bring you up to speed on what I found out this morning."

"This morning? I thought you said you'd come to the end of the trail yesterday."

"No, mi amigo, *you* said I'd come to the end of the trail. *I* have been burrowing away for the past three hours and just wait till you hear what I've uncovered."

Buchanan looked at his watch. "OK, shoot. But cut it short, Fizz. I've got a lot to do."

"You're going out for lunch?"

"Why?"

"Well, because I'm starving and I thought we—"

"You thought wrong. Get on with it."

She puckered her brow. "Tightarse."

Buchanan picked up his pen. "I've got to get on, Fizz. I'll hear all about it on Wedn—"

"OK, OK. I'll be brief." She took a plum out of her shopping bag and bit into it savagely. "I went up to the Central Library this morning and had a good read through the back numbers of some newspapers around the time of Konrad Schlegel's suicide."

"Really," Buchanan said, his interest stirred. He didn't quite see how Schlegel's suicide would help to locate the missing picture, but Fizz's manner indicated that she had found the exercise profitable.

"Uh-huh. *Quite* a story." She removed a drip of plum juice from her chin with one fingertip and sucked it off. "Evidently they were on holiday together on the island of Arran. The three of them: Konrad and the Marriners. They had rented a cottage for a week on some remote beach or other with no other habitation within miles, apart from that of the farmer who had rented them the cottage."

"So?" Buchanan waited for more, but Fizz appeared to have finished. "Is that it?"

She waved her plum indignantly. "What d'you mean, is that it? Use your imagination! You must see it's a perfect situation for a murder. No close neighbors. No police force to speak of. Obviously, it's just too much of a coincidence that Konrad Schlegel should choose that particular spot to top himself."

91

Buchanan tried not to smile because Fizz didn't like it when he took her intuitions lightly, but the idea of Teddy and/or Marcia being involved in murder was fairly amusing. "If there had been any suspicious circumstances, there would have been a lengthy inquiry, Fizz. The CID would have been called in from the mainland. Were there any newspaper reports about the matter being followed up?"

"Nope. If there was any inquiry, it wasn't reported in the press." She finished her plum and, with scarcely a glance, tossed the stone in the general direction of the waste paper basket. It was pure luck it went in. "Actually, there were circumstances that made it *seem* like a genuine suicide, but if you were going to murder someone and make it look like suicide you'd arrange all that, wouldn't you?"

"Probably," Buchanan agreed, to humor her. "What sort of circumstances are you talking about?"

She sighed and scowled at her Docs. "Well ... suicide notes," she admitted.

"Suicide notes. Plural? In his own handwriting? Mm. That's a toughie." Buchanan gave her a look that invited her to admit she was being silly but added, in the interests of good relations, "They could have been forged, of course."

"Exactly." Fizz nodded her head enthusiastically and tapped one finger on the desktop. "It's been done before. However ... there was also an eyewitness."

"An eyewitness to the suicide?"

"Uh-huh. I'm afraid so. The farmer who owned the cottage was mucking around with his cows or something on the hill above the beach and he saw Schlegel walk down the rocks—which ran out into deep water like jetties—and throw himself into the sea."

Buchanan decided abruptly that enough was enough. "And you still think it might have been murder?" he said baldly.

"It's only *one* witness," she said, sticking out her bottom lip. "He could have been bribed ... he could have been mistaken ... he—"

"But it's unlikely," Buchanan finished for her, earning himself a black look. "OK, I'll admit it's interesting, as far as it goes, but it doesn't really go very far, does it? Frankly, if I'm to suspect Teddy and Marcia of murder, I'm going to need something a little more concrete in the way of evidence—even circumstantial evidence."

"Well, maybe," she admitted and gave herself another plum. "But it does make me want to do a little snooping around that setup they're running at Lamancha. I've got the feeling we could turn something up."

"That's a royal 'we,' I hope?" Buchanan mentioned warily.

"If that's the way you want it," Fizz said, with an insouciance that Buchanan found obscurely unsettling. He didn't like it when she acted out of character and it was profoundly out of character for Fizz to let him off the hook so easily, especially when she would have trouble getting to Lamancha without wheels.

She tucked a mouthful of plum into one cheek and said, "I phoned Frau Richter last night from the hotel and she was delighted with the progress I've made so far."

"Did she recognize the description of the picture?"

"Uh-huh. She thought so. The Schluchsee is not far from where she and Herr Krefeld were born and lived till the beginning of the war, at which point, apparently, they moved to Stuttgart. She's going to send me a photograph of the lake so that I can confirm with Phillip Ure that it was the same landscape as the picture he sold."

"Good," Buchanan nodded. "So you can then take your findings to the police and tell them to get on with it."

Fizz consigned her second plum stone to the bin, with the same casual accuracy as before, licked her fingers, and gathered up her shopping. "Well, in a couple of days, maybe. Frau Richter is willing to pay me to do a little more snooping for her before I back out. I think there are lines of inquiry still to be pursued and I'm not sure the police would spend the manpower on them."

"Out at Lamancha, for instance?"

"Uh-huh. For a start."

She was altogether too blasé for Buchanan's liking. He couldn't resist saying, "You'll find transport a problem."

She got up, hefting her shopping bag. "Yes, that could be awkward, but Dennis says there's some property he wants to have a look at somewhere around there. I may be able to talk him into taxiing me over."

"Well," said Buchanan hurriedly as she walked to the door. "As I said, I can't be much of a help for a couple of days—"

93

"Forget it—"

"—but maybe later on in the week ..."

"Fine," she said lightly, without so much as turning round. "If I haven't fixed something up with Dennis by then. It's just that it's my night off tomorrow night ..."

Buchanan glared at the door as she closed it behind her. Thankless brat, he thought, and wondered at himself for dancing to her tune. Things had come to a pretty pass when she had Dennis and himself both vying for the honor of being her chauffeur.

He made a point of running into Dennis later in the afternoon and managed, via a casual reference to a new piece of real estate on their list, to bring the conversation round to Fizz.

"What brought her in this morning?" he wondered, without betraying any real interest. "Did you have her showing a property for you today?"

Dennis looked mildly affronted. "No, of course not, Tam, I'd have cleared any overtime with you first. No, she just dropped in to ask my advice about buying some stocks."

Buchanan was stunned. "Investment? *Fizz?*" He had to laugh at the idea of Fizz having money to invest. "She wanted the advice for someone else, I imagine?"

"No." Dennis opened his eyes innocently. "I got the impression that she had already spoken to you about it. Must have picked that up wrongly. I'm sure she wasn't going behind your back, though, Tam."

"No, no. I've no objection to your giving Fizz financial advice, I'm just surprised that she has that sort of money."

"Oh, it's not very much, I gather. In fact, I told her it's not really worth risking. She'd be safer in a building society."

"Mm-hmm." The only money Fizz had ever admitted to even coming close to—apart from her student's grant—was the few hundred she was hoping to earn from Frau Richter. But why she should be considering investing it in the stock market was a complete mystery to Buchanan. Investment wasn't Fizz, somehow. And why, having so decided, she should choose to ask Dennis's advice and not his, was a severe blow to his ego.

The only comfort—and why it should be such a comfort was

something he didn't even want to consider—was that it was financial advice Fizz had been getting from Dennis this morning and nothing more.

Even before she started work that evening, Fizz felt she had already put in a full and productive day.

Whatever Buchanan might say—and she was used to his habit of taking the wind out of her sails at every opportunity—the information regarding Konrad Schlegel's highly suspicious demise simply had to be considered significant. Precisely *what* it signified might not yet be apparent, but it was clear that it had to have some bearing on the case. Coincidences, like hurricanes in Hertford, Hereford, and Hampshire, hardly ever happened, and it was too much of a coincidence to have two suspicious deaths connected, even tenuously, to one painting. OK, maybe Teddy and Marcia hadn't bumped off their old buddy, but there was something fishy there all the same and Fizz meant to find out what it was.

Her second piece of research, although it had nothing to do with her missing painting inquiries, had been even more productive. The scrap of information that had caught her eye in Buchanan's *Scotsman* had said only that H.R. Wainwright, the owner and managing director of an ailing bottling plant in Hawick, had categorically denied rumors of a takeover bid from a major brewery.

As soon as she read the snippet, Fizz knew that she had heard the words "plant' and "Hawick" recently, and both of them on the plum red lips of Mrs. Wainwright. Add to that nugget of information the known fact that Dalriada Brewers—one of the biggest brewers in the UK—had their head office scarcely two miles from the property the Wainwrights had been viewing and you couldn't help but conclude that the two Wainwrights, the plant owner and the house buyer, were, in fact, one. Mrs. Wainwright had addressed her husband as "Harry," Fizz remembered, and that appeared to clinch the matter.

It was perfectly obvious that H.R. Wainwright knew the takeover was about to go through. No doubt he himself would be taken on to Dalriada's head office staff as part of the deal and he was already starting to look for a new home.

Fizz knew virtually nothing about the workings of the stock market, but she did realize that anyone in possession of this information, prior to the inevitable rush to buy Wainwright's stock, was in a position to make a very substantial killing. The moral aspect of doing so might not bear too close an examination, but such gold-edged information, coming at a time when she had a little money, was too opportune to pass up, particularly when she had access, at Buchanan & Stewart, to a wealth of professional advice.

She knew better than to ask Buchanan—who knew what he might come up with to stymie the whole plan? Phrases like "insider information" and "professional etiquette" might not *precisely* apply in this situation but Buchanan would think of something.

Even dealing with Dennis she had to be careful to say nothing specific about which shares she fancied, but that hurdle now safely negotiated, she had, with the help of her bank manager, just hazarded virtually all her ready cash and was confidently looking forward to seeing the first ever comma in her bank balance in the very near future.

She arrived at work, as usual, with enough time to grab a bite to eat before six o'clock and found Johnnyboy giving the commis chef a hard time.

"Jace, pet, how much longer are you going to be grinding that coffee? You're like the mills of God, boy, and I want this mocha filling ready before the punters start piling in. And those garnishes are still to be glazed. You needn't think I'm doing it, not on *votre vie*, my lamb. I've got enough to do, thank you very much." He caught sight of Fizz and rolled his eyes dramatically as though inviting her sympathy. "Come in, sweetie, and sit down. I've got your meal all ready. Shepherd's pie, I'm afraid. She Who Must Be Obeyed found the meat in the freezer and said to use it up for staff dinners."

Fizz was, loosely speaking, a vegetarian by nature but had learned through poverty to be virtually omnivorous. Johnnyboy set it in front of her and watched as she tasted a small forkful. "Shepherd's pie is what *she* calls it but, frankly, it could be *German* shepherd for all anyone knows! Half the stuff in that freezer has been around longer than me and she'll throw nothing out! I told her, I said, you know, Gloria, we should hire a skip one of these days and get this lot tidied out. She wasn't pleased! Didn't like it one bit, me putting my oar in. Listen, ducky, just scrape it into the bin if you don't fancy it, and I'll give you some nice ratatouille. There's plenty for tonight and she'll only want the leftovers to be incorporated into tomorrow's minestrone."

"Are you sure, Johnnyboy? I wouldn't want you to run out."

"There's a ton of the stuff, poppet, and frankly, if we run out, we run out. Gloria can self-destruct if she doesn't like it. I've had about as much as I can take from that woman anyway. Here, my love, see what your taste buds make of that. At least we know where it came from." Johnnyboy returned to his workstation and to his persecution of Jason. "When I said I wanted the carrots julienne, Jace, I meant *thin* not bloody anorexic! I could floss my teeth with these!"

Jason ignored him as he always did and carried on glazing the garnishes with no visible sign of resentment.

"Anyway, sweetie, it turns out there was a piece in the *Scotsman* about Herr Krefeld's picture," Johnnyboy proceeded, cracking eggs one-handed into a mixing bowl.

"Was there?" That was something else the boss-lady wouldn't like one bit, Fizz thought.

"Frazer saw it this morning when he was sitting where you're sitting now, having his coffee. I thought he was going to burst a blood vessel right here in my kitchen. It said the police were looking into the disappearance of a valuable painting after the sudden death of a German tourist in the Royal Park Hotel last week. Just a snippet. I'd never have noticed it. I don't see the clientele turning away in their thousands, but the way Gloria reacted, you'd have thought it was the end of the world."

"How do they get hold of these stories?" Fizz wondered, marveling at the efficiency of reporters. "I suppose they have their contacts in the police. Was Gloria annoyed?"

"Not so much annoyed," Johnnyboy paused and looked at the ceiling as though grasping for the correct term, "more what you'd call *berserk.* One was reminded somewhat of a great white shark in a feeding frenzy." He grabbed a handful of almonds and threw them into the sauce with a flourish, smiling as he did so with deep satisfaction. "Jason and I were entertained to a disgraceful exhibition of temperament, weren't we, Jace? And, of course, poor Frazer bore the brunt of it as usual. She's a bit calmer this evening, but I'd stay out of her way, Fizz, if I were you."

Fizz was, at first, inclined to take this advice to heart, but by the time she had finished her ratatouille it had occurred to her that poor old Gloria might be cheered by the news that the investigation into the disappearance of the picture was making good progress. Accordingly, before relieving Rosemary at the reception desk she made a detour to the housekeeper's room, which Gloria used as her office and where she was usually to be found during working hours.

The door was lying open and, as she approached along the passageway, Fizz could hear someone speaking, apparently on the telephone. She didn't at first recognize the voice as Gloria's because it sounded several tones deeper than Gloria's normal pitch and because she was—extraordinarily—speaking in a not-wonderfully-genuine Glasgow accent.

"No, I'm sorry, sir, but you must have the wrong number ... no, she's not here ... yes, but she's not here at the moment ... B-Barbara, I think ... no, you're wrong there, sir. Mrs. Renton's name isn't Gloria, it's Barbara. I *am* sure. No, she's from ... from Perth, I think. As far as I know, she was born there. Mr. Renton? Frank. Frank Renton, that's right. I don't know where he's from. Could I ask who's calling?"

Fizz was rooted to the spot with curiosity, but she could tell that the conversation had almost run its course and she didn't want to be caught standing in the passageway with her ears flapping. Now, clearly, was not the time to drop in for a chat and a discreet and speedy retreat was probably the best option,

It was difficult to know what to make of Gloria's charade. It appeared that she had been speaking to someone who was trying to track down both herself and Frazer—someone she most emphatically did not want to see. There had been a noticeable tremor in her voice as she answered her caller's questions, a tremor that was unlike Gloria's normal brash delivery and which indicated to Fizz that she was very, very frightened.

This discovery was both welcome and unwelcome. It indicated that, perhaps, there was more to the disappearance of the painting than simple theft, but it also made it quite clear to Fizz that she hadn't a clue what the hell was going on.

# Chapter Ten

It wasn't that Buchanan minded missing an evening's golf on Tuesday. There was a cold wind whipping in off the Firth and there looked to be a fifty-fifty chance of rain later, so he was able to assure himself that he might have done only nine holes anyway. But what really rankled was that he had been forced to admit to himself that, if he had to choose between playing golf and allowing Dennis to taxi Fizz around, the golf didn't even come a close second.

This discovery he found to be totally appalling. He could envisage no worse fate for himself than to become emotionally involved with Fizz who was, not only the most provoking woman he had ever encountered, but who would, without question, have much the same effect on his life and career as Nick Leeson had on Barings Bank. Even on the fringes of his social scene, as he was determined to keep her, she was a sleeping tiger.

Fortunately, he was able to reassure himself that his emotions were not involved. Had Dennis been other than the blatant woman-izer that he was, had he, indeed, been other than a partner in the firm, Buchanan felt that he would have had no qualms about their relationship. But, as things stood, the situation was obviously not one that should be encouraged.

Perhaps he was being a trifle dog-in-the-mangerish, but, hell, he and Fizz had been through a lot together over the past year and a certain—well, not friendship, exactly, but a camaraderie had taken root between them. When Fizz needed help with a project, it was to Buchanan that she turned and, although he might wriggle like mad when she did so, he'd be damned if he'd let Dennis elbow him aside.

Juvenile, yes; peevish, certainly; but it was better than the jealous reaction it might appear to an outsider.

"You're sure I'm not being a terrible nuisance?" Fizz said, as they drove Lamanchaward in the setting sun. She had never worried about being a nuisance in the past and certainly wasn't much bothered by the possibility right now but, as it was already too late to do anything about it, she clearly felt safe enough to make the pretence. "I thought you said you were busy till Thursday."

"Not tonight, as things turned out," Buchanan said shortly, and firmly changed the subject.

As they slowed for the turn into the Lochmore Foundation, they saw Andrew and Jean Samuel sitting outside one of the cottages that flanked the track. They had a bottle of wine on a table beside them and had evidently been enjoying a civilized end to the day, watching the sunset and the lengthening shadows on the purple September hills.

"How nice to see you again," Jean called, as Buchanan braked and rolled down the window. "Are you rushing by or have you time for a glass of Chablis?"

"Actually—" Buchanan started to say, but Fizz leaned across him and said she'd kill for a glass of Chablis.

"I thought it was Marcia and Teddy you wanted to talk to," Buchanan said to her, taking his time getting out because Jean and Andrew were dashing around getting extra chairs and glasses.

"I do want to talk to the Marriners, sure, but these two know all the gossip about Teddy and Konrad being bosom buddies; I'll bet they know all about the suicide too. One version, anyway."

Jean walked over to the gate to meet them, leaving Andrew to arrange the chairs. "Well, this is nice," she beamed, smoothing her graying beehive hairstyle. "We'd resigned ourselves to spending the evening just sitting here boring each other till bedtime, so this is a welcome reprieve! Do come in. It's not so chilly round the corner here in our little suntrap."

Andrew had opened another bottle and was filling delicate crystal glasses that were surely not part of the inventory of the rented cottage. "One of our little luxuries," he smiled, handing one to Fizz. "A good wine deserves a dignified glass, don't you think? A loaf of bread, a flask of wine, and a lovely evening like this. What more can one ask?"

"I suppose you're on your way up to see Teddy and Marcia?" Jean crossed her legs and the material of her trousers stretched tight across her leg, exposing a mid-thigh panty line. "They'll be delighted to see you again. George is there tonight. I saw his car go whizzing by just as we were finishing dinner."

"George?" said Fizz.

"Their son."

"Oh, yes." Fizz sipped her drink. "I didn't know they had a son. He doesn't live at home, then?"

"Oh, dear me, no," Jean lifted her brows in faint amusement. "He and Teddy don't get on."

That comment didn't please Andrew. He flicked a sour glance at his wife as he said, "George has a little flat over Musselburgh way, I believe. He and his daddy are like two bulls in the same field, right now. You know how it is—just the usual friction that springs up when lads reach their teens and refuse to accept parental control. It'll all have been forgotten in a few years, but meantime they're better under separate roofs."

Jean made an impatient little noise with her tongue, and her head twitched as though she had only just prevented herself from shaking it.

"You don't agree, Jean?" Fizz said immediately, taking the same meaning from the body language as Buchanan had done. She gave Jean a conspiratorial smile, apparently just making conversation. "You think it's more than that?"

Jean looked a little reticent, but only for a moment. "Teddy is patience itself with the boy—far more patient than I would be if he were mine. And Marcia! Well, all I can say is, it would do George a world of good if his parents simply told him to face up to his own mistakes instead of expecting them to bale him out every time he—"

"Well, you know darling," Andrew interrupted, passing round a plate of cheesy biscuits, "we don't know the whole story. An outsider's point of view isn't always the correct one. A biscuit, Tam? Oh, do try one, they're really very nice."

It was quite obvious that he wasn't comfortable with his wife's gossiping, but when Fizz smelled a whiff of even a mild scandal it took more than a polite hint to divert her.

"That's what dads are for: running home to when things get tough," she said, she who had never had anyone to run to. She shared a knowing look with Jean and murmured, "What sort of thing does he get up to?"

Jean made a disapproving mouth, but Andrew got his oar in first. "He's just like any other lad who's finding his feet in the world. He has the occasional beer too many, spends more than he earns, forgets to tax the car. We've all done it, and I suppose our fathers all reacted just the way Teddy does. I know mine did."

Jean gave him a hard look. She didn't like being gagged and proved it by saying, "He's spoiled rotten, that's the trouble. Both of his parents have been too soft on him all his life and now they expect him to have some self-discipline, which is silly. Marcia's biggest mistake was in buying him that flat."

"Anyway," Andrew said firmly, and just a fraction too loudly, "tell me, Fizz, how is your search for the missing picture proceeding?"

"Not wonderfully well," Fizz replied, smiling with a cheerfulness that indicated she was as happy with this topic of conversation as with the one she had just been denied. RADA, Buchanan reflected, would have been a waste of time to Fizz.

"Apparently," he said, "it's only very rarely that one of Schlegel's paintings comes up for auction."

"That's true," Andrew said, topping up Fizz's glass, which had gone down faster than anyone else's. "Actually, I think Teddy would prefer to keep the collection intact, but from time to time, presumably when the coffers are getting a bit low, Marcia insists that he part with one. I don't think she has sold many."

Marcia sells the paintings, Marcia buys the flat for George: it sounded to Buchanan as though Marcia had tight hold of the Marriner purse strings, which was scarcely surprising, knowing Teddy. He decided not to comment on this, but Fizz, whose thought processes were clearly parallel to his own, had her own agenda.

"It's Marcia who does all the business side of things, then?"

Jean gave a throaty chuckle. "I can't imagine what sort of mess their finances would be in if Teddy had a hand in them. He's such a duffer with money that Marcia has to do everything. Of course, dear Teddy is such a duffer about everything other than art. It's not that he's dumb: he's just not interested."

"They say that's the sign of a genius," Andrew smiled. "A one-track mind."

"George must be a great distraction to him," Fizz remarked in an all too patent attempt to get the conversation back to where she wanted it. Buchanan had known that she was only waiting her chance, but so, apparently, had Andrew because he was ready to head her off at the first mention of the taboo name.

"You must ask Teddy to show you the collection, Fizz. I'm sure you'd find it interesting and I know Teddy would love to show it to you."

"I will," Fizz said brightly, showing no outward sign of the frustration Buchanan could sense coming off her in waves.

Now that she knew she'd get nothing more about the George/Teddy situation from Andrew or Jean, she was itching to be out of there. She gulped down her wine as though it were Coke and then sat fidgeting and sending Buchanan hurry-up glances. Obviously, she now wanted to rush up to the farmhouse before George should depart, so that she could observe at first-hand the relationship between father and son. However, manners were important to Buchanan and he could not bring himself to swallow his wine and run, as though that had been his only reason for stopping.

Jean, seeing Fizz's glass empty, made to open another bottle. "Really, Andrew, I don't know where you can have put our nice silver bottle opener. I can't make head nor tail of this ghastly tin thing …"

Andrew held out his hand. "Here, give it to me, Jean. It's quite simple, you know."

"Please don't bother for us, Andrew," Fizz said, hurriedly. "This is lovely, sitting here watching the sky changing color, but really, I don't think we should leave it much later to drop in on Teddy and Marcia. Maybe we could take a rain check?"

"By all means, my dear," Andrew said, and if he was disappointed to see her go he hid it well. "Of course we mustn't keep you, but you know you're very welcome to drop by any time."

Buchanan drained his glass and made what apologies he could

as the Samuels walked them to the gate, but Fizz's impatience was just this side of rudeness.

"Well, that's too bad," she said crisply, when Buchanan pointed this out to her. "But I want to see this George person. He sounds like a bit of a rebel, if you ask me, which is peculiar, don't you think, considering his gene pool? Teddy and Marcia are so placid. You'd imagine they'd have a really good relationship with their offspring. Doesn't it make you curious to meet George?"

"Not really," said Buchanan. He wasn't especially keen to intrude on a family gathering, particularly if relations were currently somewhat strained, so he tried to sound repressive, but Fizz was not easily repressed.

"Well, it has *my* synapses twitching, anyway," she said. "I think we should suss out this guy and we may not get another opportunity."

"OK, I take your point." Buchanan was beginning to form an unwilling respect for Fizz's judgment in cases like this. She couldn't always explain why she felt a line of action was important, but, on occasions when it didn't cost too much in time or effort, he was finding himself more inclined to give her her head. "I just think it was unnecessary to be rude to Andrew and Jean."

She shrugged that off without trouble. "We'll drop in again sometime. Take them a liter of Spanish plonk."

Buchanan thought it unlikely that Spanish plonk would fit the bill and even more unlikely that Fizz would foot it.

They left the car in the car park and walked across to the farmhouse and it was only when they were less than ten paces from the door that Buchanan realized that Fizz had chosen a route across the grass verge so that their approach was virtually noiseless. She had heard, as Buchanan now heard, raised voices coming from the bow-windowed room to the left of the front door.

"Fizz!" he said hotly, shocked, as ever, by her shamelessness. She was on tiptoe, trying to see in at the window, but she grabbed his arm and turned on him with a glare that demonstrated the uselessness of protesting. Without wasting a word on her, he yanked his sleeve from her grasp and strode on ahead, but for the few seconds it took him to reach the doorbell, he was unable to close his ears to the altercation within.

"... trouble you've caused your mother and me! It's not two months since your last 'crisis' as you call it. You promised, then, that it would be the last time and I believed you, dammit! And now this! Do you expect to get away with this sort of behavior for the rest of your life? Answer me, dammit! Do you think for one minute that—"

"There were bills I hadn't expected," claimed a lighter voice that had to belong to George. "It's not my fault that the—"

"Well, whose bloody fault is it, then? Tell me that? I ought to take a stick to you!"

Buchanan, on the doorstep, did a quick about-turn, caught Fizz by the shoulders, and propelled her back into the gathering shadows. Caught unawares, she went with him, but her furious stare demanded an explanation.

"Fizz," he whispered, bending down to bring his lips close to her ear, "I'm not going in there tonight and I think you should think twice about it also. With that kind of row going on, you're not going to get anything out of anybody and you could end up being asked to leave, which would put an end to your investigations here. Remember, you're dependent on the goodwill of these people. You can't force them to talk to you."

She twitched her shoulder free of his hand, and if anyone can yell in a whisper she did it then. "I don't give a monkey's chunky about talking to them! I'll learn much more from listening to that row!"

She turned purposefully on her heel and was about to take off again, back to the bow window, when a footstep sounded on the gravel behind them and Dodie Galbraith hove into view. He spotted them at the same second, but, as he was about to raise a hand in greeting, the sound of the raised voices reached him and he halted momentarily before resuming his advance.

"Fkn at it again, urr they?"

Buchanan grimaced. "We intended to drop in for a chat, but maybe this isn't the best time. We'll come back later in the week, maybe."

"Aye. Therr's a fkn rammy every time George shows his face around here. Goes on fur hours."

106

"What's it about?" Fizz demanded, clearly miffed at being balked of her eavesdropping.

"Who fkn cares?" was Dodie's opinion. "No' me. Ah've got more tae worry me than Teddy an' that wee shite o' a son o' his. Fancy a drink? Ah'm on ma way up tae the fkn glasshouse fur a wee bevvy an' a wee look at the telly. Kat an' Bremner'll be there. They like their brandy in the evenin'.'"

"N—," said Buchanan just as Fizz said, "Sure, why not?"

So they all strolled across the cropped turf to where the glass-and-wood building was beginning to glow with lamplight in the gloom.

Kat was lounging in one armchair with her feet on another and her old chum Bremner McGrath was crouched on the edge of a couch beside her, reading a magazine. They had a bottle of brandy on the table between them and both of them had tumblers of the stuff, half filled and apparently neat. Neither of them looked wonderfully happy to see Dodie enter, but Kat, at least, brightened at the sight of the other two.

"Well, well, look who's here, Bremner! Visitors!" Her loud, grating voice met them on the doorstep. "Grab a pew, folks. Here, Tam, throw those papers on the floor and park yourself there where I can hear you properly. We didn't expect to see you two tonight. Didn't expect to see you either, Dodie."

"Naw, but therr's a good picture on at hauf nine—*Police Academy III*—an' ah felt like a wee break."

Kat shuddered visibly and gave herself a large injection of brandy, while Bremner buried his nose between the pages of his magazine.

"We were on our way to have a chat to Teddy and Marcia when we realized they had company," Fizz said, in a patent attempt to guide the conversation the way she wanted. "It seemed—"

"Oh, it's only George," said Kat. "He's here two or three times a week, so you wouldn't have been intruding on anything important."

"It sounded like the fkn Ypres salient," Dodie put in, opening a well-stocked cocktail cabinet. "Teddy was doin' his nut this time. Y'could hear him halfway down the track an' he was givin' George hell, ahm tellin' you."

"Dear me." Kat looked as though she were taking this seriously. "I thought, after the last time …"

Her voice trailed away as Dodie offered Fizz and Buchanan their choice of a surprising gantry. Fizz, who had no preferences but would drink anything that would make her stagger, accepted a dry Martini and Buchanan, since he was driving, settled for a dry ginger.

"Oh-ho! Intae the fkn hard stuff?" Dodie sneered, passing Buchanan both bottle and glass. "Mind that disny go tae yir head, now. Terrible stuff, the dry ginger, if yir no used tae it."

Buchanan gave him a flicker of token amusement but wasn't moved to defend his choice. If Dodie was in favor of drink-driving, that was his business.

"It's a pity that Teddy and his son don't get along together," Fizz was saying to the two brandy drinkers, though, as far as Bremner was concerned, she might as well not have spoken.

Kat wafted a deprecatory hand. "It's just a phase. George has to learn to keep an eye on the pennies, that's all. He can't expect to have Teddy and Marcia footing his bills all his life." She removed her large and dirty trainers from the armchair to allow Dodie to seat himself and turned her attention to Buchanan. "So, Tam, have you found your missing picture yet?"

"Not yet," Buchanan smiled. "Actually, it's Fizz's project. I'm just tagging along for the ride."

"Things are progressing," Fizz said, "but slowly. Actually, I wanted to know more about Konrad Schlegel's death, just in case it might have any bearing on the case. That's what I wanted to talk to Teddy and Marcia about."

"Oh dear." Kat looked at Bremner, who lifted his eyes momentarily from his magazine to meet hers. "That's not one of Teddy's favorite subjects, is it, Bremner? And when Teddy gets upset so does Marcia. They never really got over it, you see. The shock of it all. The thought, perhaps, that if they'd realized how deeply depressed he was …"

Fizz waited for a moment to see if Kat was going to continue, but when it became clear that she had fallen into a sort of reverie she said, "What was he depressed about?"

"Nobody wiz buying his fkn stuff," Dodie submitted.

"Actually, there was more to it than that." Kat rearranged the folds of the voluminous caftan-like garment she was wrapped in and glanced at Bremner for support. "He was ill. Marcia told me that he had been diagnosed with multiple sclerosis and his hands were beginning to shake. That's a terrible fate for a painter to suffer. Poor Konrad would know that his painting days were over and he must have felt that he had nothing left to live for."

"I suppose that's why they went off on holiday to Arran," Fizz suggested, helpfully. "I dare say Teddy and Marcia were trying to take Konrad's mind off his troubles. He probably just went to pieces suddenly and threw himself off the rocks."

"It wisnae that sudden," said Dodie, tilting his can of Guinness and giving himself a long, noisy swig. "I heard he wrote to his uncle an' his bank manager and left a letter for Teddy and Marcia and made out his fkn will as well. Y'don't do all that on the spur of the fkn moment, do ye? Naw. Konrad knew what he wiz doin' OK."

"Then he clearly didn't want Teddy and Marcia to stop him," Buchanan said. "If he was so determined to end his life, they have nothing to blame themselves for. It wasn't as if it was simply a cry for help, was it?"

Kat looked at her brandy, the level of which had scarcely dropped at all. "I think they both felt they should have guessed that Konrad was suicidal. They were so very close to him, and had been for so many years. Marcia said to me once that the worst thing about the business was that Konrad had not confided in them. She still feels that there must have been something they could have done to help him."

"They went to art school together, didn't they?" Buchanan remembered. "Were Teddy and Marcia professional artists too?"

"Teddy worked in advertising for a while when they were first married and I believe Marcia was in teaching for quite a few years, but neither of them was in Konrad's class as a painter. I'm not sure when Teddy became Konrad's agent, but it was certainly quite a few years before his death."

Kat looked invitingly at Bremner, who had put down his magazine and was, at least, listening to the conversation if not actually contributing anything to it, but he only shook his head to indicate that he had no information to offer. He didn't look particularly shy to Buchanan; just, perhaps, a little unsociable. Maybe he was one of those rare people who chose not to speak unless he had something to say.

For whatever reason, he surrounded himself with an impenetrable screen of reticence that even Fizz, who was not widely noted for her intuitive regard for another's privacy, apparently felt unwilling to broach. He looked at nobody directly and gave no sign of interest in what was being discussed and, while the others were being so forthcoming, there was no necessity to quiz him.

"Did they live here in Lamancha at that time?" Fizz asked.

"No, no. Teddy didn't buy this place till after Konrad's death," Kat said. "They used to have a place in Cornwall. St. Ives."

"Right cozy wee setup they had goin', so ah hear," Dodie grinned. When he did so, his leathery cheeks folded vertically in the middle, making his expression one of malevolence rather than amusement. "The three uf them shacked up thegither for years in this fkn dump of a place that used tae be a lighthouse. Miles from anywhere. All uf Schlegel's best stuff wiz done there—only time he ever got his act thegither, 'f ye ask me. That's where he did aw the seascapes an' the rainstorms that are sellin' now."

"That's true," Kat agreed. "Konrad really developed during those years. He had Teddy to thank for it, of course. Teddy knew that what Konrad needed was solitude. He needed to be focused in on himself for a time so that he could come to know himself properly and know what it was he needed to communicate in his art." Kat set down her glass and turned her head to look at Fizz and Buchanan. In the lamplight, her strong profile was like that of an American Indian. "Solitude worked for Konrad and, to a lesser extent, it worked for Teddy and Marcia too. It was a wonderfully creative period for all three of them. That's why they became set on providing a place like this for other committed artists."

"They fkn charge plenty fur the privilege while they're at it, though, don't they, Kat? If it wisnae fur what they skin aff their committed artists, they widnae be living like Lord and Lady Muck like they do here. The stuff Teddy's turning out these days isnae worth a shite. Nor Marcia either."

"Dodie," said Bremner McGrath quietly, making both Buchanan and Fizz twitch with surprise. "Mind your mouth."

Dodie, for a second, seemed ready to make some sort of retaliation to this rebuke, but in the end he did nothing but make a bored face and roll himself one of his spindly cigarettes.

"You must have known Teddy and Marcia a long time." Fizz leaned over so that Bremner had to meet her eye before he could retreat behind his magazine. "Did you know Konrad Schlegel as well?"

In the silence before Bremner answered, Buchanan distinctly heard voices coming from the farmhouse. As he glanced out of the window, a door slammed and George came bounding down the steps and strode toward a white Ford Escort that was parked by the near side of the drive. He was tall and bushy-haired like his father and, as he glanced up at the windows of the garden room, his expression was visibly surly. Apparently, he and Teddy had not parted friends.

"No, Miss Fitzpatrick, I did not know Konrad Schlegel," Bremner said, eventually, having considered the question in all its aspects for several seconds. His manner was nitpickingly precise, like that of an Oxford don as played by Alan Bennett, but his tone was caustic to the point of rudeness. "My connection with Teddy and Marcia dates from the inception of the Lochmore Foundation. Konrad Schlegel, as Kat has already made clear to you, died before this place came into being."

"Well, of course, I realized that," Fizz retaliated, smiling with suspect benevolence while regarding him like the fond mother of a retarded child. "I should have made it clearer that what I was actually asking was whether you had met Konrad Schlegel *before* his suicide. But now I know. Thank you."

Their eyes clashed, momentarily, with the force of two colliding lorries. Bremner knew he had been slapped down and made to look like a carping old grouch and he didn't like it.

"We should be going," Buchanan said quickly. He got up, lest Fizz should give him any argument, but the action gave him a view across the grass to the farmhouse and there came Teddy, striding toward the garden room.

"I saw your car in the car park," he said, rushing in and shaking hands with both of them, all hair and friendliness like a somewhat larger version of one of his sausage dogs. "Did you want to see me? Have our friends been looking after you? You've had something to drink?"

He beamed fondly at Fizz, stooping over her chair as though he would have liked to pinch her cheek. Fizz twinkled at him pertly.

"We've had a lovely time, just sitting here chatting and tippling. Actually, Buchanan was about to drag me away."

"No, no. We can't have that, Tam. You have time for another drink, surely?" He lowered his thick body onto the couch beside Bremner. "And, you wanted to talk to me, surely, Fizz? Is there news about the picture, or is it more information you need from me?"

"There's no news, I'm afraid," Fizz answered, as Buchanan sat down again. "And there's nothing really urgent I had to get from you, only we were passing by—Buchanan was giving me a driving lesson—so we thought we'd pop in just to keep in touch."

Her eyes, meeting Buchanan's in a fleeting glance, held an expression of virtue quite at odds with the lies that were tripping so blithely off her tongue.

"We did wonder, though," she went on, "if you would let us see some of Konrad Schlegel's paintings."

Buchanan wasn't too happy at being included in this request. He said, "Of course, we could come back another time if you'd prefer ..."

"Not at all," Teddy waved this suggestion away with both hands. "You're only too welcome. They view better in daylight, of course, but in fact I took out some of Konrad's Black Forest work this morning and hung it in the gallery in case it might be of interest to you. I'll be delighted to show it to you."

He led the way across to the farmhouse, talking animatedly about Schlegel and apologizing for Marcia who had gone early to bed, and ushered them down a short, paneled hallway into a locked room at the rear of the house. As he snapped on the light switch, a couple of dozen spotlights blinked on, each one illuminating an individual picture, the back glow casting barely enough light to show the stacked canvases tilted against the lower walls.

Teddy, with a sweep of his hand reminiscent of St. Peter opening the pearly gates, invited them to partake of the cultural treat awaiting them. He had the sense to leave them to it, at least for a first perusal, and contented himself with standing back in the shadows in a reverent silence.

Buchanan, as always in such situations—and Janine had, in her time, subjected him to quite a few—was embarrassingly unimpressed. He had never learned to appreciate anything other than old masters or the occasional deliberate attack on his senses like Picasso's *Guernica*, and Schlegel's work left him cold. The paintings were, without exception, either seascapes or landscapes and, while the roiling clouds and sheets of rain were well executed, as far as he was able to judge, the scenery was fairly run of the mill. When you've seen one mountain range, was his feeling on the matter, you've seen them all.

Fizz, on the other hand, was apparently enchanted. Buchanan could hear her making soft, unconscious sounds of approval as she moved from canvas to canvas. She leaned close to inspect the brushwork, she stepped back to gaze reverently at the whole. Finally, she said, "But these are surely major works, Teddy? Why have I not heard of Konrad Schlegel before?"

Teddy almost lit up the shadowy room. He opened his arms as though he would have clasped her to his bosom, and said, "Konrad's hour will come, Fizz. Already, in Germany, his early work is beginning to attract buyers from some of the major galleries. With careful management, we will see the same reaction all over the world. But these things take time."

Buchanan felt it incumbent upon him to make appreciative noises, but he was profoundly relieved when Teddy finally ended a second tour of the exhibits, this time with explanatory notes, and let them go.

"God," he said to Fizz as they drove away, "I thought he was going to make us sit a test on 'Konrad Schlegel: the man and his works.' What a bore."

"Damn tootin'," Fizz agreed, somewhat surprisingly, and yawned without covering her mouth. "But it was interesting to see the paintings of the Schluchsee. He has one landscape there that

113

must show almost the same scene that's in Frau Richter's photo-graph."

Buchanan glanced round at her curiously.

"But you enjoyed seeing the collection. You said they were major works."

Fizz gave him a look.

"Bollocks," she said, and yawned again.

# Chapter Eleven

Interesting though her second visit to the Lochmore Foundation had proved to be, Fizz had to admit to herself that, in fact, it had produced very little in the way of actual evidence. The fact that Teddy's relationship with his son was going through a bad patch was scarcely riveting, and trying to investigate the Marriner/Schlegel *ménage à trois* in Cornwall was unlikely to prove worth the effort.

However, there was still one lead that might yield something before Frau Richter ran out of patience. Phillip Ure, the art dealer who had bought the missing picture originally, had got it at a weekly auction in Comrie, a small town about an hour and a half's drive away. There was just a possibility that the auctioneer might know who had offered the painting for auction and, if so, that person could know something that would take the inquiry a stage further.

A phone call to Phillip on Wednesday morning elicited the information that the next auction was only two days away, which was fortunate but, from there on, it appeared that Fizz was going to have to make her own luck. Phillip wasn't going to the auction, so there was no chance of scrounging a lift from him, and, according to his desk diary, Buchanan was going to be in court with a client all day, so he was no use to her either.

That left public transport, which would take hours, or Dennis, to whom she definitely did not want to be beholden. Dennis would be doing her a very big favor if he took time off during business hours to drive her to Comrie—a favor that he would expect to be repaid in only one coinage—and, while Fizz would not hesitate to disappoint him, if it came to the bit, she preferred not to welch on any agreement, even an unspoken one. In her experience it rarely paid to do so, and in spite of what Buchanan claimed to believe, she did have a conscience, even if she didn't always use it.

By Thursday evening, she had still not solved her transport problems and they were weighing on her mind to some degree while she ate the courgette flower and tomato orzotto that Johnnyboy had concocted for her evening meal.

"Don't take your time with it, sweetie, will you? You know what Gloria's like about staff dinners. She's gone upstairs for a lie-down before dinner, but she could be back down again at any second. She's been up and down all day like a whore's drawers, that woman, checking up on everybody. Rosemary says she's been hanging around the reception desk, reading the register, asking about new arrivals, driving everybody barmy. And *Frazer!*" Johnnyboy lifted his shoulders and rolled his eyes ceilingward. "The man's seriously deranged!"

"What's he been up to?" Fizz asked between mouthfuls.

"Sweetie! I can't begin to tell you! *Lurking*, basically. Lurking about the back kitchens and the storeroom, lurking in the vegetable garden—Jason nearly fell over him when he went out for a lettuce a minute ago. *Looooomed* out at him from behind the compost heap, he did! Jace, I said, this is taking care in the community too far, I said. One nutter about the place is bad enough; *two*, my pet, is just too depressing! They'll be chasing him with butterfly nets next and where will that leave us? Up the Jobcentre, that's where."

"What's behind it all, do you think?" Fizz asked, making conversation while she scraped the last crumb from her plate.

"Well, sweetie, I'll tell you this, there was none of this irrational behavior before that old German chappie checked in. I was just saying to Jason, things have been going from bad to worse all week." He took Fizz's plate and tilted it to see the light flash on its shiny surface. "Looks like you could manage a little more, am I right?"

"If there's plenty, Johnnyboy, you sweet thing!"

"I don't know where you put it, love, but I certainly wouldn't like to be in a plane crash in the Andes with you, that's for sure!"

A sudden thought occurred to Fizz as she watched him serve her second helping.

"Johnnyboy ... you're off duty between lunchtime and dinnertime, aren't you?"

"If I'm lucky. Sometimes we're still serving at half past two and I'm supposed to be back in my kitchen by five thirty. Why do you ask?"

"Just wondered." Fizz ate a little orzotto and pursued her line of thought while Johnnyboy watched her with amused curiosity.

"What's going on in that curly little head, I wonder?"

Fizz smiled at him, wondering whether she'd just had a bright idea or not. His spots appeared particularly colorful today and, while she tried to think, a small, independent part of her brain kept trying to join them up like a dot-to-dot picture.

"I wonder if you'd do something really generous for me, Johnnyboy?"

"As long as it's not too kinky, sweetie."

"If you're not doing anything tomorrow afternoon, how would you like to view a des res with all mod cons in Comrie?"

Johnnyboy leaned backward from the hips and spread a delicate hand across the base of his throat. "*Moi?* Why on earth would I want a house in Comrie? I'd rather be swallowed by a whale! *Comrie*, for goodness' sake! Sweetie, there isn't even a Body Shop in Comrie! Besides, if there's money involved—any money at all—I'm not even in the frame!"

"No money involved. Just a nice run in my boss's flashy car, a quick dash round Comrie auction, and back home again. We might be able to lean on him for a drink on the way, but mainly, you'd be doing me a favor."

"Doing you a favor?" Johnnyboy looked at the kitchen spoon he was holding as though for clarification. "Just run that past me again, would you, pet? You want me to buy a house—"

"No, you don't need to buy it, just look at it. I need a lift to Comrie tomorrow afternoon. I have to drop in at the auction— just for quarter of an hour max—and the only way I can get there is for somebody to ask to view one of our properties in Comrie. We only have one, as far as I can remember, but I need you to pretend you're interested in it."

Johnnyboy opened the fridge and toyed absently with some nameless cuts of meat that were marinading on the shelf. "I don't know, sweetie, you see—"

117

"It's important to me, Johnnyboy, or I wouldn't ask."

"When you say 'boss,' are you referring to that nice Tam Buchanan?"

Fizz hesitated to blight what was clearly a fervent hope. "I'm afraid Buchanan doesn't deal with the real estate side of the business—which is just as well because he'd know you were a friend of mine and smell a rat. But Dennis is a nice guy too. A bit of a smoothie but a lot easier to bamboozle than Buchanan. Go on, Johnnyboy, it'll be a laugh."

Things were starting to hot up in the kitchen. The first of the diners were beginning to filter into the dining room and both Johnnyboy and Jason were completing their last minute preparations like actors waiting for their cues.

"What, exactly, would you want me to do?" said Johnnyboy, turning the gas up under the consommé.

"Virtually nothing. Just phone up and ask to see the property in Comrie. I'll give you all the details. Then all you have to do is turn up and be treated like a VIP. At the end of the day, you can say you'll think about it and simply disappear. No hassle."

"And what are you going to get up to at this auction you mentioned? Nothing illegal, I hope?"

"No, honestly, Johnnyboy. I just have to speak to somebody. Won't take ten minutes. I may have to get *you* to suggest stopping for a drink or something so that I can pop out and attend to my personal agenda, but that's the worst I'll ask of you. Promise."

"Well ... I'll see, sweetie. Ask me later."

Fizz left it at that for the moment, fairly confident that her transport problems were solved, and went to take over from Rosemary at the reception desk.

Rosemary was dealing with an irate guest who couldn't get his shower to work properly and, since it was still only five to six, at which time she went off duty, she opted to accompany the guy back to his room to see if he had been operating it properly.

No sooner had the lift doors closed behind them than Frazer appeared through the swing doors with his eyes popping out of his head.

"I heard raised voices, Fizz," he claimed, staring round the reception area as if he expected to find a battle in progress. "A man's voice. Who was it? Have you been having trouble?"

Fizz looked at him severely, not bothering to hide the fact that she thought he was overreacting. "No, of course not. Just one of the Japanese party who's unfamiliar with Western plumbing. He was a bit mad because he'd got himself undressed to have a shower and then had to dress again to come down and complain. Rosemary has gone up to sort him out."

"Oh ... that's all right, then. Just as long as ..." His voice died away and he stiffened as the doors swung open to admit a couple of guests.

Fizz followed his eyes, experiencing a small frisson of alarm as she did so, but it was only two more of the Japanese party, who went on through to the lounge without stopping. She turned to Frazer and looked him in the eye.

"You're not expecting trouble from anybody, are you, Mr. Renton? Because, if so, I think I should know about it, don't you?"

She saw the white of his eye as his pupils swiveled in her direction. "Trouble? No, no. Of course not. I just thought I heard something, that's all." He edged back toward the swing doors as he spoke. "I'll be checking the cold store, if you're looking for me."

Fizz watched him go with amazement. Those doors led only to the kitchen/storage area, which meant that Frazer must have been *lurking* in the store the whole time she was eating her dinner. Johnnyboy was right. The place *was* turning into a madhouse.

When Johnnyboy arrived at the office the following afternoon, work ground suddenly to a halt. The bleep and rattle of computers ceased in mid-word and the reception area became a crossroads for people who had no business to be passing through at the time of day.

Even Fizz, who was, to some degree, prepared for her confederate's panache, was awed by the exquisite thundercloud-gray suit, mint-green shirt, and chunky gold bracelet. There was a dusting of greenish shadow on Johnnyboy's eyelids and his bald head drew the eyes like a single buttock.

"Is that real?" she whispered, eyeing the bracelet as they waited for Dennis to unlock his car.

"Well, if it isn't, my love, I was stung for one pound fifty," Johnnyboy replied without moving his lips. He swiveled his kitten hips on to the passenger seat beside Dennis, leaving Fizz alone and palely languishing on the back seat.

From that point onward, Johnnyboy held the floor, elaborating on what he wanted from a home of his own and expounding on his personal preferences as to interior decorating. Dennis could do little but make polite rejoinders, but his face in the driving mirror when being instructed on how to tent a bedroom ceiling really made Fizz's day.

"Oh dear me, it *is* just a teeny bit smaller than I had imagined," was Johnnyboy's first impression of the cottage. "I mean, one thinks—four bedrooms—and one gets a picture of ... well, of a certain *size*, if you follow me. I do hope this isn't a disappointment to you in any way, but, frankly, I think I might feel a teensie bit cramped in here."

Fizz sent him a pointed look. It was rather soon to be backing off: they still needed Dennis to believe it was worthwhile wasting time in Comrie. "Wait till you've seen inside," she said firmly, leading the way up the winding path to the front door. "It's bigger than it looks and I think you'll find it would offer wonderful scope for some of your artistic decorating ideas."

"Well, dear, if you have the time so have I, but, frankly, it's so much smaller than it looked in the photograph."

Dennis gave him the grand tour, dutifully pointing out the double-glazing and the fitted kitchen but, clearly, his heart wasn't in it and Johnnyboy gave him no help. Every time she had the chance, Fizz glared her frustration at her accomplice, but he made her work for every concession.

"What about this sloping ceiling?" she demanded. "Can't you just see it tented in pink satin, the way you described on the way here?"

"Not in satin, dear," said Johnnyboy, shocked by the suggestion. "In *this* cottage? Dear me, no. *Much* too rustic for satin. Cheese-cloth, now, or even a nice sprigged muslin if you could get it in cream." Turning his back on Dennis, he dropped Fizz a slow wink. "Yes, I see what you mean, dear. With the right treatment, this room could look almost pretty. Pity the window is so small and deeply set."

"Perhaps if you were to line the window recess with mirror tiles ..." Fizz suggested, annoyed at having to work harder than she'd done with the Wainwrights.

"Now *that*," said Johnnyboy, turning to Dennis, "is an excellent idea. My word, what a creative young lady! She has certainly opened my eyes to this charming little house. Perhaps I was a little hasty in writing it off so quickly. Just let me look at the lounge again; perhaps it could be improved."

Dennis brightened visibly and beckoned Fizz to follow as he ushered Johnnyboy back downstairs. "Miss Fitzpatrick is one of our brightest employees," he claimed, flashing her one of his whiter than white smiles. "She has quite a knack for spotting the potential of unique properties like this one; properties whose charm and character have been, perhaps, degraded by a series of careless owners."

"Exactly," Johnnyboy agreed, looking about him with enthusiastically feigned interest. "Actually, this place is rather quaint—or could be with a little work. I'm rather glad I decided to look at it."

It was quite apparent that he was beginning to enjoy himself enormously, half-believing that he could be genuinely interested in buying the house, and seeing himself giving full rein to his originality in its furbishment. Which was all very well, except that Fizz's hidden agenda had its own time scale and the auction sale had started three-quarters of an hour ago.

Finally, her imperative winding-up signals got through to Johnnyboy and he allowed himself to be persuaded back into the car. Dennis was apparently heartened by renewed optimism. He launched into a lecture about the tax advantages of taking out a mortgage and was outlining one particularly favorable deal when Fizz suddenly spotted the village hall, where she knew the auction was being held. Accordingly, she poked Johnnyboy in the spine and he, responding to his well-rehearsed cue, said, "Forgive me for interrupting you, Dennis my dear, but my brain is simply not working today. All these facts and figures may be your bread and

121

butter, but they're quite indigestible to me. Why don't we stop somewhere for a coffee or something and you can explain it all to me slowly."

"Certainly," said Dennis, braking reflexively. "Or, you might prefer to wait till we get back to the office and I can show you the literature."

"Well, to be honest, dear, there's also the tiny matter of a call of nature."

"Oh, right. What about this place ... they appear to do afternoon teas."

Fizz was able to give Johnnyboy a quick thumbs-up sign before walking round the car to where Dennis was getting out.

"Dennis ... it's OK if I slip away for ten minutes, I hope? I think we passed a chemist's shop just down the road."

To Dennis, as to most young men of Fizz's acquaintance, the mention of a chemist's shop implied all sorts of private feminine functions, the names of which were never to be spoken aloud, so there was no problem with awkward questions.

"Sure. Take your time. We'll only be discussing financial matters, so it would be a bore for you anyway."

"Thanks. Won't be long."

It took only seconds to sprint back down the road to the village hall but, once there, it wasn't so easy to find anyone from the firm of auctioneers with time to talk to her. Finally, one of the porters, responding to her urgent pleas, told her to hang on for a minute and he'd find someone who could answer her questions.

There was such a press of humanity around the auctioneer that Fizz was squashed into a corner, her shoulder against a tall glass showcase full of vases and small ornaments. Among these, one tiny flagon stood out like a beacon: exquisitely shaped, delicately fluted, and finished with a dull blue glaze that held Fizz totally mesmerized. It reminded her of a perfume bottle she'd seen in the Topkapi collection in Istanbul some years back and which she'd never forgotten. It didn't occur to her to want to possess it—her years of carrying all she owned on her back had made her something of a minimalist—but she could see that, if it went to the right bidder, it would give pleasure for years to come.

When she heard herself addressed by the returned porter, she took a moment to readjust to her surroundings.

"I found Mr. Adamson," the porter said, raising his voice above the chant of the auctioneer. "If you'd like to follow me ... it's a bit quieter round the other side. Not so crowded anyway."

They wove their way through the crowd and ended up behind the auctioneer's platform, where there was little activity other than the purposeful to-ing and fro-ing of porters and young ladies with clipboards.

Mr. Adamson was a tall, elegant man in his early seventies, smoking a briar pipe and writing busily in a thick ledger. He rose from his table and shook hands as Fizz introduced herself.

"And, you are in need of some information, I understand?"

"Yes, I need to know the background of a picture that has disappeared," Fizz said, aware that her period of leave of absence was fast expiring. "I've traced it back as far as this auction room, where it was sold at the first sale in August, and now I would like to know who put it up for auction."

"Ah." Mr. Adamson stuck the stem of his pipe between his molars and grinned around it. "Not easy."

"You don't keep a record of buyers and sellers?"

"Oh, indeed we do." His eyes flicked sideways at the ledger. "But a certain discretion is paramount in this business, Miss Fitzpatrick. We don't give out names of sellers on request, you know. Oh, if it's a police matter ... a matter of stolen goods ... that sort of thing, then of course we are happy to cooperate, but normally, no, I'm afraid I couldn't do that."

"I see." Fizz nibbled the inside of her lower lip. She was not as concerned as she would have been if he had told her he didn't keep records, but she clearly had to re-think her approach. Charming as he was, Mr. Adamson was nobody's fool. He had a firm and steely glint to his eye and it was obvious to Fizz, who had made a lifetime study of the art of persuasion, that he was simply not going to be sympathetic to just any tale of woe. The sad fact was that some people had a gullibility gene and some were born without. Mr. Adamson, she suspected, was one of the latter.

123

Behind her, the auctioneer droned, "Seven pounds. Eight. Do I hear eight-fifty? Thank you sir, eight pounds fifty ..."

"In that case," she said finally, "I may have to go to the police, but I know our client would prefer not to: that's why she engaged a firm of solicitors to make the inquiries."

Mr. Adamson looked at the Buchanan & Stewart business card that Fizz had given him, but showed no sign of being impressed.

Fizz re-slung her shoulder bag and pretended to be about to leave. "Just to save time," she said, "could we establish that you do have the name on file? No point in my going through all the proper channels only to find he didn't give a name."

"Oh, he'd give a name all right." Mr. Adamson leaned over his desk and opened the ledger but kept his shoulder between Fizz and the page. "Everyone gives a name. The first auction in August, you said?"

Fizz stepped back a little as though to give him privacy. If he thought she was likely to lean over his shoulder to see the name, he wouldn't relax enough to give her the opportunity of a quick glance.

She heard the auctioneer say, "One-twenty-five. One-fifty. One-fifty. One-fifty. Do I hear one-seventy-five? Come on, ladies and gentlemen, this charming little piece is worth a great deal more than one-fifty."

Momentarily distracted, she turned her head and was amazed to see that the item currently under auction was the darling little blue flagon, the magical, hypnotically beautiful object of desire that had quite made her afternoon. She couldn't believe that, even in a cultural backwater like Comrie, the auctioneer was having difficulty in squeezing a paltry amount like one pound seventy-five out of his purblind bidders. For less than the price of a beer, they could have something that would enhance their lives and they were too obtuse to take it!

Without consciously thinking about it—without even a word to Mr. Adamson, who was running his finger down a page—she waved an imperious hand at the auctioneer and thrilled with relief when he acknowledged her.

"One seventy-five, on my left. Thank you, miss. One-seventy-five, ladies and gentlemen, for this most superb piece. Who'll give me two hundred?"

The words took two seconds to penetrate Fizz's consciousness, then the air burst out of her lungs with a sound like a death rattle. She could neither speak nor move but stood there paralyzed by shock while every drop of blood in her body, so it seemed, drained from her veins, leaving her in a state of corpselike semi-consciousness.

"One-seventy-five I'm bid, ladies and gentlemen, for an authentic Paul Leroux piece. Surely I hear two hundred?" The auctioneer paused, looking sternly around the audience, while Fizz watched helplessly, too dazed even to hope for another bid. "I have one hundred and seventy-five pounds, on my left. One hundred and seventy-five. Dear me. This piece would easily make double in Edinburgh, ladies and gentlemen. Surely, I hear two hundred? No? Then it's one hundred and seventy-five ..." Finally it came. "Two hundred? Thank you, sir. Two hundred at the back of the hall."

Sight returned slowly to Fizz's eyes and she saw Mr. Adamson staring at her in consternation. "Dear me, you don't look well at all, miss. You'd better sit down before you fall down."

He grabbed the chair he'd been sitting in and swung it round under Fizz's bottom as her knees gave way.

"It's the heat," he said, beckoning a porter with a sort of angry impatience. "Far too many people in here today. I should have done something about it earlier. Tony, run and get this lady a glass of water; she's been taken faint."

Fizz, meantime, was recovering fast. The initial shock had passed and she was able to perceive that it was unlikely she could have been made to fork out one hundred and seventy-five pounds, even if there had been no other bid. Particularly since she didn't have it. But what had an even more therapeutic effect was the discovery that, with her forehead propped on her hand like this, and her elbow on the desk, she could read the open page of the ledger.

She could scarcely believe her luck. She could have tried to fake a dizzy turn, but she'd have had to be pretty damn good to fool a sharp cookie like Mr. Adamson. However, there was no doubt that he was quite alarmed by her sudden pallor and very evident

125

distress. Moaning a little in reply to his commiserations, she quickly scanned the columns for the words "oil painting."

And there it was: "Oil painting, 16 × 22, cottage garden, unsigned. £60.00." Below this entry were listed three or four other items that had apparently been offered for sale in the same lot, but before she could find the name associated with the goods a hand fell on her shoulder.

"Here you are, miss. Drink this and you'll feel better."

Fizz groaned a bit more and tried to line up the list of items with the column of names beside it. She didn't dare turn her head to the side but had to swivel her eyes to focus on the barely legible handwriting. The hand pressed firmly on her shoulder, assisting her to straighten, and she had no choice but to lift her head.

"That's the way," said Mr. Adamson encouragingly. "There's a wee bit more color in your cheeks now. Dear me, you gave me quite a fright there."

Fizz sipped the water and tried to look as if she might have a sudden relapse, but before she could droop over the desk again Mr. Adamson pushed the book aside and, picking up a sale catalog that had been underneath it, began fanning her with quite embarrassing solicitude. That effectively put an end to her snooping, so she had little choice but to effect a miraculous recovery and sprint back along the High Street to where she had left the others.

It was disappointing to have made so little headway, especially after all the trouble she'd gone to, but on the drive back to Edinburgh she had leisure to assess the small amount of information she had been able to glean and it seemed that, just possibly, it wasn't as sterile as it had at first appeared.

# Chapter Twelve

Buchanan woke up with a premonition that his Saturday morning was going to be, once again, disrupted by a visit from Fizz, but, because he didn't believe in premonitions, he did nothing about tidying up the flat, so the place looked like a pigsty when the doorbell rang about eleven o'clock.

Fizz ignored the mess, merely sweeping a pile of discarded clothing onto the floor before throwing herself on the tortured couch. Buchanan watched her unlace her Docs, sighed, then went and made the tea.

"Letter from Frau Richter," Fizz said when she'd dealt with her immediate nutritional needs. "Came this morning."

"What's she saying? Anything of interest?"

"Nothing much. She's pleased with the effort I'm putting into the investigation. Check enclosed. Also some snapshots of the place where she and Herr Krefeld used to live way back before the war. A lake called the Schluchsee in the Black Forest."

She passed across a thin sheaf of photographs in a paper folder. Most of them showed small groups of adults and children against a background of mountains. The lake, from different angles, featured in them all, but the grainy black and white processing left much of the scenic beauty of the area to the imagination. They were, quite patently, snapshots of people, not of scenery, and had been focused accordingly.

"I take it she wants you to find out if the lake was the setting of her brother's painting?"

"Yes." Fizz fingered the neat knot of hair she had achieved at the back of her head and several strands sprang aggressively loose to dangle around her ears. "I don't suppose it will further the investigation any, but it appears to be important to her to have her assumptions confirmed. At least it proves that what she said about her brother's phone call was true."

"Well, I think we assumed that anyway," Buchanan said, stroking Selena, who had draped herself across his knees like a travel rug. "You've proved that he bought a picture and you've proved he had it valued. What you have yet to establish is that he still had it in his possession at the time of his death. At the moment, it's quite possible that he left it somewhere to be valued and it's still there, waiting for him to pick it up."

Fizz did a sort of Elvis Presley lip curl. "I thought of that, of course, and I phoned every dealer in the Edinburgh phone book, but nobody admitted to having it." She succumbed to the allure of a biscuit and nibbled it thoughtfully. "It's not really likely, anyway, is it? I mean, he was due to leave Edinburgh quite early the following morning, so he'd have been seriously pushed for time if he had to pick up the picture before he set off. No, I'll lay you ten to one he was killed for it."

"Not according to the post mortem," Buchanan pointed out. "Senile myocardial degeneration, it said on the death certificate. You can't inflict that on a victim."

Fizz's bleached denim eyes rested on him speculatively for a second as though she were about to ask how he was able to be so specific, but she said only, "Senile what?"

"Senile myocardial degeneration. It means his heart was worn out due to his age."

Fizz dismissed this explanation with. a wave of her biscuit. "That's just what they say when there's no obvious sign of death in an old person. All it means is, his heart stopped beating which, at his age, was not abnormal. It's a way of saying he died of old age."

She knew quite well she hadn't a leg to stand on but, obviously, she wanted to think she was investigating a murder rather than just a matter of lost property.

"Well, if it wasn't senile myocardial degeneration," he said reasonably, "it must have been something else, and *that* was bound to show up in the post mortem. You have a theory about that, I suppose?"

She made an unconvincing attempt to look confident. "I'm working on it."

Buchanan glanced at the clock. He had arranged to have lunch at the clubhouse with a rather charming young divorcée rejoicing in the name of Carlotta. She was the sister of a GP who was one of the regular Saturday foursome and who had brought her along the week before, and she fitted Buchanan's blueprint of the ideal woman to a T. There was still plenty of time to get to the golf course, but getting rid of Fizz was never a fast process.

"Well, I'm just dashing out to the golf course," he said, whipping the tray away before she could start eating again. "So, if that's all the news ..."

"Oh, good," she said, a trifle disconcertingly. "I was hoping you'd be heading out that way. You can give me a lift."

"Where to?" asked Buchanan warily.

"Home, of course. You will be going along the High Street, won't you?"

She knew damn well that he didn't usually take that route but, in point of fact, there was nothing—except his own irrational reluctance—to prevent his doing so. He hated to submit to the superstition—and it *was* only superstition—that Fizz acted as some kind of unconscious jinx on his social life, but it was a proven fact that at least four recent friendships had fallen by the wayside after Fizz had entered the frame. It seemed, sometimes, that he had only to mention a girlfriend to her in passing for the budding relationship to come rapidly unstuck, and usually for the most ridiculous reason. He knew he was being silly, of course, but there was no need to mention Carlotta anyway.

"All right, as long as we don't waste any time. I have a lunch appointment at one thirty."

Fizz opened her eyes a notch and he was sure, just for a moment, that she was going to ask who he was meeting. Wiser counsels prevailed, however, and she just nodded and bent to tie her laces.

She sat quietly reading his *Financial Times* with a worried expression on her face till he got changed and then followed him downstairs to the car without saying very much. The lunchtime traffic was no worse than usual, so it was still only twenty to twelve when they reached the High Street.

"Tell you what," Fizz said, out of a long silence. "I'll just stop at Phillip Ure's shop and show him these photographs. It's just round the corner at the foot of Blackfriars Street."

Buchanan was happy to comply. Parking in Blackfriars Street was marginally easier than finding a place in the High Street, especially on a Saturday.

"I don't know about this Phillip Ure," Fizz confided as he backed into a "Resident's Only" parking spot. "I know he *said* he bought the painting at auction, and he seemed very straightforward when he was telling me about cleaning and restoring it and all that stuff but—I don't know, I keep getting this funny feeling about him."

Buchanan looked at her with interest. "Well, we may have swallowed everything he said a bit too readily because he put you on the Lamancha trail but, when you think about it, that hasn't exactly been wildly profitable so far, has it?"

"No, that's what I mean," Fizz nodded, puckering her brow. "I'm beginning to wonder if he handed us a red herring to keep us from looking too closely at his own part in the scenario. And also, who knows whether he was lying when he said he got the picture at an auction? There may have been a middle man."

"That's something you could check."

"Mmm. I've tried sussing out the auction situation, but the auctioneers aren't giving anything away. Tight as a duck's arse, the guy I spoke to. Maybe I'm just imagining things. I don't know. But there's just something about Phillip Ure that rings a bell somewhere. If you met him, you'd know what I mean."

Buchanan looked at his watch. He had at least twenty minutes to spare. "I've got a couple of minutes," he said. "I shouldn't leave the car here, but I don't mind chancing it if you want me to come in with you and take a look at him."

The idea appeared to strike Fizz as a good one. "If you're sure it won't make you late for your appointment."

Even as he locked the car, Buchanan was regretting giving way to his curiosity. It wasn't even his case, dammit, so why was he so keen to have had a hand in it? Who was he hoping to impress with his talent for character assessment? Fizz, for God's sake?

The shop was tiny and badly lit and smelled of linseed oil and mothballs and beeswax, and of chrysanthemums, a tall vase of which flanked the doorway. Much of the free space was crammed with tables and dressers and bookcases and every flat surface was piled with old books, pictures, bric-a-brac, old linens and laces, and a wealth of total junk. As the door closed behind them, an orchestra of clocks chimed the three-quarters.

"Hi," said Fizz to the young man who was lounging in a wing chair reading a book.

He looked up and smiled, sliding a pair of reading glasses down his nose and squinting over the frames. He had a thin, intelligent-looking face and wispy black hair over a narrow head.

"Oh, it's you again. Hi. How's the investigation going?"

"Not wonderfully," Fizz admitted, and indicated Buchanan. "This is Tam Buchanan. He's helping me."

Buchanan shook hands, looking for signs of shiftiness or unease, but was disappointed. Phillip appeared genuinely pleased to have someone break the monotony of his day.

"I got these photographs this morning from Herr Krefeld's sister," Fizz said, opening the folder and laying the snapshots, one by one, on the chest of drawers at Phillip's elbow. "She thinks the picture her brother bought might have been painted around this area and she wondered if you might recognize the lake or perhaps these mountains in the background. It's the Schluchsee in the Black Forest."

Phillip slipped his glasses back into place and leaned over the picture, taking his time with each of them in turn. "I think … yes, I'm sure it's the same area. These mountains look …" He picked one up by the corner and nodded positively. "Yep. This is definitely the same place. This one is taken from exactly the same angle as the painting. Well, more or less. The beach, the jagged ridge beyond, this rocky escarpment at the side. Yes, I think I could swear to it that this is almost the exact scene, apart from the clouds and … I seem to remember the artist had included a group of dark rocks—probably for contrast—and I don't think those trees were included, but if you ignore the artistic license it's identical."

He was clearly happy to have been of help. There was absolutely no reticence in the way he spoke and the way he met Fizz's eyes showed he had nothing to hide. Buchanan felt he had seen enough and since he had already been illegally parked for five minutes there was no point in pushing his luck. He was about to excuse himself when he heard Fizz say, "It occurred to me that when you bought the picture at the auction there might have been other items in the same lot. Do you happen to remember if there were?"

This struck Buchanan as an interesting piece of lateral thinking on Fizz's part and he paused to hear Phillip's reply.

"Actually, yes, there were one or two other things. Let's see ..." He pushed down his spectacle frames again and his dark eyes scanned the cluttered table tops. "That old hand mirror came with the picture. And the photograph in the silver frame—well, it's silver plated, actually. So's the bottle opener, it was part of the lot, and so was the racing trophy beside it. None of it of particular interest to collectors but, considering what I got for the painting, it was quite a bargain lot."

Fizz was subjecting the racing trophy to a close examination, but Buchanan was more interested in the bottle opener. "How much is this?" he asked Phillip.

"A fiver. Like I said, it's only silver plated."

Buchanan was aware of Fizz's curiosity as he fished a fiver out of his wallet. As an objet d'art the bottle opener was unlikely to appeal to her any more than it appealed to him, but he rather thought its interest might outweigh its lack of charm. It might be purely coincidental that Andrew and Jean Samuel had lost a silver bottle opener recently, but it was certainly something that should be checked.

"I have to go now," he told Fizz. "I'll talk to you on Monday."

If he told her about his suspicions right now, he would find himself taxiing her down to Lamancha tomorrow, and he had other plans for his Sunday—or would have if today's luncheon was the success he hoped for.

Fizz lifted a finger, holding his eye with her own. "Just give me a second, OK? I need to have a word with you before you disappear."

Buchanan looked at his watch and ground his teeth. The spare twenty minutes he had counted on had now dwindled to five and if the traffic had built up in the interim he could find himself with nothing to spare.

Fizz put the snaps back in her shoulder bag and made ready to leave. "And that was everything that came in the same lot?"

"All the rest was junk," Phillip nodded.

Fizz snapped on a quick frown. "You threw it out?"

"I'm afraid so. Some of it may be in that rummage basket there. Just odds and ends." Phillip scrabbled among a collection of small objects and brought forth a strip of leather. "A racing bridle. That was in the box. Also, I seem to remember, a couple of racing prints without frames. I sold those quite quickly."

"Fizz ..." said Buchanan.

"Yes, I'm coming," she spun round and her elbow caught the vase of chrysanthemums, carelessly set atop a narrow bookcase. Buchanan saw what was coming and tried to leap sideways, but his movement was restricted by the knowledge of the damage any violent reaction could cause in that welter of glass and thin china. He managed to catch the vase in time to prevent it smashing to the floor but the spout of stale, evil-smelling water that exploded from it soaked Fizz from shoulder to waist.

"Shite!" Fizz cried, staggering back, her T-shirt adhering like clingfilm to her otherwise—quite obviously—naked torso.

Buchanan was transfixed, first with astonished appreciation and then with horror and embarrassment. Phillip was stuck in the appreciation stage and making the most of it and Fizz was still too shocked to realize that she was making his day.

There was nothing Buchanan could do but interpose himself between Fizz's virtually exposed breasts and Phillip's concentrated stare and proffer his hankie. It took several minutes of infuriated swearing from Fizz and pointless faffing around and apologizing from Phillip before Fizz could be extricated from the situation and chivvied out into the street.

"Here," said Buchanan, when they reached the pavement. "You'd better borrow this till you get home."

He hauled off his best cashmere golfing sweater and handed it to her, but she waved it away.

"I'm not cold."

"You're not decent."

She glanced down at her delightfully pert bosom and picked the clinging fabric away from her skin with her fingertips. "I don't smell too good, either," she said, showing not the slightest sign of embarrassment, "and if I get your cashmere sweater all stinky I'll have to get it cleaned—which costs money."

"Don't be silly—"

"No. Thanks but no thanks. It's not necessary." Her sudden smile, straight into Buchanan's eyes, was uncomfortably perceptive. "I'll keep loosening my T-shirt. Promise."

Buchanan looked hurriedly at his watch. "I have to—God! Look at the time!—I have to get a move on, Fizz. I'm late already and I—" The words withered on his lips as he registered the slip of paper tucked under his windscreen wiper.

"Oh, dear," Fizz murmured, following his tortured gaze. "Not a parking ticket?"

There were times when Buchanan envied Fizz's talent for swearing. The cathartic outpouring of invective such as she had just demonstrated in the antique shop had to be so much more satisfying than the silent grinding of teeth which was all Buchanan could permit himself in public. "I could have done without this," he muttered.

Fizz grabbed him by the back of his shirt and pointed up the hill toward the High Street. "Look, there he is. The traffic warden. I say good morning to him every day." She whirled round suddenly, slung her shoulder bag across Buchanan's shoulder, and, with a careless "Hang on a sec," she disappeared into the crowd of Saturday shoppers like a gazelle.

"Oh great!" Buchanan closed his eyes, wondering what more the Fates had in store for him today. If Fizz hadn't left her bag with him, he'd have driven off without even taking his leave of her, and to hell with the fine. Even if she managed to get the parking warden to agree, he'd have to write to the city council traffic department to have it squashed, and he knew he wouldn't bother.

Right now, time was more important to him than money. He was going to be at least twenty minutes late getting to the golf club—even if the bloody car didn't break down or the road cave in beneath him en route and, even supposing Carlotta hadn't gone ahead without him, there would be barely time for a quick snack before they were due to meet up with the rest of the group.

He started to stride up the hill after Fizz, but he had only gone a few paces when he saw her returning, her small, smug smile advertising her success. It was difficult to look properly grateful, but he made all the right noises as briefly as he could and roared away from the curb with no more than a very small twinge of conscience at leaving her standing there, soaked to the skin.

She had a huge talent for looking waiflike and vulnerable and not even the certain knowledge that anyone who accosted her on the way home would be walking knock-kneed for a fortnight could quite negate it. Buchanan knew that there was no need for him to run her back to her flat, but he couldn't clear his head of the image of her watching him drive away, her hand raised in a wave and her T-shirt already starting to snuggle ... to flow ... to smooth ... over her—

"Bloody hell!" He turned his head sideways and sniffed.

The God-awful smell that had been hanging around Fizz had not all been coming from her. He too had received his share of the stagnant water and his shirt was now stinking like a dead rat.

# Chapter Thirteen

Fizz had been toying with the idea of going for a walk on the Pentlands in the afternoon but, by the time she had showered off the smell and dried her hair, it was too late. She spread out her Law books and notes on the kitchen table and tried to do a bit of studying, but her mind kept drifting away.

She was going to have to phone Frau Richter some time over the weekend because the old lady was impatient to hear whether her assumptions about the photographs matching the painting had been correct, and she wasn't looking forward to it. The truth of the matter was that, for all her effort, she had produced very little that she could use to bulk out her report.

OK, she had established that Herr Krefeld had indeed bought the picture he had told his sister about, but, as Buchanan had pointed out, there was no proof that he'd had it in his room on the night he died, so there was still nothing she could use to ginger up the police inquiry, even if she had wanted to do so, which she certainly didn't.

She was perfectly convinced, in her own mind, that the painting had been stolen from the hotel. Furthermore, the bad vibes she had experienced on her first sight of Herr Krefeld's body were just as strong as ever. OK, he had died of a heart attack, you couldn't get round that, but even that fact was suspicious. There was something rotten in the circumstances surrounding the painting's disappearance that was stinking worse than her T-shirt, but she was no nearer putting her finger on it than she had been a week ago.

The fact that the guy who painted the picture had committed suicide simply had to be significant. So did the behavior of Gloria and Frazer since Herr Krefeld's demise. It looked very much, at first glance, as if the Rentons knew more than was good for them and that someone was threatening them to ensure that they kept that knowledge to themselves. What didn't tie in to that scenario was the way Gloria had been trying to make out to her telephone caller that he or she was speaking to the wrong Rentons—not Gloria and Frazer, but Barbara and Frank—two quite different people. Now why would she do that? Surely whoever was threatening them knew exactly who they were and where to find them?

A brief interview with Gloria, or even Frazer, might clarify matters a little as to who the mystery caller might be, but she would have to be very clever to get anything worthwhile out of either of them if they didn't want to tell.

Neither Gloria nor Frazer, however, was around when she got to the hotel that evening, and not even Johnnyboy had been subjected to their company all day.

"For which I am profoundly grateful, I can tell you, sweetie," he informed Fizz as she tucked into her vichyssoise, "because I've had about enough of that woman and so has everyone else. She had a huge row with Rosemary this morning and she practically snapped the face off poor Jace here—didn't she, pet—just because he left the back door unlocked when he came in from picking some parsley."

"What was the row with Rosemary about?" Fizz asked.

Johnnyboy's tall hat wobbled, exposing an inch of bald occiput, as he twitched his head. "Nothing at all, dear, as far as I can make out." He continued slicing a cucumber into a hundred or so transparent slices. "Something about putting a telephone call through to Frazer after he had told her he wasn't to be disturbed. Poor Rosemary was in tears by the time Gloria had finished with her."

Fizz had never experienced Gloria's temper, but she had heard enough from the other members of staff to know that it could be awesome. "Vicious, was she?"

Johnnyboy shrugged. "I've seen worse." He cleaned his knife thoughtfully and then added, as though he felt compelled to be factual, "But then, I've seen *Reservoir Dogs*."

"Gloria can be a total shite sometimes," Fizz said.

137

"Well, yes, if you want to employ a euphemism I suppose you could call her that. Just be glad you don't have to put up with her twenty-four hours a day."

Fizz scraped her plate. "You should get a place of your own, Johnnyboy. Living-in is always a pain in the backside."

"Tell me about it." Johnnyboy drooped his eyelids wearily, studied the plate of seafood salad he was composing, and added a judicious radish before passing it to Fizz. "When I win the lottery, I'll get myself a little pied-à-terre like yours in the Royal Mile, or maybe a country cottage like that one we looked at yesterday. I must say, my love, I rather enjoyed being a prospective house-buyer."

"You were superb, Johnnyboy. I'm sure Dennis thinks I'm a born saleswoman."

"You are, poppet. Don't let anybody tell you different. You could sell a lead weight to a drowning man—and, listen, that boss of yours is simply panting to get into your knickers, do you know that? I could see it in his eyes before we even left the office."

"Mm-hm," Fizz said with her mouth full.

Johnnyboy paused to look at her, one hand on his hip and the other resting on an invisible, shoulder-high walking stick. "Just don't tell me you go for that sugary sweet-talk he was whispering to you when he thought I wasn't listening? Sweetie, he's as smooth as Egyptian whisky, but he really isn't in your class. I mean, *is* he, love? Take my advice and grab that lovely Tam Buchanan. He's the alpha male in that setup, no question."

Seeing the conversation beginning to go downhill, Fizz skipped pudding, which was, in any case, only a fruit compote that was dangerously close to its sell-by date, and went to take over from Rosemary. She had hopes of learning more about that morning's Rosemary/Gloria bout, but the receptionist was in a hurry to strike the gyves from her ankles and lost no time in grabbing her coat and getting the hell out of it.

Apart from three or four check-ins, the first part of the evening passed comparatively quietly. Gloria drifted by once or twice but didn't linger, and on her last transit of the foyer she paused only to say that she and Frazer were going up to their quarters and didn't want to be disturbed.

"If anyone is looking for me tonight, I'm not on the premises. Absolutely no exceptions, have you got that, Fizz?" Gloria was as hard-nosed as ever, but you could see that the strain—whatever its cause—was starting to get to her. "That goes for Mr. Renton, too. We're going to get an early night."

Fizz was momentarily tempted to ask, "What if any more guests pop their clogs?" but decided that Gloria might not see the humor in the remark.

She had never, in the eleven weeks she'd been working at the hotel, known anybody to ask for either of the Rentons in the evening, and she didn't envisage any problem arising in the immediate future, so she said only, "I have to make a short phone call to Frau Richter this evening."

"Oh, go ahead," Gloria said, as she marched impatiently away. "I told her you could phone from here, so do it by all means, though what bloody good it'll do now ..."

The rest of her remarks were lost to Fizz as the curve of the staircase hid her from sight, but she was left wondering why her boss's eagerness to help Frau Richter had begun, so suddenly, to evaporate.

Unable to find an answer to this enigma, she got out her notebook and dialed Frau Richter's number.

"Yes? Elsa Richter here." As usual, she sounded crisp and decisive and ready to be critical.

"Good evening, Frau Richter. Fizz Fitzpatrick calling."

"Ah, Fizz. I have been hoping to hear from you sometime over the weekend. You got my letter and the old photographs? They were not very good, I'm afraid. I hope they were of some use?"

"Yes, they were, Frau Richter. I showed them to the antique dealer who sold your brother the painting and he was able to say, quite confidently, that the painting was of the Schluchsee."

"Ah ..." Frau Richter's voice sounded a little breathy for a moment. "I am so glad to know that." After a brief pause, she added in a new tone, "From which direction was the picture painted?"

"It showed a beach, I understand, with a ... a ..." Fizz groped for the right word and finally settled for "a sort of rocky cliff at one side and a low, wooded hill in the background. Exactly the scene in one of your snapshots, except that the artist had added a few dark rocks on the beach to balance the composition, I think."

"Ah, yes," Frau Richter sounded pleased to have this extra confirmation. "When Bernd and I were children, there were no rocks on the beach, but there are rocks now, yes, and many boats on the lake and they were building big new houses on the cliff when I was last there a few years ago. Things change, my dear, and seldom for the better. That is why my painting is so valuable to me."

"Well, at least we know it existed," Fizz said, "even if we haven't found it yet. But I *did* find out that other items auctioned in the same lot as the painting were handed in by the same person, so I'm hoping that I can get some sort of lead through tracing them to their source. I'm still very hopeful that we'll be able to determine what happened to the picture."

"And get it back?"

That was the question Fizz had hoped she wouldn't be called upon to answer. "There's no way anybody could guarantee that, Frau Richter," she said with unwilling honesty. "But I don't think we should give up just yet."

There was a silence that went on and on, punctuated only by hissing on the line. Finally, Frau Richter drew an audible breath and said crisply, "Good. If you are willing to give your time, Fizz, I am willing to pay for it. This painting is worth more than money to me, you understand? So, we will do our best to get it back, right? I will post you another check at the end of the week unless I hear from you before that."

Fizz smiled at the mouthpiece. "Very good, Frau Richter. I'll keep you posted."

It was no longer a matter of the money—if, indeed, it had ever been—but of wanting to get to the bottom of the intriguing facts of the case. However, as leads dried up around the hotel and the artists' retreat at Lamancha, it was beginning to look as though it might be necessary to spread the investigation farther afield, and that would cost more than she could personally afford—especially now that her paltry fortune was invested in the stock exchange. Which was something else that gave her palpitations when it occurred to her in the dark watches of the night.

If anyone had told her she would ever hazard her last penny on anything whatsoever, she would have laughed in their face. Only the thought of a prolonged lentil diet could have prevailed upon her to gamble, even on the sort of certainty that the Wainwright deal appeared to be, and she was now finding she didn't really have the bottle for it. Had she realized how long she was going to have to wait for confirmation of her inspired guess, she would have thought a bit harder before committing her cash. As it was, she was likely to be doolally with worry before she learned the outcome of her stupidity.

The thought of her finances reminded her, in a roundabout way, that she would be back at university in another couple of weeks and therefore it might be a good idea to spend some quality time with her Law books. She didn't mind studying; in fact, she rather enjoyed it—especially when, as at present, she was actually earning money at the same time. From about nine thirty onward, she was virtually uninterrupted and had put in a good hour and a half on *McDonald's Criminal Law* when the street door swung open to admit a character who immediately had all her attention.

He was probably in his late fifties, built like a piece of earth-moving equipment and with a face that would have looked ugly on a warthog. The black leather trousers and jacket and the steel-capped boots he wore said "biker" to Fizz, but bikers didn't usually carry folding umbrellas.

A single glance was enough to inform Fizz that this was no average guest. He was carrying no baggage and his manner was neither tentative nor indicative of the satisfaction that identifies the weary traveler reaching his longed-for destination. It took him perhaps ten or twelve strides to reach the reception desk, and well before he reached it Fizz knew he was trouble.

"Mr. Renton around?" he asked in tones that fell short of being dulcet.

Fizz shook her head, her suspicions confirmed. This was the Rentons' worst nightmare, come to haunt them, and the only thing she could do was try to head him off.

"I'm awfully sorry," she said, with her smile on full beam and half her thoughts on cursing the Rentons. "I'm afraid they're not in just at the moment. Is there something I can help you with?"

"Not in?" demanded the pseudo-biker, widening his already somewhat protuberant eyes, the better to see her with.

"No, I'm afraid you've missed them."

He leaned across the counter in a swift movement that had a powerful diuretic effect, and said in a distinctly menacing tone, "You're sure about that, missy? I wouldn't like to think you were just fobbing me off. I've come a long way to speak to them."

For a moment, Fizz wondered if she could be making a mistake in keeping this guy at bay. What if he were a genuine caller and the Rentons went bananas when they heard that she'd given him the bum's rush?

She could think of only one way to be sure he was the same guy who had scared Gloria on the phone.

"No, indeed not, sir," she said earnestly. "Barbara and Frank are very rarely in the hotel at this time of day, but you can usually catch them any time between nine and five."

His chivlike stare wavered immediately and Fizz could see his tongue probing the inside of his cheek while he considered this development. Abstract intellectual exercise was clearly not his strong suit and Fizz could tell he was finding the opacity of the situation quite challenging.

"Right," he said finally, but with profound suspicion. "I'll … um …"

But the effort of planning his next move being, all too apparently, too much for him, he turned on his heel and left without another word. Fizz watched him go and listened for the sound of a motorbike fading into the distance, but she could hear nothing.

Grabbing the phone, she punched in the code for the Rentons' apartments and kept her finger on the buzzer till they answered.

"For goodness' sake," Gloria's voice crackled down the line. "I'm not deaf, dammit! You don't need to wake the entire building!"

Fizz gripped the receiver as though it were her boss's neck. "I've just had a very ugly customer at the reception desk, Mrs. Renton. He was rude, he was popping mad, and he was looking for you. I got rid of him, this once, but I want you to know that I won't be doing it again, OK?"

"Dear me." Gloria sounded vaguely concerned, but neither apologetic nor conciliatory and, before she said another word, Fizz already knew she was lying. "Who was this person? Did he leave a name?"

"No, he didn't," Fizz said angrily. "He was in no mood to leave a name."

"I hope you don't mean he was abusive, Fizz?"

Gloria was either a whole lot jumpier than she sounded or she was taking the whole business much less seriously than, Fizz felt, was appropriate to the circumstances. "Well, no," she had to say, "he wasn't abusive, exactly, but he was in a real bad temper."

"But not with you, Fizz."

Fizz brought the phone round in front of her eyes and glared into the earpiece. If Gloria was trying to imply that she was over-reacting to what had been just another irritable customer, she could think again.

"We are talking about a thug, Mrs. Renton. A seriously intimidating thug. And, what's more, I think you were expecting him."

Gloria wasn't ready for that revelation. She went down for a count of nine but then recovered enough to respond, "Oh, surely it can't have been Mr. McPherson? Dear me, what will the man do next?"

Fizz waited for an explanation but was forced to ask, "Mr. McPherson? Who's he?"

"Just a terrible man that did some building work for us last year. He never finished the job, so we're refusing to pay him till he does so and I'm afraid he's taking it very badly." Gloria was now sounding as Thatcherish as ever and even managed a trace of condescension as she added, "I'm sorry you've had this to deal with, Fizz, but you were quite right to send him away. He should have known better than to call outwith business hours."

Deeply grateful for this pat on the head, Fizz said firmly, "I won't be doing it again, however, as I said earlier. As far as I'm concerned, relief reception duty, which is what I signed on for, does not include manning the drawbridge."

"No, no, of course not, dear," said Gloria in a voice so sickly sweet Fizz could feel it attacking her dentine. "I'll have a word with our accountant in the morning. I'm sure you'll have no more trouble."

Fizz had to be content with that assurance although, when she thought it over, she was far from convinced that Gloria was telling the complete truth. One could well understand why, if they were expecting a visit from Mr. McPherson, both she and Frazer had been keeping low for the past few days. He was patently not the sort to engage in peaceful negotiation when he could get quicker results from the application of a steel-capped boot. However, that didn't explain why he would be put off by Gloria's appropriation of the two fake Christian names.

No. If Gloria was telling the truth, it was certainly not the whole truth, and the likelihood was that her whole story was a load of complete codswallop.

# Chapter Fourteen

If Buchanan had known when he left home on Tuesday morning that he would be spending part of the afternoon at Musselburgh racecourse, he would have worn something less formal than a sharp business suit and restrained tie. He wasn't quite sure what Fizz hoped to gain from their visit, but if her intention was for them to melt into the crowd she should have given him some warning because he stuck out, as she herself remarked, like a third nostril.

Other than the uniformed sector—the jockeys in their silks, the trainers in their tweeds and trilbies, the hangers-on in their green wellies and waxed jackets—the crowd was in casual gear to a man and a spirit of carefree festivity prevailed. Fizz, in her navy blue Oxfam number, apparently felt perfectly at home, but that, Buchanan surmised, was because she didn't give a damn what she wore as long as it protected her from the elements.

"Take your jacket and tie off and leave them in the car if you're uncomfortable," she recommended, leaning on the fence of the saddling enclosure and licking her ice cream. "It's warm enough."

Buchanan all but shuddered at the suggestion. "The idea is to look casual," he said, "not shabby-genteel. I'd as soon wear a knotted handkerchief and a string vest."

This apparently painted a picture in Fizz's mind that amused her so much she got ice cream up her nose and had to borrow his hankie.

"We don't have a lot of time to waste," he said, when she had finished choking. "The last race is in about half an hour, so if you're going to find someone who can answer your questions you'd better get a move on. There's probably a security office somewhere in the main building."

"Mmm. In a minute." Fizz bit into her double nougat and watched the line of braided and burnished mounts that were being paraded by their stable lads, many of whom were either female or seriously long in the tooth. "You don't fancy a flutter, I suppose?"

"If you mean, do I wish to finance your choice for the next race, then the answer is no."

"Thought not." She licked her fingers and wiped them on his hankie. "C'mon then, Scrooge, let's get to work."

"I can't say I'm wildly hopeful that this part of today's exercise is likely to be much of a success," Buchanan said as he shepherded her through the crowd. "In fact, I'll be honest with you, Fizz, you're playing a real long shot, so don't build up your hopes. Just because one of the other items that Mr. X offered for auction with the picture turns out to have been stolen, it doesn't mean that the others were also hot."

"Well, if you're going to be nit-picking about it, you still don't even have any proof that the silver bottle opener was stolen from Andrew and Jean, do you?"

Buchanan refused to let her irritate him. "No, but if you'd told me you were planning this expedition, I'd have checked it out before we set off."

"Exactly. You'd have been mind-blowingly pedantic as usual. But, why waste the time when you know it has to be the same bottle opener they were looking for last week? It's our most valuable clue so far. It ties the painting to Lamancha, and the horse-racing gear that was in the same lot ties it to Musselburgh racecourse."

She had a facility for nipping through the press of people that left Buchanan struggling to stay within earshot, but she kept chatting over her shoulder without worrying about whether he could hear her or not.

"What about Perth racecourse?" he said, catching up with her for a moment. "Or Hamilton? Or Kelso?"

"Too far away," she said, with a confidence he found very misplaced. "If we're looking for someone based at Lamancha, we have to think local. If he pinched the bottle opener, he may have pinched the racing gear too, which would suggest to me that he is somebody who can get close to the action." She cannoned into a glowering man in a Barbour jacket, gave him a sunny smile, and received instant absolution. "I reckon he's a regular racegoer. Somebody who's not going to miss a race meeting if he can help it. Whoever put that picture up for sale, I'll bet you two things: he has connections with Lamancha, and he's here!"

Buchanan wished he could share her conviction but, in the meantime, the sun was shining, the atmosphere was exhilarating, and he had escaped, if only for a couple of hours, from behind his desk.

They found the security office just inside the lobby of the main building and Fizz wasted no time in ingratiating herself with the gray-haired man behind the counter who, when Fizz had put him in the picture, passed them on to a tall, elegant woman in her late thirties, who introduced herself as Mrs. Mathieson.

"Let me just get this straight," she said, ignoring Fizz and addressing her remarks to Buchanan. "You suspect that the other items in the same lot in the auction sale might have come from here?"

"Actually—" Buchanan began to indicate Fizz, but Fizz didn't need his help.

"Well, not all of them, no," she said, with the bright, affectionate smile that she kept for people to whom she had taken an instant dislike, "but perhaps the racing bridle and the cup."

Mrs. Mathieson turned her head slowly as though just registering Fizz's presence. She had an aristocratic, high cheekboned face and distinctly—but not unattractively—prominent front teeth, so she was good at looking disdainful. "You don't have the name of the seller?"

"No, I'm afraid not," Fizz said, with frightening humility, and her smile became even warmer. "But I thought there was just a chance that you might be able to tell me who would be disposing of such items at the present time. Maybe a stable that's closing down? Somebody who's retiring, perhaps? Someone who might have inherited some bits and pieces of racing gear that he didn't want? No?"

Mrs. Mathieson thought not. She returned her attention to

Buchanan, drooped her eyelashes, and gave him the benefit of a distinctly fetching pout. "I'm sorry to be of so little help, but I'll certainly let you know if I hear anything of interest."

Buchanan hesitated, waiting for Fizz to continue, and then was tempted to take a more active part in the conversation. Mrs. Mathieson wasn't wearing a wedding ring and he had always had a weakness for autocratic women.

"There is another possibility," he said, adopting a cozier tone. "Would you know if either the racing bridle or the cup had been reported stolen?"

"If the theft had been reported, yes, I'd know about it," she said, straining to keep her top lip tucked carefully over her teeth as she smiled back at him, "but, I'm afraid there are a lot of unreported thefts on the course. It's so unlikely that we can do anything to actually retrieve stolen goods that, unless it's something expensive, people don't bother to tell us when something goes missing. They simply put it down to experience."

"That's too bad." Buchanan nodded as though he could understand that attitude, and she gave him a long, pensive look.

"I'll keep my ear to the ground, of course," she said, holding his eyes. "Actually, I could ask around and see if anyone has heard anything. You never know. Why don't you give me a ring sometime next week?"

"That's very kind of you," Fizz chimed in, fairly glittering with amicability. "I'll do that. Around Wednesday or Thursday? Would that be OK?"

Mrs. Mathieson tried freezing her with a glance, which bounced harmlessly off Fizz's smile, and then admitted, with another lingering look at Buchanan, that Wednesday would be fine.

It was turning out to be even less of a wasted afternoon than he had calculated, Buchanan reflected as they emerged into the sunlight. He rather thought he might take up Mrs. Mathieson's kind invitation since, thanks to the collapse of his date with Carlotta last Saturday—a total fiasco from beginning to end—he was, once again, uncommitted.

It amused him to see Fizz still churning with irritation but, for once, she forbore to comment. It was a momentary impulse that incited Buchanan to tease her by commenting, "A rather attractive lady, didn't you think?"

Fizz flicked him a quick glance. "Gave you a woody, did she?" she asked politely. "Well, I'd have thought it would take more than a woman's ability to eat an apple through a letterbox but, there you go. Whatever turns you on, old buddy ..."

Buchanan recoiled, unable even to summon up a careless chuckle and silenced by Fizz's innate ability to douse his enthusiasm at the first flicker. He headed back to the stand at a quick march, but Fizz caught him by the sleeve.

"Why don't you go and have a look at the queues around the bookies' stances and the Tote. I'll check out the stand and meet you back at the rails for the off."

Buchanan was quite happy to go along with that. He had seen a very nice little chestnut in the saddling enclosure and, although he knew nothing about form, he rather thought he might slip a fiver on it when Fizz wasn't looking. Mindful of her instructions to keep a low profile, he had a good look round before putting on his bet and then found a vantage point from where he could scan the other punters while keeping out of sight behind a notice board.

There were about a dozen bookies, so it was difficult to keep an eye on all of them, but Fizz had insisted that he bring the office camera, used for taking photographs of their real estate properties, so he ran off what was left on the film by snapping wide-angle group shots that Fizz could study later if she so chose. After about ten futile minutes of this chore, he considered his duty done and made his way back to find a place at the rails beside Fizz.

The crowd that had been milling around the saddling enclosure and the forecourt was now filling the stand and lining the rails, binoculars at the ready. The grooms were coaxing the horses into the starting boxes and the air of tense expectation was so pervasive that Buchanan began to feel almost jittery with excitement.

Even discounting the fact that he had money on the outcome, he couldn't help being swept up by the experience: the sheer power and beauty of the horses, the thudding rush as they passed by only feet away, the yelling of the spectators, and Fizz's uninhibited instructions to the jockey of her choice.

"Oh, well," Fizz said wistfully, as they turned away. "Pity we didn't put money on it. My choice came in first."

Buchanan looked at her closely. "You're kidding, Fizz?"

She raised her eyebrows and looked at him but, as she was opening her mouth to speak, her eyes slid past him and focused on something behind him.

"Well, flip me gently. Will you look who's here."

Buchanan turned to look over his shoulder but, since Fizz then grabbed him and dragged him into the cover of the crowd, it was a moment before he could see who was the focus of her attention.

"Look! Over there at the corner of the stand—behind the woman in the orange jacket. Wait a minute—he has moved back … There! See him now?"

It was Andrew Samuel in his B-movie tweed jacket—probably the last of the retreat's guests whom Buchanan would have expected to see—if he had expected to see any of them, which was by no means the case. Andrew was taking very little interest in what was going on about him, merely leaning against the corner of the stand and cogitating deeply while his eyes followed the lucky winners who were beginning to queue up to collect their winnings.

If Buchanan was staggered, Fizz was bubbling like Andrews liver salts. "What did I tell you?" she demanded, making an obvious effort to refrain from jumping up and down. "You see? It wasn't so much of a long shot, was it? There *had* to be someone from Lamancha here."

"Only if your entire theory were correct," Buchanan muttered. He found himself staring at Andrew with such intensity that it wouldn't have surprised him if the guy had sensed his regard, turned round, and stared back at him. "If Andrew is the guy we're looking for, it means the bottle opener wasn't stolen from him. It means he sold it—together with other items that were probably his to sell—and without telling his wife. Seriously, Fizz, does that fit your picture of Andrew?"

"You have a better explanation?" Fizz demanded. "He's here, isn't he? Just as I predicted. He's the boyo who sold the painting OK. No question."

"It's curious, I'll grant you that," Buchanan admitted, "but Andrew doesn't fit the profile. Think about all the other items that were in the same lot. Surely, if they're not the pickings of an opportunistic thief, they must be simply a collection of bits and pieces from someone's attic. They're obviously not the sort of thing Andrew would have by him during his stay at the retreat."

She hated to be thwarted, especially by anything remotely approaching logic, and her face reflected all the ire of which it was physically capable, which wasn't a great deal.

"Well, stuff you, Buchanan," she started to say and then stopped as Andrew suddenly jerked his shoulders away from the wall and started to walk toward them.

There was little chance that he had spotted them since his eyes were on the ground and his bent head was only visible in brief flashes as he wove through the crowd, but Buchanan was ready to duck down as he moved past them.

"Don't lose sight of him," Fizz hissed in his ear, her view of their quarry being more impaired by the throng than Buchanan's. "He may be meeting someone."

Buchanan grabbed her elbow and stayed doggedly on Andrew's heels, but their luck had run out for the day. Andrew merely skirted the stand and strolled out of the racecourse gates and down the road to where he had his car parked. He spoke to no one and did nothing at all that might have been construed as suspicious and, as they watched him drive away in a direction that would lead him to Lamancha, Fizz was muttering imprecations beneath her breath.

"If we had parked the car round this side, we could have followed him and seen where he went," she said, and gave Buchanan a look that made it clear who was to blame for this omission. "Shit. Why did it take us so long to spot him? We could have watched to see if he spoke to anyone or if he was just here for the racing."

"Maybe he didn't want to be seen," Buchanan said reasonably. It seemed to him, now that he thought about it, that Andrew had been keeping very much in the thick of the crowd as he made his departure. Anyone would have expected him to have taken a less densely packed route to the exit than the one he chose, but perhaps that just didn't occur to him at the time.

As they started to walk back to the car park, there was a sudden exodus of people from the racecourse, indicating that the last race of the day had been run. In a couple of minutes, the streets of Musselburgh would be jammed solid and there would be bumper to bumper traffic all the way back to Edinburgh. It would be touch and go whether they'd make it in time for Fizz to start work at six o'clock.

"You don't think Andrew might have seen us earlier, do you?" Fizz said, twisting her brows.

"I don't know, but I have a very slight and unreliable suspicion that he might have been acting just a trifle shiftily. I don't know how you happened to spot him behind that woman in orange, but there wasn't much of him showing, was there? Nor did he have to be tucked away in that corner where he had a very narrow view of the field. There was plenty of room just behind him in the stand."

Fizz digested that for a minute or two and then said, "But he wasn't doing anything. He was just standing there. Why hide?"

"You tell me," Buchanan suggested. "It's your case, old chum."

Fizz muttered under her breath. Buchanan couldn't have sworn to what she said, but it sounded suspiciously like, "*Smartass!*"

# Chapter Fifteen

Fizz was frustrated to find that Buchanan wasn't in the office the following afternoon when she turned up for her usual Wednesday stint. According to The Wonderful Beatrice, Guardian of the Diary, he was in Glasgow and unlikely to show his face till tomorrow morning.

This was particularly irritating because Fizz was still totally mystified by Andrew's appearance at the racecourse the previous day and wanted to do a bit of brainstorming with Buchanan to see if, between them, they could come up with something that might account for his being there.

The fact that one of the Foundation's residents had fulfilled her prophecy and turned up at the races was a source of satisfaction, but at the same time she could have wished very heartily that it had been almost any of the other residents. If one of them was up to something nefarious, as seemed likely, Fizz's prime suspect would have been Dodie Galbraith because she could have believed almost anything of Dodie, given his background and his current attitudes.

Even Kat would have been easier to picture as a petty criminal. She might be no spring chicken but she gave the impression of being something of an iceberg, with nine-tenths under the surface, and she was certainly every inch an individual. If she had showed up at the rails, yelling and waving her stick, it would have been a surprise, sure, but not utterly incomprehensible. Encountering her pal Bremner, for that matter, would not have surprised Fizz all that much—not because of anything he said or did but because he was such a dark horse. Who could tell what kind of person he really was or what he might be up to?

But *Andrew?* Andrew, with his gentlemanly air and his middle-class values and his staid, unexceptional lifestyle, maintained in the face of the other residents' laid-back nonconformity? And, even more to the point, Andrew on his *own*: not taking Jean for a pleasant day out and a bit of a flutter, but skulking around—she was now sure he had been skulking around—as though he knew that Fizz and Buchanan were there looking out for him. It simply didn't figure.

Shit.

The enigma of Andrew's obvious involvement in the mystery weighed her down while she showered and changed and got herself to work that evening. It was still taking up most of her concentration while she ate her dinner and Johnnyboy took her silence as a personal insult.

"Here I am," he told anyone who happened to be listening, "stuck in this *bloody* kitchen all day and I can't get a word out of anyone! I don't think it's too much to ask. Just an occasional 'Uh-huh' or the odd 'Really?', that's all I expect. But no! I could have gone deaf days ago and I wouldn't know it! I'm talking to myself in the *mirror*, for God's sake! I'll be inviting Jehovah's Witnesses in for coffee next!"

"You've got Jason," Fizz pointed out.

"Jason! You don't need *me* to tell you about Jason's wealth of anecdote and witty repartee, my love, you've had experience of it yourself. It's like listening to a tape of Marcel Marceau in here of an evening! If I don't get some social intercourse—and, yes, I *do* mean social, poppet—I'm going to go completely gaga."

He stared moodily out of the window at the depressing display of garbage containers in the distance and fingered his spotty brow as though he were reading a message in Braille.

"I'm sorry, I'm not at my most fascinating tonight," Fizz said. "I've got a lot on my mind."

She was tempted, just for a moment, to talk things over with Johnnyboy. He might know something about the Rentons' part in the mystery which he hadn't considered worth telling her, but it was extremely unlikely. Johnnyboy's brain was not a storehouse, it was a conduit. All cerebral activity, other than that necessary for day-to-day survival, was channeled straight out through his lips and, besides, Fizz had not lost sight of the fact that he too was a hotel resident. It might be hard to imagine him launching Herr Krefeld into eternity, for the sake of his painting or for any other reason, but he'd had the same opportunity as the Rentons had had, so he was ruled out as a confidant.

She had made up her mind not to tell Johnnyboy about the Rentons' sinister visitor—the alleged Mr. McPherson. While she was unsure whether Gloria's version of the facts was genuine or not, it had seemed unnecessary to worry him with the possibility that he might become involved. However, it made for an interesting topic of conversation and it was the only one she could think of at the moment.

"There is something I meant to tell you about," she said, scraping her plate and looking wistful in the hope of a second helping. Johnnyboy complied with a motherly smile.

"And what was that then, flower?"

"There was a nasty looking individual asking for Frazer and Gloria the night before last. A real heavy-duty hombre with a broken nose and a disposition like a shark with receding gums."

"Looking for the Rentons?" Johnnyboy draped himself across the workbench like Pavlova in the closing moments of the "Dying Swan." "Now that's *interesting*, sweetie."

"Interesting for you, maybe. Bum-clenchingly scary for me, I can tell you. The guy was carrying one of those collapsing umbrellas and I'm bloody sure it was weighted with lead."

Johnnyboy did a nimble jeté and started to wave his arms about. "Just *what* is going *on* in this place? Will somebody tell me what's going on? It's like the run up to the St. Valentine's Day massacre! Jace! Come and listen to this, pet. We're all like to be murdered in our beds!"

"I don't think so, honestly, Johnnyboy," Fizz said, wishing she hadn't mentioned it. She had anticipated that he might be a little concerned but not that he would organize a mass walkout, as seemed imminent. "The guy was only interested in the Rentons and I got rid of him quite easily."

"But he could come back," Johnnyboy squawked, showing the whites of his eyes. "He could walk through the back door at this very minute!"

155

"So keep it locked," Fizz told him curtly, suddenly tiring of his histrionics. "He doesn't constitute any threat to you, Johnnyboy. Gloria says he's just some building contractor they're in dispute with over some work he never completed. She promised she'd see her accountant yesterday and get it all straightened out."

"What building work?" Johnnyboy demanded, planting his hands aggressively on his hips. "There hasn't been any building work done on this place since that offensive overwrought-iron balustrade that Gloria insisted on having put around the patio. And if she refused to pay for *that* piece of architectural vandalism, there's not a jury in the land would convict her. Somebody should swing for it."

"Well, I'm going to ask her about it tonight," Fizz told him. "I want to get to the bottom of this business."

"Not tonight you're not," Johnnyboy smirked. "They've gone out."

Astonished, Fizz swallowed a lump of roast duckling unchewed and it went down like an open umbrella. "How come they've gone out? They never go out in the evening—well, almost never, and certainly not till after dinner's over at any rate."

"Well, they have this evening. Now, you tell *me*, sweetie—is that a coincidence or are they expecting trouble?"

His deep pleasure at the thought of Gloria's adversity appeared, for the moment, to have driven all thought of personal safety from his mind, and a small catlike smile curved his lips as he waited for Fizz's opinion. Fizz, however, was as much in the dark as he was.

It looked very much as though the Rentons were now running scared, which would indicate that Mr. McPherson had paid them another visit. But, surely, if he had turned up at the reception desk again, either Rosemary or Hollis would have mentioned seeing him. Hollis came in at six on a Tuesday night so that Fizz could have a night off, but no doubt McPherson would have thought twice before trying to bully Hollis the way he had tried to bully Fizz. Hollis was an ex-policeman—twenty years ex, to be exact, but still able to bar the way of Mr. McPherson and his like, lead brolly notwithstanding. Rosemary, on the other hand, was unlikely to be much of a deterrent, but if she had been annoyed by a second visit from the builder she would have told Fizz about it in case he came back while Fizz was on duty.

It was, of course, possible that McPherson had been in direct contact with the Rentons, but as long as he wasn't likely to be calling in person, Fizz wasn't over-worried about that. However, just to be on the safe side, she armed herself with a mini-aerosol of hairspray that she habitually carried, purely for protection, in her shoulder bag. It might not have the knockout effect of Mace, but she had herself been on the receiving end of an accidental squirt of hair lacquer in the eye and she knew how it hurt. More to the point, there had been times in the past when circumstances had forced her to be in the wrong place at the wrong time and when she had found the presence of that little canister a profound comfort to her nerves. She had never actually needed to use it, so she wasn't sure how long its effect might last but, if the worst came to the worst, it would at least give her a running start.

During the first part of the evening, she was kept busy handing out room keys, answering queries, booking in new arrivals, and sorting out minor problems, but things quietened down by about ten thirty, so she was able to get her books out and pretend to herself that she was catching up with her vacation projects.

The constant half-expectation of seeing Mr. McPherson again wasn't exactly an aid to concentration, however, so she made very little headway and was just about ready to call it a day when the door slammed and there he was, leaning over the counter.

He had covered the distance between the door and the reception desk in the time it took Fizz to turn her head, but he wasn't fast enough to prevent her fingers closing round the can of hairspray which, inapprehensive or not, she had kept right there on her lap, just in case. She flipped off the lid and let it roll to the floor as she stood up, holding the can out of his line of sight.

"Hello again," she said, grinning like a Steinway.

Mr. McPherson looked no prettier than he had done on his previous visit and did not return her smile.

"Right, missy," he said, grinding his teeth in a way that even Buchanan, a teeth-grinding *aficionado*, could have predicted would do irreparable damage to the dentine. "I want to see the Rentons and I want to see them now, got that? I don't want any more of your little porky-pies about them being out or being called Barbara and Frank or any other rubbish. Just get them out here."

Fizz held on to her grin like a buoy in a storm. "But … but, they *are* called Barbara and Frank, sir," she said in girlish tones, stalling desperately in the hope of putting him off his stride again, as she had done before. "Why should I lie to you about something like that? At least that's what the staff call them and that's what they call each other and I—"

Mr. McPherson put an end to this load of codswallop by pushing his face half across the counter and fixing Fizz with a stare that burned its way to the back of her skull. "Well, they may have fooled you, missy, but they haven't fooled me, so just get on that phone there and tell them they're wanted."

If the Rentons had been on the premises, Fizz would have delivered them to him on a plate: indeed she was now deeply sorry that she had not done so when first requested. The breath fluttered in her throat and her finger found the button of the aerosol as she said:

"I'm sorry to have to tell you this, sir, but I'm afraid you've missed them again. I understand that you're keen to speak to them but—"

With a dull thud, Mr. McPherson laid the end of the folding umbrella (which again formed a conspicuous part of his color-coordinated ensemble) on the edge of the reception counter. The atmosphere, which had not been cozy to begin with, was now like liquid hydrogen.

"I wouldn't lie to me again if I were you, missy. I really wouldn't. I don't like people who waste my time and you have been giving me the runaround for days. You'd better speak up now before I start losing my temper."

Fizz quickly made her eyes round and guileless and quivered her bottom lip a little. She had long ago realized that Fate had short-changed her in the self-defense department. She had neither the fangs of the hunter nor the speed of the hunted. All she had was her wits and the face of a motherless child, but she knew how to use them both.

"I don't lie for the Rentons," she said, with a nervous but oh-so-gallant little lift of the chin. "They don't pay me enough."

Mr. McPherson hesitated, his scowl drooping a little at the corners and his eyes searching her face. "You sure about that?"

"I am. I saw them go out that door this evening with my own eyes and they told me they wouldn't be back till about one a.m."

As she spoke the words, she uttered a silent prayer that Gloria and Frazer would not, in fact, arrive back at that precise time. Admittedly, they would have Hollis here to protect them if they did, but it could be messy even so.

Mr. McPherson's brows lifted a millimeter. "One a.m.?" he repeated, with keen interest. "You absolutely sure about that?"

"That's what Barbara told me as she went out, sir. She sounded quite precise about it. I'm sure you'll catch her then, if you're in a hurry to speak to her. I'll leave a message on the board for her, if you like, and she'll see it when she comes in."

"No," Mr. McPherson said, loud enough to make Fizz twitch. "Don't you do that, missy, you hear me? No notes." He paused momentarily and then his eyes tilted up a little at the outside corners, giving him a sly look. "Mrs. Renton wouldn't want that. I'll … I'll leave it till tomorrow evening. Maybe about nine o'clock. But, no notes. You can give her the message in the morning."

Fizz nodded, projecting abject willingness to please. Mr. McPherson's acting talents being what they were, it was fairly obvious that he planned to return around one o'clock and catch the Rentons as they came in, but she wasn't going to interfere with that. Anything that happened between the hours of midnight and eight a.m. was Hollis's problem and she'd have plenty of opportunity to put him in the picture when he arrived to take over the helm in about five minutes.

"Don't worry," she said sunnily, "I'll make sure she gets the message. Who will I tell her to expect?"

"Mr. A-A-A-Albert," mumbled Mr. McPherson—if even that was his name—and brightened the room just by leaving it.

It took Fizz several seconds to prize her clenched fingers off the aerosol and calm down. She was really angry, because that was the way fear affected her, and she felt an immediate need of someone to shout at, but by the time Hollis clocked in she was past that stage and even beginning to wonder if she hadn't been overreacting after

159

all. The trouble with Mr. McPherson was that he didn't actually say or do anything that could be quoted and it wasn't easy to make Hollis understand that it was the *way he said it* that took the edge off one's enjoyment of his company.

The blame, of course, lay fairly and squarely at Gloria's door. She had promised that this sort of thing would not happen again and she fully deserved the tongue-lashing she was going to get when Fizz caught up with her tomorrow. Had there been more than a week or two till the end of her contract, when she was due a substantial completion bonus, Fizz would have told her what to do with her job, but she was going to have to settle for an apology and a guarantee that there would be no more incidents of this sort.

She was already phrasing the complaining phone call she planned to make to Gloria when she let herself out into the night and started to walk down the poorly lit drive toward the gate.

She didn't see the figure detach itself from the shadows of the pillared porch and barely registered the sound when, behind her, a man cleared his throat.

# Chapter Sixteen

Buchanan had spent his day in Glasgow in conference with other lawyers sitting round a table and drinking too much coffee and breathing in the cigarette smoke of an advocate he didn't want to insult by complaining. He had also missed his Wednesday-lunchtime squash date, so he arrived home feeling not only seedy but seriously in need of exercise.

Selena thudded on to his shoulder as he came through the doorway, purring rapturously and uttering small squeals of delight as she caught the whiff of king prawns from the takeaway he had picked up, together with his dry cleaning and his other shopping, on his way in.

They ate in companionable silence on the couch, watching the six o'clock news and letting the stress of the day ebb away. Buchanan rearranged his meal to allow Selena a tinfoil container to herself and donated a king prawn or other tidbit every time she indicated that her appetite was not yet appeased. She ate her main meal sometime during the morning on weekdays, but had such a predilection for Chinese food that she was in danger of developing a monosodium glutamate dependency.

In the back of Buchanan's mind as he ate was a general acceptance of the idea that he would go out later for a game of golf, but he started to read the *Scotsman*, which he had not yet had time to open, and an hour disappeared before he knew it. Even then, he would have had time for nine holes before the light went had not his eye fallen on the newly developed film that he had brought in with him. He knew there was nothing of interest on it, but he looked just the same and was immediately captivated by their vivid evocation of his day at the races.

Buchanan had never interested himself in photography, but it was amazing how the gaiety and excitement of the occasion came across in the casual shots of the bookies and the queues of punters. He found himself smiling as he studied them, remembering the flavor of the day, the fresh wind off the Firth of Forth, and the warmth of the September sun through his formal suit.

He wasn't even looking at the faces that were caught forever in that frozen moment. He was simply appreciating the scene as a whole, so when he found a face he knew staring back at him it took him a moment to recognize it.

"Bloody hell," he said, straightening so unexpectedly that Selena lost her balance and fell off his knee.

After a minute he got up, found a magnifying glass, and took the entire film across to the window to examine every print. The same face was in two of them, not staring directly into the lens as he had at first feared, but focusing on something in the distance, something that was probably nothing more interesting than the starting gate. At the time he had taken these shots, Buchanan remembered, the riders had been lining up for the off, so there was probably a bit of a rush on to get bets laid before the starting bell.

The discovery that Andrew Samuel was not the only suspect to have turned up at Musselburgh races put all thoughts of golf out of Buchanan's head for the time being. He needed to think about the implications of this new piece of evidence and—the thought occurred to him—he really ought to share it with Fizz as soon as possible. She wouldn't be in the office again till Friday afternoon and if she found out that he'd been sitting on such interesting information for two days there would be no living with her.

Finally he decided to kill two birds with one stone by going for a late-evening run in Holyrood Park so that he could meet Fizz at the hotel on the way back, by which time she would be finishing work. The idea appealed to him on a subconscious level also, because he had never liked the idea of her walking home alone at midnight and this would give him the chance of escorting her without having to admit—either to her or to himself—that he was doing his old mother hen act again.

He left home at about twenty to eleven, which gave him plenty of time to do the whole circuit around Arthur's Seat before ending up at the Royal Park Hotel. It was, by then, just on five to twelve but, since he was steaming with sweat and dressed in his baggy old track suit, he stayed outside, walking up and down in the porch, waiting for Fizz to emerge.

An odd character in black leather charged through the lobby door just after he arrived, sending him a close and suspicious glare as he passed by, and then a hefty gray-haired chap went in, but there was no further traffic till Fizz rushed out, at her usual break-neck pace, and sped down the drive before he could attract her attention without alarming her. He cleared his throat as he strode after her, to let her know he was there, but she took no notice and he heard her quick intake of breath as he drew level with her.

"Bloody hell, Buchanan! What d'you think you're doing—creeping up on people at this hour of night? You might think what you're about once in a while!"

That was the thing with Fizz: you couldn't win.

Buchanan was used to getting a waspish reaction every time Fizz got a fright but couldn't help thinking that she seemed a lot more jumpy than usual. "What's the matter with you?" he said, trying to see her face properly in the half-light. "I did cough, you know, to let you know I was behind you. What's with all this hysteria?"

She piped down immediately but didn't bother to offer any apology. "What're you doing here anyway?"

"Forget that for the moment," Buchanan said. "You're not usually like this. What's got into you?"

"Nothing," she said impatiently and set off down the drive with a purposeful stride.

"Don't give me that, Fizz," Buchanan insisted, keeping pace with her. "Something has happened to make you jittery and I want to know about it. Has somebody been bothering you?"

Fizz glared at him, pressing her lips together. "Listen, Buchanan, I don't want you interfering. It's nothing I can't deal with by myself, OK?"

"No, it's not OK!" The idea of somebody frightening Fizz filled Buchanan with fury and alarm. "It's not a matter of whether you can handle it yourself or not. It's a matter of ..."

He wasn't quite sure what it was a matter of; all he knew was that he had to know about it. Fizz didn't scare easily, he'd had plenty of opportunity to judge that, but although he respected her ability to look after herself he had to be sure that she could, indeed, handle this one on her own.

"It's no big deal," she said, clicking her tongue with exasperation. "It's just a guy that the Rentons owe money to. A builder called McPherson. He was there at the hotel, just before I came out, thirsting for their blood and I thought, just for a second, that it was him behind me."

Buchanan laid a hand on her shoulder to slow her down a bit, but it had little effect on her speed. "A guy in a black leather jacket? Right. I saw him. He came out while I was waiting for you. He didn't threaten you, I hope? If so ..."

"No, he didn't threaten me, Buchanan. Don't get your Y's in a twist. I told you: it was the Rentons he was gunning for and they weren't in. End of story."

"But he scared you. Don't tell me he didn't, Fizz."

"Goddammit, you do go on, you know that? OK, he's a scary dude, I admit it, but he's not really going to lie in wait for me outside the hotel. That was just ... I just wasn't thinking ... and when you popped up like Orpheus from the Underworld, it just threw me a little, that's all."

The heels of her Docs made solid rubbery thuds as she marched up the slope of the Royal Mile. There were still a few people walking about, but the traffic had slowed to a trickle of private cars and the odd taxi.

"You're sure this guy—McPherson?—is who he claims to be?" Buchanan asked. "You're not suspicious that he has some connection to Herr Krefeld's picture, are you?"

Fizz didn't answer for a moment, then she said, "I can't see how there could be any connection but, basically, all I know is what Gloria told me. Who knows whether she was lying or not?"

"Gloria already knows about him?" Buchanan ducked his head to see Fizz's face. "You mean, she was expecting McPherson to arrive? You mean, this wasn't his first visit?"

He could see from her expression that she was annoyed with

164

herself for letting the cat out of the bag, but he was even more annoyed—nay, infuriated!—to discover that the Rentons were putting her in such a dangerous position.

"This is preposterous, Fizz," he said, grinding his teeth as an aid to keeping calm. "I can't imagine why you're allowing this to happen. The Rentons are totally out of order—"

"Oh, for heaven's sake, let it lie, will you?" Fizz snapped. "I need the money, Buchanan, OK? I know this is an entirely new concept for you to grasp, but some people have to do things they don't particularly revel in so that they can enjoy such luxuries as food now and again. I have another two weeks to go to complete my contract and I'm not going to risk my bonus by telling Gloria to stuff her crummy job at this stage in the game."

"But you shouldn't have to put up with this thug making you scared to go out in the dark—"

"Listen." She stopped by the tall iron gate that sealed the passageway to her flat and turned to face him. "I'll talk it over with Gloria tomorrow night. She promised me that she'd get her accountant to square things with McPherson yesterday, but obviously it's taking a little time. I'll be firm with her when I clock on tomorrow night." She took out her bunch of keys and jangled them impatiently, making the point that she was in a hurry to get home to bed. "You still haven't told me what you're doing here. Has something happened?"

Buchanan was still far from happy about the staff safety standards at the Royal Park Hotel, but he could see that nagging on at Fizz was not going to solve matters. Shelving the problem for the moment, he took out the folder of snapshots and handed them to her.

"These are the photographs I took at the races. I think you may find one or two of them very interesting indeed."

"Really?" She slid the prints out of the folder, but there wasn't enough light to see them clearly. "What's interesting about them?"

Buchanan couldn't resist grinning. "Andrew wasn't the only suspect who was at Musselburgh that day. There's another face in the crowd that will give you food for thought."

"Well, who is it, for God's sake, Buchanan? Don't be so bloody annoying!"

"It's Teddy's son. George. He was waiting in a queue to put a bet on the last race."

She looked at the folder in her hand for a second and then turned her head and stared away up the hill toward the spire of St. Giles, sticking up above the rooftops. Buchanan waited patiently, rather hoping that she would have some light to throw on this unfathomable piece of information, but she disappointed him.

"What the hell?" she asked, turning back to him and wrinkling her nose in exasperation. "Were they together, do you think? Andrew and George? Surely not."

Buchanan shrugged. A cool wind had sprung up, turning his sweat-soaked tracksuit into an ice bag and he was in a hurry to get moving again. "I've been thinking about it all evening, but I'm as much in the dark as you are. Anyway, you can study the snaps and think it over and I'll talk to you on Friday."

"But I want to talk to you about it now," she said irritably and looked up and down the street again as though searching for an alternative to the obvious solution. Finally she bit the bullet and said, "Come up and have a coffee."

Buchanan was deeply sensitive to the honor he was being granted. In the full year he had known her, she had never allowed him—or anyone else he knew about—to pass through that iron gate, even to press her buzzer on the entry phone beyond. On the odd occasion when he'd had to pick her up at home, she had watched for him from the window rather than allow him entry.

He was, therefore, curious enough to take note of his surroundings as they passed through the arched entry into a small courtyard beyond and then climbed four flights of stairs to reach her tiny eyrie on the top floor. From the landing window, he could see the lights of Princes Street and, away beyond, across the Forth, the streetlights of Fife were draped across the dark hills like diamond necklaces.

He followed Fizz into a bare white room that was more like a small farmhouse kitchen than a lounge. Some kitchen units were crammed into what had once been a bed recess and the rest of the furniture consisted of two armchairs, a table, and two chairs. There were textbooks on the bookshelves, some photographs of her

166

grampa and his second wife, Auntie Duff, on the mantelpiece, and a clay pot of parsley on the windowsill, but otherwise the place looked exactly as it must have looked when she moved in last July.

By the time he realized that she was monitoring his scrutiny, it was too late to hide his dismay and it was clear she expected a comment of some sort.

"What can I say?" he shrugged. "Champneys it isn't."

That, oddly, appeared to please her more than if he had tried to dissemble. "Oh, I know it's not to your taste, Buchanan. But the fact is, the less junk you collect, the less dusting you have to do." She took a kettle out of a half-empty cupboard and held it under the tap. "For the eight years before I rented this place, remember, I carried everything I owned on my back. If I lived in a place like yours—with every drawer and cupboard crammed with stuff, and a hi-fi and a telly and a *cat*, for God's sake, it would feel like a ball and chain."

Buchanan could appreciate that her background was different from his, but that didn't stop him feeling depressed by her Spartan lifestyle. She'd never *had* any comfort in her life, that's why she didn't miss it. She'd never had a real home since the age of fourteen when she'd been sent away to school, never had a mother or father since she was three, never had the cash to buy the little comforts that he himself considered the bare necessities of life. The fact that she neither needed them nor wanted them somehow failed to cheer him up. She could throw all her possessions into her rucksack and be on the first tramp steamer out of Leith docks before he knew she was gone.

She had a good look at the photographs while she waited for the kettle to boil and then said, "What do you think, then? Were Andrew and George there together or separately?"

Buchanan shook his head thoughtfully. "Not together, surely? I just don't see Andrew and George as bosom buddies, do you? In fact, I wouldn't have thought that Andrew would have been into horse racing at all. Somehow he doesn't strike me as the type to travel all the way from Lamancha to Musselburgh for a day at the races. He might go with a party, perhaps, for a day out, but I wouldn't have thought he'd go on his own, or—even less likely—with George."

167

"Exactly what I was thinking," Fizz agreed. She put three spoon-fuls of brown sugar in his coffee, without asking, and topped it up with plenty of milk, the way he liked it. "I'm sure those two haven't much in common and they certainly didn't travel home together. I wonder if they each knew the other was there."

"I've been thinking about that." Buchanan drank half his coffee in one go, replacing some of his depleted body fluids, and began to thaw out a little. "You remember we thought that Andrew might have been acting a little strangely—keeping in the thick of the crowd, etc.? Well, if he was hiding from somebody—"

"—was it George?" Fizz finished for him. She thought for a minute and then put both hands to her face and gave it a brisk rub as though to encourage the flow of blood to her brain cells. "I'll tell you something, Buchanan: this bloody case gets more complicated every day instead of the other way round. A couple of days ago, I was telling myself I'd have to pack in because I had no suspects and no real leads. Now I have more suspects than I know what to do with and more leads than a plate of spaghetti. Shite! They can't *all* be in it, can they? We're not dealing with a bloody conspiracy?"

Buchanan looked at her curiously. "How many of them are you classifying as suspects?"

She set down her mug and held up a hand of spread fingers. "OK. We have the Rentons, who may or may not be telling the truth about Mr. McPherson. We have Andrew and we have George, one or both of whom must have put the picture up for auction. We have the Marriners—"

"The Marriners?" Buchanan was surprised into interrupting. "What have you got against them?"

"Well, nothing concrete, but they knew Konrad Schlegel before his suicide and it may not have been a suicide. OK, OK!" She flapped a hand at his expression of severe doubt. "I know there's evidence that it was genuine, but I'm keeping an open mind like you're always nagging me to do."

"OK. So that's—what?—six suspects?"

"Yes. But if you add in those who had opportunity but no proven motive you have to include Johnnyboy, who was on the premises when, presumably, the picture disappeared from Herr Krefeld's room. Then there's the person—probably one of the Foundation residents—from whom George or Andrew stole it."

"*If* they stole it," Buchanan pointed out. He had been going over this same ground all evening and had already explored that particular cul-de-sac. "It could have belonged to either of them. You've really no reason to conclude that any of the auctioned items were stolen."

"The bottle opener was stolen," she said, holding up a declamatory finger. "Andrew and Jean simply thought it had been mislaid."

"Did they? Jean thought so, I think, but maybe Andrew hadn't told her that he'd got rid of it. Maybe he'd never liked it. Who knows?"

Fizz fell silent, chewing the inside of her bottom lip and staring blindly at her Docs. Her hair was three-quarters loosened from the toggle at the back of her neck and clustering around her cheeks in a tangle of wispy ringlets and dancing gold springs. She looked pale and sleepy, the last of her summer freckles as clear as if they had been dotted across her cheekbones with a sharp eyebrow pencil.

"You're tired," Buchanan said, standing up and putting his mug on the mantelpiece beside a snap of her grampa's farm, where he had spent his recuperative fortnight last spring. "We can discuss this at the office on Friday if you want to."

He stopped halfway to the door, remembering that the problem of Mr. McPherson had not yet been settled to his satisfaction, but before he could speak she said, "No, Friday's too far away, Buchanan. I want to go back to the Foundation tomorrow and quiz Andrew—and maybe George, if he's there. We have to establish whether the bottle opener is actually his and I think we should also see what happens when we tell him we saw him at the races."

Buchanan never failed to be amazed by the scope of her demands on his time. "I've already taken half an afternoon off this week, Fizz, and the work is piling up. If you want to take time off in the evening, that's a different matter but—"

"You know I can't do that," she said, sullenly pushing out her lips as though he were being totally unreasonable. "Who'd man the reception desk?"

"Listen, Fizz. I don't want to interfere, I really don't, but Gloria has no right to ask you to deal with people of Mr. McPherson's stamp and she has no right to withhold your bonus if you resign early because of him." Buchanan tried to speak reasonably in case she suspected that he was taking the matter a little too personally. "Please will you do me a favor and let me speak to her? Maybe she'll feel it easier to tell me the truth of the matter, rather than an employee."

Fizz's face was like a brick wall. "No way. I don't need a man to fight my battles, Buchanan. I—"

"Don't think of me as a man, think of me as your legal representative. I can negotiate some leave of absence for you till she gets this matter cleared up."

"On full pay?" Fizz muttered, the scowl melting a fraction.

"Of course."

Silence.

Buchanan sighed inwardly and upped his offer. "I should at least be able to get you an evening off tomorrow."

"And you'd run me over to Lamancha?"

"I suppose so."

She smiled, her sullenness a thing of the past. "OK. I was planning on cornering her tomorrow morning anyway, so you can tag along with me and put in your two cents' worth if you like. But I don't want her to think you're there as my honorary daddy, OK? Your only reason for being there, as far as Gloria is concerned, is in finding out if Mr. McPherson has anything to do with the missing picture."

"It's a deal," Buchanan was happy to say.

It felt, at the time, like a minor victory, but as Buchanan was jogging home along Princes Street he realized that Fizz had also got precisely what she'd wanted out of the arrangement. Considerably more than he had, when you balanced it out.

# Chapter Seventeen

It took Rosemary the best part of five minutes to find the Rentons and tell them that they had visitors, and it was another five minutes at least before Gloria came striding into the TV lounge, where Fizz and Buchanan were waiting.

She seemed to Fizz to be holding herself rigidly together. Everything about her was stiff: her well-lacquered hair, her well-corseted bum, her set expression, her politely extended hand.

Buchanan, ever the gentleman, rose to receive her.

"I hope this isn't an inconvenient time for you, Mrs. Renton. We won't keep you many minutes."

"Not at all, Mr. Buchanan. Jason has gone to look for Frazer; I'm sure he'll be here in a minute. Good morning, Fizz." She lowered herself into the corner of a couch and clenched her hands in her lap. "Has there been some development?"

"Not really," Buchanan said, stretching out his legs and crossing his neatly black-socked ankles. Both his tone of voice and his body language were tranquil and soothing, and Gloria relaxed a little in response. "Fizz has been making steady progress, of course, but I don't think we're quite out of the wood yet."

"Well, these things take time," Gloria said as Frazer appeared in the open doorway, heralded by an invisible aura that was around sixty percent aftershave and forty percent whisky. "Ah, there you are, Frazer. Where on earth have you been all morning?"

"Garden," Frazer answered shortly, shook hands with Buchanan, greeted Fizz, and sat down beside his wife. "Something happened? Not bad news, I hope?"

Fizz kept her mouth shut. Buchanan was good at this sort of thing. He knew how to keep things cool and neutral, and she was content to let him set the tone of the conversation before she started complaining.

"No, nothing like that. Just a small point I want to clear with you to get it out of the way, so to speak." He smiled at Gloria as though asking her permission to go on.

"Of course. Anything we can do," she said, returning the smile, but her face froze again as Buchanan went on.

"Mr. McPherson." He raised his eyebrows and looked from Gloria to Frazer and back again. "Fizz mentioned that he had called more than once, demanding to see you and clearly in a violent frame of mind. Forgive me, but one can't help wondering if, perhaps, there could be some connection to the matter we're investigating."

"No, no. Nothing of the sort." Frazer jumped in immediately while Gloria was still choking in her spleen. "My wife explained all that to Fizz at the time—surely Fizz must have told you? The man's a cowboy builder who disappeared without finishing the job he was doing for us. Nothing to do with Herr Krefeld or his painting or any of that business, I assure you."

"What was it he was building for you?" Fizz asked.

Frazer swung his head round to look at her. "What?"

"The building job. What was it?" After waiting a moment for Frazer to think of an answer, she added, "Because I don't see any evidence of recent building work around the place. Certainly nothing half finished."

"It ... ah ... it was ..." The veins on Frazer's nose swelled visibly and he started sweating pure Scotch.

"Really, Frazer," Gloria said suddenly, sitting forward and laying a hand on his arm, "this is all very silly. We should have been frank with Mr. Buchanan from the beginning. Perhaps he could have been able to help us."

Frazer said nothing, but there was a pathetic glint of hope in the way he looked across at Buchanan.

"Please," Buchanan said, "feel free to tell me as much or as little as you choose. As I said, if it has nothing to do with the matter Fizz and I are interested in, then, of course, it's none of our business, but I'm happy to give you any advice that might be of assistance."

He caught Fizz's eye and gave his head an infinitesimal jerk toward the door, apparently suggesting that she should offer to withdraw, but Fizz was having none of that. Not unless Gloria insisted on it.

Gloria, however, was too keen to share her troubles to quibble. "I was afraid this would happen," she said, re-clenching her hands in front of what had once been her waistline. "We did everything we could to keep Herr Krefeld's death and the theft of his painting out of the papers. If it hadn't been for that dreadful woman—his sister!—insisting on making headlines out of it, no one would have been in the least interested!"

She took an embroidered handkerchief out of her jacket pocket and blew her nose angrily, giving Frazer time to say, "Mr. McPherson isn't a builder, of course. He's Jim Cox, Gloria's ex-husband."

Fizz had expected almost anything but this. She was surprised into an involuntary expletive and couldn't help but admire the calm way Buchanan nodded and murmured, "I see," as though the matter were of only academic interest to him.

"I can't tell you what I've had to suffer from that man," Gloria stated grimly, cutting across Frazer's next remarks as though what he had to say couldn't possibly be of any interest. "He has been a violent beast since we were on our honeymoon and so jealous that I was afraid to even speak to another man. He knocked a salesman down the front steps once and if the poor man hadn't fallen into a snowdrift he could have broken his neck. And as for the brutal treatment I myself had to put up with, you wouldn't believe it."

Fizz, for one, found it difficult to view Gloria in the role of a victim. The way she bullied everyone around her—and poor Frazer in particular—would have led one to suppose the boot had been on the other foot.

"Jim Cox is a psychopath," Frazer said, fixing his bloodshot eyes on Buchanan as though to impress on him the seriousness of the claim. "He put Gloria in hospital four years ago."

Fizz tried to exchange a covert glance with Buchanan, but he avoided her eyes and nodded understandingly at Gloria.

"So you left him?"

Gloria dropped her eyes and breathed heavily, lifting her shoulders in a half-shrug. "I met Frazer in hospital."

"I wouldn't allow Gloria to go back to that situation," Frazer said with a machismo which was rather touching since he had probably had little say in the matter. "She moved into my house as soon as she was discharged from hospital, but it was only a matter of weeks before Cox tracked us down there and we had to disappear."

"I don't know *what* he'd do to Frazer if he got his hands on him," Gloria burst out, grabbing Frazer's arm and squeezing it till her knuckles whitened.

"*I* do," Frazer muttered as she paused for breath.

"Frazer and I live in constant fear of opening the door and finding Jim on the doorstep. He tracked us down again after we moved to Peebles—he actually came face to face with Frazer in the post office!"

The reference affected Frazer visibly. "That was a nasty experience," he whispered, and swallowed thickly as though he were suddenly nauseous, "but, thank God, he didn't know who I was."

"But that's what made us decide to make a clean break, to start a new life here in Edinburgh. We thought it would be easy to disappear in the big city. It never occurred to us for a minute that he would eventually trace us here."

Neither of them seemed willing to carry the conversation any farther at that point. Their faces were both set in identical expressions of misery and Gloria was having difficulty in maintaining her rigid self-control. After a moment, Fizz opened her mouth to prompt them, but Buchanan raised a finger an inch off his chair arm and she took the hint.

Finally it was Frazer who went on, "We don't know how he got on to us. Very few people knew that we'd moved to Edinburgh and no one knew our address, but he found out somehow and we suspect he's been here for months trying to find us. We were—"

"You knew he was here?" Buchanan interposed as Frazer showed signs of omitting this information.

Gloria said, "I saw him on Princes Street. They say you'll see all the world on Princes Street if you sit there long enough." Her cheeks wrinkled crisply as she forced a smile. "That was back in … oh, May or June, I think. We knew he wouldn't give up easily, but there was nothing we could do except hope he wouldn't stumble across us. We'd been much more careful this time—there's no entry in the phone book under Renton, our rates listing is under the name of the hotel, and so on. But we hadn't counted on getting our name in the papers, which, of course, is what gave us away."

Fizz couldn't help but feel some sympathy for them, particularly for poor old Frazer, who was, basically, a nice guy and must, for years, have been regretting coming to Gloria's assistance.

Buchanan uncrossed his legs and sat up. "You've been to the police, I assume? You should be able to get an injunction to prevent Mr. Cox from approaching either of you."

Gloria emitted what would, in anyone less determinedly correct, have been a snort. "I've been to the police more times than I can remember, Mr. Buchanan. They are full of legal solutions, but none of them will stop my husband from mauling Frazer—or worse!—the minute he gets the chance. If he had known who Frazer was, that time he met him in Peebles post office, there's no way the police or an … an injunction or anything else could have stopped him. Oh, we could have charged him with assault, of course, but what good would that do if Frazer had to walk with a stick for the rest of his life? The police won't give us round the clock protection, so, you see, there's no solution to this sort of problem, Mr. Buchanan."

"Well, no easy solution, perhaps," Buchanan said. "But I don't think you have to give up just yet. Let me think about it for a minute."

He got up and walked over to the window bay, sticking his hands in his trouser pockets and staring out into the front garden. Frazer eyed his back hopefully and Gloria eyed his cute bottom with equally concentrated interest.

Fizz cleared her throat to reclaim their attention and asked, "What happened last night after I left? Did Mr. Mc—I mean, did Mr. Cox come back?"

"I don't think so." Gloria transferred her gaze to Fizz's face and her expression hardened. Clearly she wasn't too pleased about the part Fizz had played in dragging her dirty washing out into the public domain, but that, as far as Fizz was concerned, was just tough luck. "Hollis told me, of course, that you had warned him to expect trouble, but if my ex did come back he certainly didn't approach Hollis."

"I told him you'd be back around one a.m., so maybe he just

waited for you outside. Hollis would have locked up by then if all the guests were in."

Gloria inclined her head regally, indicating that she had no further comment at this stage.

"So," said Fizz brightly, "what about tonight? I assume you're not expecting me to man the drawbridge again, are you? I mean, I don't want to be unhelpful, but I'm not going to get into an argument with a leaded umbrella, Mrs. Renton, not even for you."

"No," said Buchanan's voice behind her. "That's certainly not going to happen, is it, Mrs. Renton? I'm sure I don't have to point out that you have a duty of care toward your employees and, really, Fizz already has considerable grounds for complaint."

"Oh, absolutely," returned Gloria obediently and Frazer, looking considerably alarmed, seconded this energetically.

"What I would suggest," Buchanan said, coming back to his seat, "is that you give Fizz a few days off till we deal with the immediate problem of Mr. Cox's persecution. Over the weekend should be enough. I'm confident that she could safely resume her duties by Monday night."

Gloria and Frazer looked at him with tremulous hope, encouraging Fizz to say firmly, "On full pay, of course."

"You think you can do something?" Frazer said gruffly. "God, I hope you're right, Buchanan."

"I think ... indeed I'm quite sure I can," Buchanan nodded. "I'll contact a couple of ex-policemen who have done some inquiry work for me in the past. They'll be happy to hang around for a few hours till Mr. Cox turns up and prevent him doing anyone any harm. With their evidence, you'll have no trouble having him arrested and I can assure you that a few months in jail will make him think twice before annoying you again."

For a second, Fizz was sure that Gloria was about to cast herself upon him and cover his face with kisses, but she contented herself with leaning across and laying her hand over his.

"If you can get rid of that man," she murmured, in tones that suggested severe laryngitis, "I'll be forever grateful. You really think a few days will be enough?"

"If Mr. Cox turns up over the weekend, Mrs. Renton, he'll be attended to once and for all, I promise you." Buchanan stood up, probably to rid himself of Gloria's hand, and looked pointedly at his watch. "Let me make a few phone calls and I'll get back to you this afternoon. And the arrangement with Fizz ..."

"Of course," Frazer hastened to assure him, and slipped a fatherly arm around Fizz's shoulders as they walked to the door. "No problem about that, we can get Hollis to come in early and cover for her over the weekend. She deserves a few nights off and it's the least we can do."

Even Gloria managed to crack a smile, in the end, and when Fizz looked back from the doorway she had squared her shoulders and was headed for the kitchen, probably for a celebratory bout with Johnnyboy.

Fizz had rarely felt so well disposed toward Buchanan as she did on their way to Lamancha that evening. He might be pedantic, unimaginative, faultfinding, prim, and mentally trapped in the 1960s, but occasionally, just occasionally, he could transcend all that and justify his existence. She curled up in the passenger seat of his Saab and smiled at his austere profile.

"You're some banana, Buchanan, you know that?"

"You're too kind."

"Nope. You're a silver-tongued wizard. A whole weekend off *with* pay is a helluva settlement. I don't know how you did it."

Buchanan said nothing, but with an air of great modesty.

"And the way you managed to get Gloria pouring out her soul to you like you were her shrink. I've got to hand it to you, muchacho, you're hot stuff."

Buchanan hooked a suspicious eyebrow at her. "I hate it when you're nice to me, Fizz. It usually ends up costing me money."

"Ah, but this time you've paid in advance," she said magnanimously, luxuriating in the thought of three consecutive days to herself. She watched the panorama of rolling farmland beyond the windscreen for a while, tuning over the morning's revelations in her mind, and then said, "And what about old Gloria, then? I'm still in shock. Imagine Gloria as the victim of a bullying husband. I mean— *Gloria*, for God's sake! She has a temperament like a Rottweiler."

"Overcompensation, maybe," Buchanan suggested. "She's making sure it doesn't happen again. It's hardly surprising if, as Frazer says, Cox was responsible for putting her in hospital."

"Mm-mm. He didn't say *how* though, did he? For all we know, she broke a tooth on his shin. I must say, that would be more in character. Or maybe she got one of his testicles stuck in her throat."

"You met the guy, I didn't," Buchanan said, "but if he's as violent as the Rentons are making out, I imagine even Gloria would have a hard time with him."

Fizz thought that was probably the case. Her one regret was that professional ethics prevented her sharing the story with Johnnyboy. His thoughts on the matter would have been worth hearing.

There was little sign of life around the Foundation buildings when they arrived. Neither Andrew nor Jean was in their cottage and their little suntrap corner was deserted, the chairs tipped up against the table and the wind chimes chattering like maracas in the breeze. The lights were on in the garden room, but they could see from a distance that Dodie was in sole possession, watching the television and working his way through a six-pack of lager.

"Well, bloody great," Fizz said, as they walked from the car park to the farmhouse. "They must all be in there with Teddy and Marcia, which means that we won't be able to talk to Andrew alone without making a big deal of it."

"Just a minute," Buchanan halted and stood peering into the gathering dusk. "Isn't that Andrew over there by the goat pen?"

It was indeed Andrew, pacing along slowly with his hands behind his back and his eyes on the path in front of him. Much relieved to get him on his own, Fizz hurried forward before someone else could turn up and interrupt her. He looked up when she was a few paces away and halted in surprise.

"Hi, Andrew."

"Well, well. How are you, Fizz? And Tam. Looking for the Marriners, are you? I've just left them at Kat's cottage."

"We wondered where everyone was," Fizz said. "The place looked like the *Marie Celeste* when we came in. Nobody to be seen except Dodie watching TV."

"Which is why everyone is round at Kat's place," Andrew said, in a sort of mumbled undertone which, no doubt, salved his conscience. "Why don't you go on round there? I'm sure they'll be glad to see you."

"We might do that," Buchanan said easily, propping his behind against a handy wall as if he was in no hurry to move on. "If you're sure we won't be intruding."

"Not a bit of it." Andrew assumed a more relaxed stance, clearly accepting that the conversation was likely to last longer than a few polite remarks in passing.

Fizz said, "We almost ran into you at the beginning of the week."

"Huh?" It was a most un-Andrew-like monosyllable and showed his surprise.

"Mmm. At the races. But you disappeared before we could attract your attention."

"Oh … at the races? You were there, were you? Dear me, what a pity I didn't see you." His cool was now firmly back in situ and he smiled as he said, "A great day, wasn't it? Were you lucky?"

"Yes," said Buchanan cryptically. "I rather think we were, actually, in one way or another. Are you a regular racegoer?"

"No, no. Not what you'd call regular."

"Tell you who else we saw there," Fizz remarked, watching his face. "Teddy's son. George."

"Really?" The reply was prompt enough, but there was a lot of fast thinking going on behind Andrew's eyes.

Buchanan said, "You didn't see him yourself?"

This time the reply was delayed a second while Andrew decided how much to admit. His smile was gone now and Fizz could see that he was caught in a dilemma: had he himself been watched while he was watching George, or could he safely deny seeing him? Finally he chose the safer route.

"I believe I did see the lad, but I didn't speak to him. Frankly, we don't get along too well, George and I." He straightened, shivering slightly as though he was feeling the bite of the wind, his body language indicating that he had other things to do.

"Before you go," Buchanan said, taking the bottle opener out of his jacket pocket. "I have something here that could possibly belong to you."

Andrew took it from him and turned it over in his fingers, but not with any particular consternation. He looked merely surprised and pleased as he looked back at Buchanan. "Where on earth did you come by this, Tam? Jean has been accusing me of throwing it out with the rubbish for the last month."

"I think it was stolen from you," Buchanan said, sidestepping the question.

It was perfectly clear to Fizz, from Andrew's sudden stillness, that he knew this was the truth. She said quickly, "And, of course, Andrew, you know who took it."

He looked at her, frowning a little, and then turned his eyes to Buchanan, but he made no reply.

Buchanan said, "We'd be very grateful, Andrew, if you could tell us what's going on here. It may appear to you to have nothing to do with the missing picture, but if someone is stealing from a Foundation resident we ought to know about it."

"Dear, dear, dear. This is bad," Andrew muttered. "This is very bad. I really don't think I should discuss it." He walked away a few steps, walked back, and shook his head. "I can't see any connection ..."

"It was George, wasn't it?" Fizz said, making it a bit easier for him. "Was that why you were watching him at the races?" She felt Buchanan twitch irritably at her elbow, but wasn't in a mood to be patient with Andrew's qualms of conscience.

"I should speak about this to Teddy first," he muttered.

Buchanan got up off the wall. "Teddy may not need to know. It might cause less upheaval if you just put us in the picture. If it has nothing to do with our investigation, you can rely on our complete discretion. No one else need know anything about it."

Andrew's head turned from side to side as though a solution to his dilemma might be found hovering in the evening air, then, to Fizz's utter surprise, he said, "Let's go over to the atrium. We'd better talk to Dodie."

# Chapter Eighteen

As they passed along the glass wall to the door of the garden room, Buchanan could see Dodie still lounging in front of the television set, the waistband of his jeans undone and his bare feet cushioned by the magazines on the coffee table. Evidently Dodie noticed their approach, however, because by the time Andrew ushered in his visitors he was at least decent.

"Hullo doll," he said to Fizz, affording Buchanan scarcely a glance as he dragged a chair closer to his own and indicated it with a flourish. "Things is lookin' up! C'mon in, ya wee stunner, an' give us yer chat."

Fizz moved the chair back a couple of feet and sat down, paying him no more attention than she would to a stain on the carpet. Andrew swung round a chair for Buchanan, but didn't himself sit down.

"Dodie," he said, leaning down to switch off the television set. "Fizz and Tam … they want to talk to us about George."

The pleased expression slipped from Dodie's face, leaving it blank. "What about George?"

Buchanan left that question to Andrew, which was a mistake because Fizz took the opportunity to leap in and stretch the truth more than was strictly necessary.

"We have a fair idea of what George has been up to," she lied placidly, "but we need you and Andrew to tell us what you know about it."

Dodie's eyes narrowed as he looked sharply at Andrew. He was a thoroughly unsavory looking character at the best of times, but right at that moment he looked a bit crazy too.

"I thought we should talk to them together, Dodie," Andrew said.

He was clearly under a fair bit of stress and his manner toward Dodie was both nervous and placatory. "We don't want the matter to go any farther, do we? This way there's no need to involve Teddy and Marcia."

"We'll treat any information you give us with the strictest confidence, of course," Buchanan said, falling back on formality in an attempt to keep things cool. "Nothing you tell us will go any farther than this room unless you give your permission."

Dodie took a long look round the gallery of faces, sank about a third of a can of McEwans lager, and shrugged. "I don't give a bugger who knows," he said. "George is a wee shite, a complete waste of space, an' if Teddy disnae know that already it's time he fkn found out."

"It would break Marcia's heart," Andrew said, apparently underlining his desire for secrecy. "She knows he's difficult to control, naturally, but she doesn't know he's a thief and a crook."

"A crook?" Buchanan wasn't quite sure what Andrew was intending to convey by that label.

Andrew stuck his unlit pipe between his teeth and walked about a bit in a confused way, then skirted the circle of chairs to prop himself against the windowsill. He clearly wanted Dodie to do the talking and Dodie was quite happy to do so.

"He's dead keen on the horses, George is, did y'know that? Fancies his chances as a fkn punter. As long as I've been here—near five months—he's been putting money on wi' the bookies three or four times a week." He smiled grimly at his beer can and gave himself another long pull. "All the time he's sittin' in here, reading the racing papers, talking about starting prices, flashing his fkn winnings. I used to get him to put on a few quid for me now and again—well, it started off as now and again, but then it got to be once a week at least. Then, when Andrew moved in, he started having the odd flutter too."

"Never more than a tenner," Andrew put in. "Maybe twenty pounds if George said he had a sure-fire cert."

"Did you win anything?" Fizz asked, irritating the hell out of Buchanan. She could never wait for information to come to her, she had to go and get it every time.

182

"No' fkn much," Dodie told her, "but enough to keep us going."

"It provided a little excitement in a somewhat monotonous environment," Andrew said, chewing his pipe stem. "There was precious little else going on around here. Of course, there's nothing to stop us going up to Edinburgh for a night out, or that kind of thing, but it's not encouraged. We're supposed to be on a sort of self-imposed retreat and the others—Kat and Bremner and the Marriners—well, they don't say anything, but you can sense their disapproval."

"Stuff them," Dodie muttered.

Andrew glanced at him and smiled. "I don't feel it much of a drag, really, but then, I'm up in town anyway, once a month, taking Jean to see her doctor, but our little weekly flutter on the horses seemed quite harmless. We—at least *I*—never dreamed that George was financing his own betting by ripping us off."

Buchanan had experienced a sort of premonition that something like that was coming, so he wasn't surprised, like Fizz, into a muttered, "Well, flip *me!*"

"He got away with it for weeks," Dodie growled, crushing his empty can in one fist with a controlled violence that made Buchanan doubt George's wisdom in trying to bilk him. "But he got too fkn greedy. He came up with a hot tip one day about the middle of July. Daddy's Girl in the three thirty at Musselburgh. Neither me nor Andrew here bothered wi' studying the form, but the odds were good, so we gave George twenty-five quid each. Well, the wee beauty came in first. Fkn George must've been crappin' hisself. He was gonny have tae cough up an' he didnae have that kinda money."

"Nearly a hundred and thirty pounds each, we reckon," Andrew said, grinning around his pipe. "Not such a great amount, I dare say, but it made up for all the bad weeks we'd had."

"Only the wee bastard never showed up with it," Dodie said savagely. "We never saw hair nor hide of him for the next week, so we knew he'd never placed our bet. Maybe he'd never placed any of them—just paid us out of his own pocket once in a while when we happened to win." He straightened and threw his empty can into a cane basket full of magazines. "It wisnae the money. Ah jist canny stand being shafted by a wee shite like him."

183

"So, what did you do about it?" Fizz prompted, meeting Buchanan's quelling frown with a glint of impatience.

"Dodie put the fear of death into him," Andrew started to say, but Dodie drowned him out.

"I didnae say nuthin'. Aw I did was leave a wee message on his fkn answerin' machine sayin' that if we didn't hear from him by the end of the week we'd be up to see him. I didnae have to spell it out—he fkn knew he'd better cough up."

"And did he?"

Buchanan ground his teeth. There was no shutting her up.

"No' for near a week. Then he came swanning in saying he'd had the 'flu and handed over the money as cool as you like."

Andrew moved away from the window, pulling a chair round and sitting down next to Fizz. "I believed him, actually," he said, looking a trifle embarrassed. "He's such a persuasive young man and we had no real reason to think he'd been duping us all these weeks. And even you, Dodie—you weren't really convinced, were you?"

"I'm no as daft as I'm cabbage-lookin'," Dodie claimed, almost convincingly. "I mebbe let him run a couple of weeks, but I was fkn sure he'd get what was coming to him if I caught him at any joukery-pokery."

"That's why I was at the races," Andrew said, confirming what Buchanan had already guessed. "He'd told us about another 'nap,' as he called it—Palermo—a certain winner that was running in the last race at Musselburgh that day. Once again, the odds looked suspiciously high for a horse that had any chance of making the first three, so Dodie and I decided to find out if he was really putting our money on or pocketing it."

"And the twisted wee pluke fkn pocketed it!" Dodie exploded, going red in the face and punching a fist into the arm of the chair. He grabbed another lager can, wrenched off the tag, and gulped furiously. "Fkn Palermo's still fkn runnin', but, by God," he said with a belch, "he'll think twice before he does it again when I get my hands on his scrawny neck! I'll teach the wee bastard a lesson he'll no' fkn forget."

"You haven't seen him since Tuesday?" Buchanan had to ask.

184

Dodie seemed too angry to speak, for a moment, but his fierce glare in Andrew's direction told Buchanan what to expect.

Andrew gnawed nervously at his pipe. "I was very angry with the lad, but by the time I got back here I was more afraid that, when Dodie learned the truth, he'd ... well, I thought a cooling-off period would probably be a good idea. I'm afraid I phoned George and told him to disappear for a while."

There was a long silence, which even Fizz seemed unwilling to break. Andrew fell to cleaning the dottle out of his pipe while Dodie sizzled quietly and muttered under his breath.

One could see now why George had been driven to petty larceny round about the end of July. He may have had a little cash in reserve and he may have managed to borrow a little more from his parents, but clearly the unexpected success of his hot tip had left him with a shortfall that could not be made up any other way.

The Samuels had contributed, albeit unwittingly, the silver bottle opener, and he had probably managed to pick up the sporting prints and the racing cup from somewhere around the racecourse. Unfortunately, there was still no clear pointer to where he had poached the oil painting.

"So, you can see why we'd prefer to keep it from Teddy and Marcia," Andrew said after a while. "They don't like George's interest in the racetrack—in fact, I'm quite sure they have no idea just how addicted the lad is—and they would, perhaps, infer that Dodie and I had, in some way, encouraged him. I'm sure they would be quite shattered to think that George was duping their guests, and our relationship with both of them would be bound to suffer."

"Actually," Fizz remarked, "he wasn't just duping the guests, Andrew. He was robbing them. He stole your bottle opener and he may have stolen from other people here as well. In fact, it looks very much as though he stole the oil painting we're looking for from somebody here and sold it at auction, together with the rest of his booty."

Dodie, who was beginning to succumb to the effects of at least four cans of lager in rapid succession, mumbled something incoherently, evidently threatening dire consequences if he himself turned out to have been among George's unwitting (fkn) sponsors.

"I think we asked you about the painting on our first visit," Buchanan said, "and you were unable to help us. But perhaps we didn't make it clear that the original Konrad Schlegel oil painting had been overpainted with a cottage garden scene. Does that sound familiar to you? You may have seen it in someone's cottage, or in the farmhouse, even. It's quite important to us to know who George stole it from."

Andrew sketched a humorless smile. "Cottage garden scenes are pretty thin on the ground around the Foundation," he said. "I can't imagine one finding wall space even in the storerooms and I doubt very much if any of us here would have had that sort of chocolate-box art in our possession, but you'd have to ask George."

"Aye, but you'd have to fkn find him first," Dodie added in a growl. "The wee shite."

Fizz got up and looked out of the window. "We should go now," she said to Buchanan. "It would be better if we didn't run into Marcia and Teddy. We'd only have to make excuses for being here."

"Kat's having a little show of her summer's work," Andrew said, "but I expect they'll all be wandering back this way shortly."

"Right then, we're out of here," Fizz decided and made tracks for the car, Buchanan at her heels.

"So, now we know what all the family rows were about," she claimed, throwing her bag on the back seat. "George must have been running back to them for a handout every time he backed a loser. I wonder if they knew what drain all their money was going down."

"I suspect not," Buchanan said. "If they had, I doubt if either of them would have continued to finance him. Though, who knows? Maybe Teddy could be just soft enough. Anyway, if you keep asking questions there's a good chance they'll be finding out pretty soon what George has been up to. Somebody must have missed that picture by now, wouldn't you think?"

"Just what I was thinking," Fizz nodded. "If that picture was stolen from somebody here—either Bremner or Kat, for my money—it means that he or she must be keeping their mouth shut to protect George from his parents' wrath."

"Don't forget Jean," Buchanan pointed out. "But, remember, as far as anyone knew, it was only a scrappy cottage garden scene. It could have been lying around unrecognized for twenty years. Even George didn't know what he was nicking."

Fizz looked displeased by this possibility for a minute or two and then gave an unwilling nod. "You're probably right there. I keep forgetting that it was painted over. But if it was just something that had been brought here with the rest of Konrad Schlegel's possessions, after his death, the whole trail we've been following is leading us up a blind alley."

Buchanan tried to think of something heartening and optimistic to reply to that remark, but failed.

# Chapter Nineteen

Fizz had all but given up trying to get into the filing room without Dennis spotting her. If he had been deploying pressure pads, heat sensors, and photo-electric cells, he could not have been more alert to her coming and going, and she rarely managed to get her jacket off before he was right there, leering at her round the door.

"Back to the grindstone, Fizz?"

She didn't even turn her head. "That's right. I've got a lot to catch up with this afternoon."

"You're quite a workaholic, you know." He edged his way around the filing cabinet she was working at so that he could see her face. "Slaving away every evening at your hotel job, putting in two busy afternoons here every week, and having virtually no time to yourself. Don't you ever get fed up?"

Fizz allowed a few seconds to elapse to show him that she was having to concentrate on what she was doing and then said, "I don't have time to get fed up."

He leaned an arm on the filing cabinet and brought his face down to her level. "Guess what?" he said, when she was forced to look at him. "Wainwright has completed."

"What?"

"Wainwright—the Wainwrights—the couple we showed round Greydykes—they've completed the deal. The missives were exchanged this morning."

"Oh yes? Great."

Dennis looked bleak. "I thought you'd be fractionally more euphoric, I must say. After all, you played a major part in getting rid of the dump."

There was, Fizz supposed, a certain gratification in having found Greydykes a loving owner, but the boost to her ego was totally outweighed by the reminder that she was still out on a limb as far as her investment in Wainwright's firm was concerned. The confirmation that Wainwright was, indeed, resettling in the Edinburgh area wasn't really much of a comfort because she'd been certain of that all along. What she needed now was to see a public announcement of Dalriada Brewers' takeover of his bottling plant.

"Aren't you pleased?" Dennis insisted.

"Sure, I'm pleased. But it's no big deal."

Dennis was crushed but not defeated. "Well, *I'm* pleased. I'm pleased we've got rid of a property that's been on the books for the best part of a year, I'm pleased we got a better price for it than the owner had any right to expect, and I'm pleased that we have an employee who looks like making a real impact on the conveyancing side of the business."

Well, that makes one of us, Fizz wanted to say, but she resisted the impulse and tendered a sixty-watt smile. "Good," she said, filing steadily. "It's nice to be appreciated."

Dennis straightened huffily and looked at the duplicating machine with an inquiring expression as though he would have been interested in its opinion.

"I *was* going to offer to buy you dinner," he said. "It seemed to me that some sort of celebration was in order."

"Well, that would be nice, Dennis, but I don't have a window in my diary at the moment." Fizz slammed a drawer shut, narrowly missing his fingers. It would have been such a luxury to be able to tell Dennis to flush himself down the nearest loo, but who could tell when a free meal would become a fundamental necessity, regardless of who she had to look at while she ate it? Asking for cash in lieu wouldn't go down at all well with Dennis, so one had to be diplomatic. "I'm planning to go home to Am Bealach for the weekend, actually, and I don't know when I'll next have a night off. Any chance of a rain check?"

That cheered him up for the moment anyway. "Just let me know when you have the time, Fizz."

"I will. Thanks," Fizz told him, praying silently that she would

never be that hungry. Quite apart from Dennis's personal repul-
siveness, the whole idea was a no-no. There were three things a
smart girl did not do: use a hairdryer in the bath, vomit into the
wind, and fraternize with her boss. Well, not the junior partner,
anyway.

Which prompted her to wonder how long it would take the
senior partner to congratulate her on her talents. It was Buchanan
who would decide on whether to employ her as an apprentice in
two years' time, so it was his opinion that mattered.

For some reason, there was twice as much filing to do as was
normal on a Friday, so it was almost four fifteen before she got
round to cornering Buchanan.

He did a bit of eye rolling as she cleared a place to sit down on
the corner of his desk. "Ten minutes maximum, Fizz, OK? I've things
to do."

"I just want to pick your brains for a minute before you disappear for the weekend."

"All right. But talk fast. What's bothering you?"

"Well, the whole setup out at Lamancha, basically." Fizz gestured
helplessly. It wasn't easy to be explicit, especially with a time limit
on her explanation. "Right up till Gloria spilled the beans about her
husband yesterday, I had her down as one of my main suspects. I
was sure—well, fairly sure—that she and Frazer had to be involved
somehow with the disappearance of the picture. But now we're
sort of narrowing in on George and the Foundation, and I realize
we should have been doing a lot more nosing around out there,
seeing what we could turn up."

"This 'we' you're referring to being you and me?" Buchanan
inquired, but Fizz paid that remark the attention it deserved. He
might like to pretend that he was keeping firmly to the sidelines,
but there was no need to encourage him.

"So," she said, "what we should now be doing is finding out
what we can about the Foundation's guests. Have any of them any
connection to the Black Forest? Did any of them know Konrad
Schlegel? Were any of them beneficiaries under his will?"

Buchanan got up from his desk, wiggled his shoulders, and did
a few neck exercises. He was in the wrong job, really, you could see

that at a glance. He liked to be out of the office, moving around, talking to people. It was obvious he had been raised to accept that he'd be following in his daddy's footsteps when he left school and had never even asked himself if that's what he really wanted to do with his life.

"The Marriners would probably be your best source for that kind of information."

"Yes, but I'm playing it cool," Fizz said impatiently. "Teddy and Marcia definitely did know Schlegel before his so-called suicide—"

Buchanan interposed a groan.

"—and I'm not forgetting that. They have to be included in the list of suspects. In fact, I need to know more about their life in Cornwall."

"You think that could have some bearing on the case?" Buchanan frowned, still wandering restlessly about the room. "How, exactly?"

Fizz hated it when he pinned her down like that. Her vague suspicions couldn't be translated into words, especially words that would mean anything to someone like Buchanan, for whom everything had to be logical.

"I just think the whole business stinks," she said. "If the three of them lived in each other's pockets for years, the way they claim, the situation was a bomb waiting to go off. It's not natural."

"So they bumped him off?"

Buchanan's attempts at keeping his face straight were not always as successful as he evidently thought they were, but at least he tried.

"I didn't say that. But we should surely be trying to talk to somebody who knew them in those days."

Buchanan came back to the desk and sat down. "You have someone in mind?" he asked warily.

"No. Do you know anyone in St. Ives? I imagine the three of them were fairly well known—if not in person then by reputation."

Buchanan didn't even bother to think about it. "No," he said immediately. "I've no connections in that part of the world."

Fizz regarded him patiently. "You're not trying. What about lawyers? People you were at university with? You must know estate agents at least, because we've sold houses for people who moved here from Cornwall."

"Indeed? And how did you come by that information?" Buchanan closed his eyes and inclined an ear for her answer.

Fizz looked at his face and resisted slapping it. "I looked up the files, that's how. And don't start on about it because it's not exactly classified information and I did it on my own time." She put a scrap of paper in front of him. "I made a few notes. These are the phone numbers of two estate agents we've dealt with in the past few years."

Buchanan barely glanced at the paper. "I don't know these people, Fizz. I can't—"

"Sure you can. I've checked them both myself to see how long they've been in business and they were both around when the Marriners sold up twenty years ago. There weren't many estate agents in St. Ives at that time, so there's a good chance that one of them sold the lighthouse where they used to live. You'd think a property like that might stick in their minds if nothing else did."

Buchanan looked at his watch. "Fizz—this is really a waste of time. If you want to go ahead and do it yourself, I've no objec—"

"That's no use, Buchanan! You know they'll tell me to take a running jump." Fizz slid off the desk so that she could scowl at him more successfully. "Just give them a quick ring and put out a few feelers. Please. It won't take you a minute. I really need you to do this for me. And Buchanan—if the wind changes, your face will stick like that."

"I wish you wouldn't involve me in things like this, Fizz," Buchanan muttered, glowering at the phone numbers. "What is it, exactly, that you want me to ask?"

"Nothing specific. Just see if you can locate someone who knew of the Marriners and Schlegel. Were there any rumors about them? Any gossip? Were they really as close as they make out or was Marcia, perhaps, jealous of Teddy and Konrad's relationship? Any suggestion of homosexuality? Or were Marcia and Konrad closer than they should be?" Fizz spread her hands. "Just get in there and rummage."

Buchanan pushed the paper about a bit and then pulled the phone across to him and leaned back in his chair. "OK. But you can take yourself off while I do it. I can't stand having you putting your oar in all the time and telling me what to say."

This was less than satisfactory, but Fizz had little room to maneuver. In any case, she knew he would only stick a finger in his ear as he always did when she tried to interfere in his telephone conversations. She left him to it for ten or fifteen minutes and then stuck her head round the door. He was still talking and scribbling on his notepad, but there was a winding-up tone to his voice, so she went in and tried to look invisible till he hung up.

"Success?" she said, reading his face.

"Yes and no. This guy Pengilly," he tapped the paper with his pencil. "He didn't know the Marriners personally, but he knew a fair bit about them, albeit at second hand. His ex-partner had been a financial adviser at one time and Teddy was one of his clients."

"So what's the catch?"

"Nothing in particular. Just that nothing he could tell me actually amounted to much." Buchanan swung his chair round and stretched out his legs. "There was a little gossip about the three of them living together all those years, but nothing that had any basis in fact, as far as anyone was aware. The lighthouse was a few miles outside St. Ives and they weren't at all well known locally. He couldn't tell me anything about either Marcia or Konrad and all he knew about Teddy, really, was that he was a painter himself and that he thought Konrad Schlegel was the greatest artist since Michelangelo. There's absolutely no question about his affection for Schlegel. He virtually supported the guy and, according to Pengilly's ex-partner, he felt privileged to do so."

Fizz thought about that and decided that if Schlegel was such a brilliant artist he should have been earning enough to support himself, which didn't say much for Teddy's ability as an agent. That figured, of course. You need a certain toughness to sell anything, and Teddy had shown precious little aptitude in that department. He couldn't even browbeat his own son with any degree of success.

"And that's all you got?" she asked.

"I fear so," Buchanan ran the end of his pencil down the page of notes and nodded. "Not a great deal, but it does confirm to some extent the claim that they were very close, Teddy and Konrad."

"Mm-mm. I suppose so." Fizz stood up and stretched. It was almost five and she was looking forward to her weekend off. "I

193

ought to phone Frau Richter this weekend, but I'll put it off till Monday, I think. That'll give me time to look up Konrad's will first, on the off chance that he left some of his work to someone other than Teddy. I want to fit in a visit to Grampa over the weekend, but I'll have to have something to report to Frau Richter, or the money will stop coming."

"She's very keen to get this picture back, isn't she?" Buchanan remarked, looking at his watch with a grimace as he spoke.

"Well, it was her brother's parting gift, so to speak. You can't blame her." Fizz felt herself wholly in sympathy with the old dear. "Also, she seems to see it as a sort of window into the past, I reckon. Apparently, the scene is all changed now. Commercialized. Sailing schools on the lake, houses crowding the beach, etc. Her snapshots, so she says, don't do it justice."

"Mm-hm." Buchanan had both elbows on the desk and was holding his pencil in both hands, rolling it under his nose like a Corona.

"Mm-hm?" Fizz prompted, wondering what was going on in his head.

"I was just thinking … the painting wasn't a slavish depiction of the lake, was it? Why did Schlegel omit the stand of trees that were quite immature in Frau Richter's snapshot? They must still have been standing, even thirty years later. And why include a pile of black rocks?"

"Artistic license," Fizz said, with the confidence bestowed on her by one session at Edinburgh College of Art.

"You think so?" Buchanan wondered. "The trees, yes. They probably weren't particularly attractive and they obscured part of the vista. But, the rocks? I just don't see the need to paint in rocks beneath it, despite what Phillip Ure said about contrast. Why would Schlegel do that?"

"Because they were there," Fizz suddenly remembered. "Frau Richter said there are rocks there now that weren't there when she was a child."

Buchanan scratched his jaw and looked at her vaguely. "Did she say where they came from?"

Fizz, personally, couldn't see that it mattered much. "Apparently it's all changed now, with houses on top of the cliff. They'd probably have to level the cliff top if they wanted to build on it, so the rocks probably fell to the beach at that time."

"Recently? Did Frau Richter tell you that?"

"Uh-huh. Well, quite recently, I suppose. She said they were building new houses on top of the cliff when she was there a few years ago."

"Because Schlegel died more than a few years ago," Buchanan said, frowning with concentration.

"So?" It wasn't clear to Fizz where his thoughts were leading him, but she suspected he was off down one of his dead ends. "The rocks he painted could have been pure artistic license, like Phillip said in the first place."

Buchanan raised his brows. "Which would make him clairvoyant. If the recent construction work resulted in a pile of rocks at the foot of the cliff—and, from what you tell me, that seems very possible—Schlegel foresaw their position nearly twenty years ago."

It wasn't like Buchanan to look for a supernatural explanation for mysterious events, and such an explanation certainly didn't appeal to Fizz. But, on the other hand, Frau Richter had not been surprised by the revelation that the painting had shown rocks in that particular spot. She knew the beach had changed radically in the last few years. And, if it had …

"What you're saying is that the painting must be a fake, is that it?" she asked Buchanan, and when he didn't rouse himself to respond she carried on thinking aloud. "Well, it must be. If the rocks only fell to the foot of the cliff 'a few years ago'—which must be taken to mean within three or four years at the most—the picture must have been painted since then, and that rules out Konrad Schlegel."

"And yet," Buchanan muttered, nodding his head at her to underline his point, "it was good enough to fool the art experts. Barry Williams thought it was probably genuine and so did his colleague Trickett, apparently."

Fizz began to get excited. "Someone must have been making a nice living by selling fake Schlegels, but the one Herr Krefeld picked up was their big mistake. If that picture shows a scene that can be proved to be post-Schlegel, the cat's well and truly out of the bag." She considered this scenario for a moment. "Would it be worth the forger's while to kill Herr Krefeld to get the picture back?"

"How would the forger know he had it?" Buchanan hedged.

"He must have phoned the Foundation to speak to Teddy about it. Anyone could have taken the call."

Buchanan leaned back in his chair and swiveled it from side to side. "I'm beginning to like this storyline, Fizz: the idea that someone at the Foundation faked a Schlegel, that he or she painted a trashy piece of artwork on top—probably to hide it—and that George stole what he thought was a bit of unheeded rubbish to turn into ready cash. It has a ring of truth about it, don't you think?"

The small flutter of excitement Fizz had been experiencing under her diaphragm was now making her feel like she had swallowed a live chicken. "I have to phone Frau Richter," she stated urgently. "I have to know when those rocks came on to the beach."

Buchanan's reply was to slide the telephone across the desk to her, his lack of hesitation proof that he was as excited as she was, though, typically, you'd never have known it from his face.

Fizz had to look up her notebook for Frau Richter's number and her fingers could barely function as she turned the pages and dialed the code.

"Frau Richter? It's Fizz. This has to be a brief call, I'm afraid—I'm using someone else's phone—but there's one small detail I have to check with you."

"Yes? What can I tell you?"

"The beach at the end of the Schluchsee—you remember you mentioned that there were rocks on the beach last time you were there? Do you know how long they had been there?"

Frau Richter took ages to answer. She seemed thrown by the question and sounded hesitant as she replied, "How long had they been on the beach? Ah, yes, I see what you mean. I believe they fell when the cliff was leveled for building. That would be … oh, five years ago now. Why, is it important?"

"I'm not sure yet," Fizz said. "I'll let you know when I phone you next week."

She rang off as quickly as Frau Richter would let her and turned to Buchanan. "Looks like you were right, oh Fount of All Knowledge. The rocks came down when the cliff was leveled for building five years ago. Schlegel could never have seen them."

Buchanan was probably as pleased as hell, but you could never be sure. He looked at his watch.

"Right. Can I go home now or have you more chores in mind for me?"

"No. You've earned a break, compadre," Fizz said, "unless you feel moved to give me a run home?"

Buchanan cleared his desk by sweeping everything into his brief-case. "You're not on," he said, predictably. "But if you're ready to go, I'll take you up the hill as far as Princes Street."

Fizz settled for that, since it halved her walking time, and they continued to toss ideas around while they walked to the car.

"I wonder if either Andrew or Jean has the talent to forge a Schlegel so efficiently," Buchanan said as he slid behind the wheel. "Kat is basically a potter—though, of course, that doesn't mean she can't paint as well—and Dodie's style is strongly individualistic. Have you seen any of Bremner McGrath's work?"

"No, but in any case, anybody with a good art education could turn their hand to forgery—particularly if they had a painting to copy. And, remember, there are virtually identical paintings in the collection."

"Yes, but without the rocks."

"I'll tell you what's really niggling me," Fizz admitted. "Why, having forged the damn thing, would somebody then paint a crappy garden scene on top of it?"

"You think it was the forger who did that?"

"You don't?"

"I have an open mind on the matter."

Fizz's own suspicions—unlike Buchanan's—had to encompass her belief that there was something fishy about Konrad Schlegel's death. It was hard to imagine the Marriners as murderers, particularly in view of their proven affection and admiration for Schlegel, but they certainly knew him at the time of his suicide and they probably knew more than they had ever admitted.

They were waiting for the traffic lights to change at the corner of Princes Street when the truth hit Fizz like a cannon ball.

"Oh, my God, Buchanan," she yelled, pounding the dashboard with a triumphant fist. "Schlegel's still alive! The Marriners are hiding him!"

# Chapter Twenty

Buchanan had fond memories of the island of Arran. He had visited it several times before, but only for the day, so he had seen little of the island apart from Brodick, where the ferry put in. Fizz didn't know the island at all, but she claimed to be perfectly confident that they'd have no trouble finding Camusfergus beach, where Konrad Schlegel had committed suicide.

"We'll stop on the way and buy an Ordnance Survey map," Buchanan said as they headed for Glasgow on the motorway. "The last ferry from Brodick to Ardrossan is four forty on a Saturday, so we won't have any time to waste on orienteering."

"It's not all that big an island," Fizz said airily. "You'll probably find that the first local you meet will be able to give you directions."

"Yes, but I want to see if I need to take the car over or if there's likely to be public transport to where we want to go."

There was something a little unnerving about taking off into the unknown with Fizz. A five-minute error in their timetabling would result in a missed ferry at the end of the day, and the idea of spending a night under the same roof as Fizz was not one that Buchanan could contemplate with equanimity. She was perfectly able to cause trouble in an empty house and the devastation she could wreak in such potentially combustible circumstances beggared the imagination.

"There's bound to be some sort of bus service on the island," she said, "but even if we have to take a taxi it's still going to be cheaper than taking the car over on the ferry."

Buchanan was unconvinced, but they were beyond Glasgow and heading for the west coast before they left the motorway and found a place to buy a map.

"There you go," Fizz said, pointing ahead at a blue notice that listed Parking, Information, Toilets. "They'll have maps at the tourist office."

"Sure to."

"Information toilets," she mused as Buchanan slowed and pulled into the slip road. "I suppose they're something like a speak-your-weight machine. I wonder what sort of information they give? 'Eat more fiber,' maybe. Or, 'This sample is seventy-eight percent lager.'"

She went in to check out this assumption while Buchanan bought a map and reappeared as he was spreading it out on the bonnet of the car.

"Guess what," she remarked, in a voice that must have been clearly audible to the group of bus tour passengers in the next parking space. "I'm pregnant!"

Aware that some fifty pairs of eyes were awaiting his reaction to this announcement, Buchanan had to force an exaggerated laugh, which evidently shocked Fizz more than his usual frigid reaction to such typically indelicate humor.

"Isn't modern technology wonderful?" he said, returning his attention rather abruptly to the map. "The lady at the information desk says there is a bus service that goes right around the island. Two or three buses meet the ferry, so if the beach is not too far from civilization we should have no trouble getting to it."

Fizz held down the two corners of the map closest to her and bent her head to within four inches of the paper, blocking Buchanan's view and tickling his face with her hair. "Lots of beaches," she remarked, running a forefinger round the bean-shaped shoreline. "But most of them are fairly close to the road."

From what little Buchanan could see of the map, there appeared to be one main road, which ran right around the island, plus two roads that ran across its width, dividing it roughly into three. The northern end looked fairly mountainous, but to the south the terrain was more pastoral, with low hills and wide, empty stretches of moorland. Many of the beaches were ribbed with low basalt dikes, a legacy of the outflow from the volcano that had originally formed the island, and on one of these Fizz's stalking finger halted.

"That must be Camusfergus beach. Look. There's Camusfergus Farm, and the beach below it fits the details that were in the newspaper report: long rocky promontories, deserted but for a single cottage. That's it OK."

Buchanan measured the distance to the main road. "Less than a mile and a half. That's not too bad. And it's ... what? Not more than ten or twelve miles from the ferry port, which means we can get away with leaving the car at Ardrossan."

"What did I tell you?" Fizz said dismissively and got back in the car before he could argue.

The ferry crossing took less than an hour, just time enough for Fizz to consume two bacon rolls, two buttered scones, two cups of coffee, and half of Buchanan's pot of tea. She had, she claimed, missed her breakfast, owing to Buchanan's insistence on making an early start but, in spite of assuring him that she would pay her own expenses for the day, she made no attempt to pick up the bill. Frau Richter's expenses checks apparently went straight into the bank, which, knowing Fizz, came as no surprise.

The wind picked up quite noticeably during the journey, but once they entered the shelter of Brodick bay it was pleasant enough on the lee side of the deck and they were able to enjoy the scenic approach to the island and the bustle of docking and tying up.

"I wonder what attracted the Marriners and Konrad Schlegel to a place like this?" Fizz wondered as their bus meandered slowly southward through scattered villages and lush pastureland. "You'd have thought they'd get enough sea and sand around their lighthouse in Cornwall."

"Arran has always been a favorite haunt of artists," Buchanan said, remembering his first visit to the island as a boy, which must have been around the time of Schlegel's alleged suicide. "It used to be quite a hippy place in the sixties and seventies, I believe. My mother used to swear that, with the wind in the right direction, she could smell the hash before the ferry left Ardrossan."

"Really?" Fizz looked thoughtful. "I wonder if they were into the hard stuff, the three of them?"

Buchanan couldn't see that possibility having much bearing on whether Schlegel was, indeed, still alive and that was the question uppermost in his mind at the moment. In spite of himself, he had become intrigued by the case and, now that it looked as if the tangled skeins were beginning to unravel, he couldn't leave it alone. That, he had decided, was his main reason for being here, heavily outweighing the fact that if he hadn't accompanied Fizz she'd have made the trip anyway, and probably not alone.

There was only one way of discovering whether it would be possible to fake a suicide on Camusfergus beach, and that was to go and see it for themselves. With luck, they might also be able to talk to the farmer who claimed to have witnessed Schlegel taking the plunge. It wasn't the sort of thing that could be done by telephone, and besides, it was a pleasant enough day out. He'd had to cancel his golf arrangements, of course, but that might prove to be a wise move. If Carlotta turned up and found him absent, she might regret the way she had frozen him out last weekend. Maybe he'd give her a ring at the beginning of the week and find out.

The bus dropped them off about a mile inland from the beach on a single-track road that curved gently downhill between hedges of hawthorn and fuchsia. The fields beyond were mainly pastureland, but some had been cropped for hay and the black polythene-wrapped bales were still lying around like—as Fizz pointed out—the droppings of some Martian caterpillar. The shoreline was hidden by low hillocks and, at first, they could see only a stretch of choppy sea, a distant line of hills that might be the Mull of Kintyre, and a couple of sailing yachts in the distance. A herd of black-and-white cattle provided the only sign of life, regarding them without much interest as they marched past.

"There," said Fizz, pointing down toward the shore. "Chimneys. I bet that's the cottage."

It had to be. There was no other habitation in sight, and as they wound their way down to sea level it was clear that it stood virtually on the beach itself, as per the newspaper report.

Camusfergus beach was a horseshoe of white sand, backed by a fairly high bank of round, white pebbles, and separated from the road itself by a strip of sheep-cropped turf. On the opposite side of the road, the ground rose so steeply that only low scrub and bracken clung to the slope and it continued to rise, in a series of tilted fields, to a long flat-topped ridge. On a calm and sunny summer's day, the shallows would be turquoise blue over that pale sandy bottom and the distant hills would be as magical as Bali Hai. Even today, with white horses on the water and gray clouds building up to the north, it looked a wonderful place to lose oneself for a week or two.

"I don't know," Fizz argued when Buchanan voiced his thoughts. "I don't know that it was such a good idea to bring Schlegel here, not if he was as depressed as they say he was. You don't want to be locked up inside your own head when you're depressed with nothing to do but focus on your own troubles. You need stimulation and company. Activity. A counter-irritant, even. If I'd been trying to help Schlegel regain some sort of balance, I'd have signed him on for a week of hell on one of those sail training ships. He'd have been so bloody glad to get back to terra firma afterward that everything else that was worrying him would have paled to manageable proportions."

Buchanan looked at her curiously, but her face was hidden by a commotion of whirling hair. "That sounds like the voice of bitter experience," he suggested, but she merely grunted, as she always did when he evinced any curiosity about her past life.

"What I'm saying," she insisted, "is that bringing a suicidal person here would practically guarantee their deciding to commit hara-kiri."

Buchanan had to grin at her inconsistency. "You can't have it both ways, Fizz. Either the Marriners murdered Konrad Schlegel by encouraging him to end it all or the suicide was a fake and he's still alive."

"Oh, he's still alive all right," she said with calm conviction. "I don't believe the Marriners' intentions were at all evil—because, in fact, I wouldn't even be surprised if Schlegel wasn't actually suicidal in the first place. I reckon he came here with the deliberate intention of faking his own death. I'd put good money on it."

Buchanan was rather inclined to agree with her. Camusfergus beach was just about as remote a spot as one could find without traveling another hundred miles up the west coast. There were no houses in sight, other than the holiday cottage itself, and there was probably very little traffic along the single track road since, according to the map, it led only to a few houses, somewhere out of sight around the headland to the south, before looping back to the main road.

Fizz took off along one of the two spurs of rock that formed the arms of the bay, her Docs scraping and slipping on the basalt. "I reckon this is where he did it," she yelled back to Buchanan, who was following at a pace more suited to the preservation of his suede shoes. "He walked along here, took off his jacket and sweater, and took a dive off the end into deep water. It's pretty darn deep too, down there, even at this state of the tide, and I guess it has still quite a bit to go before it reaches slack water."

Buchanan got as near to the end of the rocks as he could without getting soaked by the spray. There was certainly enough depth there to hide someone swimming underwater. It was pitch black and long ribbons of reddish seaweed streaked the surface, indicating a hidden forest beneath.

"What d'you think?" Fizz said. "Is there anything to be learned from checking out the cottage, or should we take a toddle along to the farm now? I'm starving, and the farmer might offer us a cup of tea."

Buchanan looked at her upturned face and was momentarily irritated by her thrashing hair. He took his hands out of his pockets with the intention of holding it back from her face but stopped himself just in time, alarmed by his own folly.

"The farm," he said, stepping past her. "You talked me into it."

There were sometimes quite lengthy periods when Fizz rather liked living in Edinburgh, but she was always glad to get away from the noise of traffic and the press of crowds. The smell of manure and diesel fuel that met them as they approached the farm buildings reminded her of home—if Am Bealach could still be called home after more than twelve years of non-residence. There was also, however, a strong odor of silage, which was less evocative, and the mud and cow shit that plastered the cobbled yard would never have been tolerated by Grampa or Auntie Duff.

Two chained border collies announced the arrival of guests well before they could reach the door of the farmhouse and, as Fizz raised her hand to knock, a voice behind her said, "Yes?"

There were two people standing in the open end of the horsebox at the corner of the building: a big man with a mallet and a short woman with bowed legs. Fizz was immediately struck by the possibilities of a game of croquet, but the man didn't look in the mood.

"Somethin' you want?" he said.

Fizz let Buchanan do the introductions; he was better at that than she was and always managed to impress people without putting their backs up. As he spoke, the couple got down from the horsebox—which looked as much like a dirty protest as the yard did—and came toward them.

The farmer—whose name was McFarlane, if Fizz's memory served her correctly—was built like Battersea power station. He was three or four inches taller than Buchanan, who was probably knocking six feet, and he was considerably wider all round, particularly his neck, which appeared to be just an extension of his head. He was younger than Fizz had expected—maybe about forty or forty-five.

Mrs. McFarlane came up to his shoulder. She had lank black hair that fell over her face in strands and her wide gray eyes held an expression of abysmal stupidity. You could tell from the way she perked up halfway through Buchanan's preamble that she was thrilled to be asked about what was probably the only exciting thing to have happened around that neck of the woods since the arrival of the last Viking longboat.

Her husband was also pleased, but he hid it a little better.

"Och, I was thinking you were a couple o' they bloody ramblers," he admitted, wiping his hands on his overalls, which were already filthy. He appeared to be wearing most of his breakfast as well as a representative sample of every animal on the premises. "They come stravaiging through here as though they own the place, wantin' to buy milk an' eggs. We could see them far enough."

"... far enough," Mrs. McFarlane supplied, as though she had been singing a duet with her husband but had finished just a fraction later.

205

"It was you who witnessed Konrad Schlegel's suicide, wasn't it?" Fizz thought it better to make sure in case they were talking to the witness's son.

"Aye. I watched the whole thing from the top o' the brae there." He waved one pit-prop arm in the direction of a field of cows. "I didn't know what he was up to at the time, mind. You can't be up to they foreigners, you know. They wouldn't think twice about going in for a swim wi' their clothes on, some o' them, so I never gave it another thought."

"… thought," Mrs. McFarlane nodded, smiling at her husband with awe and encouragement.

"When did you realize what had happened?" Fizz asked. It was clear they weren't going to be invited in for a cup of tea and she wasn't a bit sorry.

"Well, he never came up, you see. I kept looking for his head appearing and it never did. I couldn't believe it." It was clearly not the first time he had related this story, but he was far from averse to repeating his performance. "It was a flat calm that day and I'd have seen him if he came up, but it turns out the chappie wasn't a swimmer at all. Couldn't swim a stroke, Mr. Marriner told me."

Buchanan folded his arms and propped a foot on a heap of bricks that were piled beside the doorway like a piece of installation art. "Did Schlegel know you were watching him, do you think?" he asked. "Did he wave or anything?"

"No' him," the farmer snorted and gave a short bark of laughter while his wife echoed the words. "A right dour character he was. Never looked the road I was on. No' like Mr. and Mrs. Marriner."

"You saw the Marriners a lot?" Buchanan said.

"Oh aye. A nicer couple you couldn't meet in a month of Sundays. Always had time for a wee chat when they came up for their milk. None of yer toffee-nosed English, these two. I was heart sorry for them when they came back that day and found out what had happened."

"Came back from where?" Fizz asked. She directed the question equally at both of them, but Mrs. McFarlane merely turned her worshipping eyes to her husband and waited for him to answer, her lips, as he did so, moving silently in sync with his.

"Brodick," he said. "They gave me a wee toot on their car horn as they went past the foot of the brae just about half an hour before the German chappie appeared out of the house. Away to see Brodick castle, they were. They told Moira here when they were up for their milk that they were going for a run."

Moira nodded at him and then at Fizz and Buchanan, her pale eyes glowing with importance.

Fizz looked at the field of cows that bordered the hilltop. "Would you mind if we took a walk down? Just to see what the beach looks like from here."

"Aye, right. We'll go with you and keep the beasts out yer way. They're about ready to be milked and they'll be out the gate the minute you open it."

"... open it," Moira smiled and, grabbing a stick that was leaning against the wall, she marched on ahead with her husband, making no attempt to circle the deeper pools of manure or taking any thought for the hens and chickens that darted about her wellie-booted feet. From the rear, the two of them looked, to Fizz, like Tarzan and Cheetah, but when she shared this insight with Buchanan he wasn't at all amused.

Together the McFarlanes drove the clustering cows back from the gate and untied the piece of binder twine with which it was secured. "Mind your feet," mentioned Moira kindly, if a little too late, and laid about her with her stick till she had a path cleared through the herd.

"I was clearing out the burn that day," her husband said. "Over there next to the hedge. It gets choked up wi' leaves and makes that whole corner into a right quagmire. I'm always at it."

"And how long did that take you?" Buchanan asked him. "Were you working here all day?"

"Aye. I was out here from right after the milking. I had to put in a bit o' a drainage ditch to help drain this boggy bit here, see, so I was only about half finished when the German chap appeared, in his orange jumper, walking along the rocks down there. About half past two, it was."

Fizz had to stand on tiptoe to see over the hedge. Below her, Camusfergus beach was clearly visible from end to end, pale and unblemished save for the odd wreath of seaweed and the two black lava arms that enclosed it. She said, "So, the Marriners set off for Brodick about two o'clock and then, half an hour later, Schlegel came out of the house, walked along the rocks, took off his orange jumper, and plunged into the water. Is that right?"

Both the McFarlanes nodded confirmation.

"That's right," said he, while she watched him intently. "Stood there at the point for a minute, just staring down at the water, then up with his arms a wee bit, like this, and in he went, feet first."

"And that was the last he saw of him," said Moira unexpectedly, though, clearly, this was a phrase that was traditionally part of her husband's monologue and she was simply supplying it out of a need for ritual.

Buchanan turned up his jacket collar against the wind. "That stand of birch trees beside the cottage," he said. "Was it there twenty years ago?"

"Oh aye. They're older than I am, those trees. I never mind of them lookin' any different. Why're y'askin'?"

Buchanan gave an evasive answer, but Fizz knew what was in his mind. With those birches standing there, in line with the cottage, anyone swimming around the dike into the next bay could emerge and run up the beach, unseen by any watcher on the hill above.

This was what she had hoped to demonstrate by viewing the scene for herself and, as far as she was concerned, it was conclusive proof that Konrad Schlegel had not died in Camusfergus bay.

Not even Buchanan could argue about that.

# Chapter Twenty-One

The gale that had begun to build up while they were on Arran had, by Sunday morning, developed into such a storm that there was no question of golf. Fortunately, Buchanan had brought enough work home with him on Friday evening to keep him effectively occupied for much of the day, which meant that by Monday morning he was as ahead with his current work as he had been for weeks.

The Wonderful Beatrice was able to deal with most of his mail without bothering him for more than a signature, so he was able to forge ahead with some matters pending and enjoy the unaccustomed luxury of a real tea break instead of a mug of coffee at his desk.

In this absence of cerebral activity, the thought of Schlegel's faked suicide flourished like chickweed. There had to have been some very pressing reason for the man to abandon his real identity and live the rest of his life in what amounted to virtual purdah, and although they had discussed the enigma all the way back in the ferry, neither he nor Fizz had been able to come up with a feasible explanation.

Schlegel was a bachelor, so he wasn't escaping from an unloved wife. There were no grounds to suspect that the police were after him or that he was in serious debt. But, whichever way you looked at it, for Schlegel to resort to such a course, and for the Marriners to abet him, as they must have done, there must have been no other choice open to any of them.

And where was Konrad Schlegel now? Hidden in some cottage at the Foundation? Or was he, in fact, openly going about his business there, but hiding behind a fake identity and supported by Teddy and Marcia? Any of the male Foundation residents could well fit Schlegel's profile, Buchanan supposed. Neither he nor Fizz had thought it necessary to ask the Marriners what their friend had looked like, and it was possible that the Marriners, if asked, would have been loath to answer.

Wherever Schlegel was, he was still painting—or had been up till a few years ago: still producing work that had to be hidden in a cellar or store room, daubed-over, for extra security, with some rubbishy scene.

Buchanan drummed his fingernails on the telephone. Maybe he hadn't asked that Cornish estate agent the right questions. Maybe it was time to be more explicit about what he wanted to find out. He hesitated for a couple of minutes, telling himself yet again that it wasn't, strictly speaking, his case, but he couldn't resist having one more stab at it.

"Yes, of course," David Pengilly acknowledged when Buchanan got through reminding him who he was. "I was speaking about your call to my ex-partner, Martin Shearer, over the weekend, but I'm afraid his recollections of Konrad Schlegel are even less valid than mine."

"Ah, yes. You mentioned him on Friday." Buchanan searched his memory. "I think you said he was an accountant."

"A financial adviser, in fact, but he never actually met Schlegel and only knew of him through Teddy Marriner."

Buchanan sighed, abandoning his hopes of finding someone who might tell him what Schlegel looked like. "I don't suppose, being a financial adviser, he might know anything about Schlegel's will, would he?" he persisted. "Whether Teddy Marriner was the sole beneficiary?"

"Oh, I believe Marriner inherited everything," Pengilly returned, having evidently covered this topic in his recent conversation with Shearer. "It wasn't a great deal, but Martin tells me he was able to advise some good investments that yielded well."

"Enough to allow the Marriners to move away and start their artists' retreat here in Scotland." Buchanan nodded to himself and doodled a curly pound sign on his notepad. "They did that pretty quickly, didn't they? One wonders why they were in such a hurry. Was there anyone dunning them—or Schlegel—for money? Or did

Schlegel have any other attachments—a girlfriend, perhaps—who might have expected a share of his estate?"

Pengilly took a moment to assimilate that question. Then he said, "I don't think the Marriners had any reason for moving away other than as a means of dealing with their grief. If Schlegel had any other friends or close family, I certainly never heard of them, and I never heard my ex-partner refer to them either. You have some reason for thinking different?"

"No, not really, Buchanan said hastily. "No reason at all. It just struck me as … well, what you might call a hasty decision, that's all. It's really only Schlegel's background that interests me."

"Well, as I said before, he wasn't at all well known in St. Ives and I'm afraid I don't know anyone who can be much help to you."

Pengilly's voice was beginning to betray a certain paucity of willing cooperation, so Buchanan took the hint and let him off the hook. It was obvious he could be of little help and was not likely to do any free asking around.

Before getting back to the grindstone, he gave way to another impulse that had been growing in pressure over the weekend. He said nothing about his suspicions to Fizz, who was liable to go off at a tangent at the first inkling of dubiety, but he was now beginning to wonder if Herr Krefeld's death had been, in spite of all the evidence to the contrary, entirely natural.

It now appeared likely that Schlegel had stolen the painting from the old man's room, so either he had frightened Herr Krefeld into suffering a heart attack or he had killed the old man by some means not detectable by a post mortem examination—if such a means existed.

This was something that should have been checked out earlier and Buchanan blamed himself for that. If he hadn't been so dismissive of Fizz's "bad vibes," she would probably have gone ahead by herself and made sure that there could be no mistake. However, sourcing such information was easier for Buchanan and he felt it now behooved him to do so.

Dialing the Procurator Fiscal's office, he asked for a solicitor he met occasionally at the squash club.

"Douglas? Tam Buchanan here. I need to pick your brains."

"Pick away, Tam. I do a reduced rate for squash players."

"Very droll," Buchanan returned, drawing smiley faces in all the Os in his notes. "Here's what I want to know: is there any unnatural cause of death that might not be picked up in the course of a post mortem examination?"

"You're talking about murder, are you? You want to murder someone and you want me to tell you how to get away with it?"

Buchanan allowed himself a small smile. "If you wish to put it like that, yes, Douglas. That's exactly what I want you to tell me."

"Hm-mm. Well, you won't find it easy, Tam, I can tell you that." Strange sound effects seemed to suggest that Douglas was scratching his mid-morning stubble. "It would depend on who you're planning to murder, where he or she is likely to be found, whether there were visible signs of violence or other suspicious circum-stances."

"OK. Let's say he's over seventy, found in a hotel bathroom as though he fell out of his shower, and there's no other suspicious circumstances."

"Uh-huh. Well then, you might just get away with it," Douglas admitted. "If there were no obvious signs of internal or external trauma, no toxic substances, and no reason to suspect foul play, it's possible that the death would be attributed to old age. Senile myocardial infarction is the usual get-out. It's unlikely that the coroner would feel it worthwhile to test for a massive overdose of insulin, for instance, which you should be able to lay your hands on fairly easily."

"Insulin?" Buchanan stopped doodling and sat up. There was a cold feeling in the pit of his stomach. "You're saying an overdose of insulin might be overlooked unless it was specifically tested for?"

"Correct. It's the only substance I know that would get by a standard PM, but of course, the puncture wound would give you away." Douglas hummed abstractedly for a moment and then went on, warming to his theme, "You'd want it to work fairly quickly, I'm assuming—at least within a quarter of an hour or thereabouts—so you'd have to go for a major vein. We had one case of this about three years ago where the killer tried to hide the puncture wound by injecting his wife in the back of the throat, but she went into a coma and was still alive when she was found."

"I'll worry about that aspect of it later," Buchanan assured him. "You've given me enough information to be going on with for the moment. Thanks Douglas."

"No problem." Douglas dropped the bantering tone for a moment. "Why are you asking? Is this something I'll be getting to hear about in due course?"

"Maybe," Buchanan said evasively. It was still way too early to be sharing his suspicions. He faked a chuckle. "Not unless I make any silly mistakes."

Douglas sniggered obediently. "Well, good luck. Just remember, if you get had up for this—we never spoke to each other, OK?"

"I never even heard of you," Buchanan assured him and rang off.

He sat for a while looking at his scribbled notes, and remembering Fizz's description of Herr Krefeld's naked body. He had been carrying a glass, she'd said, and it had smashed, cutting his wrist.

Cutting his wrist … and destroying the telltale puncture wound?

The realization that he ought to relay this information to Fizz without delay reminded him that he should have phoned the hotel to see if there had been any developments there over the weekend. He dialed the number and got Rosemary, the receptionist, who put him on to one of the minders he had installed over the weekend.

"No action at all," Mr. Buchanan," he was told. "Graham and I have been taking turns to keep an eye on the reception area and round the back, like you said, but there's been no trouble at all. It looks to us like the guy's been scared off. There's no way he could have spotted us hanging about—we're not daft—but we haven't seen hide nor hair of him."

"OK, but we'd better make sure. Our best chance of putting an end to Cox's threats is to catch him in the act, so I want you there till he turns up. Fizz will be phoning in this afternoon to find out the state of play, so you can tell her to stay away till further notice. In fact, ask her to phone me as soon as she can. You'd better let me speak to either of the Rentons, and I'll square the new arrangements with them."

Fortunately, it was Frazer who came to the phone and it was

easy to impress on him that the continued employment of the two minders was money well spent. There was no question of Fizz going back to work till Cox had been neutralized, but Frazer was not the man to argue about that.

It was ten past eleven by the time Buchanan got off the phone, and Beatrice's raised eyebrows as she deposited a bundle of files on his desk told him it was time he started earning some money around here.

Fizz's Sunday had been less productive than Buchanan's. The little studying she had managed to accomplish had been interrupted by long periods of bitter reflection and not a little despair. She had really counted on getting that bonus from Frau Richter and now she knew, beyond any shadow of doubt, that it had gone up in smoke.

It was silly to berate herself for not realizing sooner that she was flogging a dead horse. It was quite natural to assume that if a person wanted a picture enough to steal it they wanted it to keep, not to destroy, but she was certain that Schlegel would never have taken the chance of anyone else seeing it. It constituted incontrovertible evidence that he had still been alive when the rocks fell, less than five years ago, and he would not have dared to keep it. It was gone, and so was her five hundred pounds.

I have seen the future, she thought with painful resignation, and it's lentils.

She kept seeing Herr Krefeld lying there on his bathroom floor. If the autopsy hadn't proved otherwise, she'd have believed Schlegel to be a murderer as well as a thief. As it was, it was probably the alarm caused by finding an intruder in his room that had caused the frail old man to drop dead. Reprehensible on Schlegel's part, of course, but not in the same category as deliberate homicide.

In fact, when you looked at it coldly, Schlegel wasn't even a worthy quarry. He wasn't even a thief, in the truest sense of the word, because he had only been taking back what had been stolen from him by George in the first place. If he had been a murderer, there might have been some glory in nailing him, but, in all probability, he had never meant to harm Herr Krefeld and his sole desire, originally, had been merely to kick over the traces and

214

carve out a fresh life for himself away from whatever was bothering him—which was exactly what the Rentons were doing, when you came right down to it. One could almost—almost—sympathize with the guy.

The whole business had been a waste of valuable time and energy and all she had made out of the experience was the few quid she had scrounged off her expenses. Bugger!

Furthermore, there was still nothing in the papers about the Wainwright deal, and it was beginning to look as though she had made one hell of a mistake there. It made her physically sick to think about it. All she could do was to keep telling herself that no news was good news and to keep hoping that nothing would rob her of the next two weeks' earnings at the hotel, plus her end-of-contract bonus. That would just about put the tin hat on it.

She went out at about one thirty on Monday afternoon and phoned Gloria, as she had arranged to do, to find out if Cox had turned up over the weekend, and it was a bit of a bummer to find that the status was still quo.

"He didn't even turn *up?*"

"I'm quite sure he knows we're getting protection," Gloria claimed. "Or perhaps he saw Hollis taking your place at the reception desk."

That really pissed Fizz off. She said, "Surely the minders knew better than to make their presence obvious?"

"The whole business is ridiculous," Gloria complained, "and it's getting us nowhere. Frazer and I are living in a state of siege here! It's costing me a fortune to keep those two bruisers hanging around reception all day, and I'm having to pay Hollis over the odds to get him to cover for you in the evenings."

Fizz watched the rain sluicing down the glass of the phone box and felt her spirits sink. The words "We're going to have to let you go," were obviously hanging on Gloria's lips, ready to usher another couple of hundred quid down the plughole. A little encouragement was clearly called for to keep Gloria's shoulder to the wheel.

"He's bound to turn up soon, Mrs. Renton," she cried, in Churchillian tones. "And surely this is worth spending money on if anything is."

"It's not just the money." Gloria drew a somewhat ragged breath and took a moment to steady her voice. "It's the strain of keeping going. Frazer is utterly prostrated ..."

*Drunk*, Fizz translated mentally.

"... and Rosemary can't do any overtime because of her children, and now Hollis has gone down with flu. It's all becoming too much for me. I'm afraid we're going to have to—"

"Tell you what," said Fizz quickly, "Suppose I come in, at least for this evening, and give you a break? Even if your ex does show up—well, it's what we want, isn't it? And your two minders will be right there to nab him."

Gloria, clearly, couldn't believe her luck. "You'd do that, Fizz?"

"Frankly, Gloria," Fizz told her straight, "I need the money."

Actually, that wasn't the entire truth. There was only so much Fizz would do, even for money, and had she felt there was any real danger involved she would, at the very least, have thought twice about putting herself at risk. What came as something of a surprise, however, was the discovery that she had developed a real respect for Gloria, bitch though she was. The woman had worked hard and suffered long to throw off the past and, as far as Fizz was concerned, one didn't turn one's back on a sister with man trouble.

"Mr. Buchanan would never allow it."

"Buchanan doesn't need to know about it," Fizz said. "He's not my keeper. I'll see you about half-five."

She felt good about it as she left the phone box and ran down to the mini-supermarket for a loaf. It was obviously the way they should have played it from the beginning. If Cox had thought he had only a bimbo to get past at the reception desk, he'd have tried his hand days ago, been nabbed by the minders, and the whole business would have been over and done with.

Rajinder, who owned the supermarket, was an old friend of Fizz's. The first shop he had opened on his arrival from Pakistan twelve years ago had been close to Fizz's boarding school, and as fellow strangers in a busy city they'd had much in common. Now he had moved up in the world, but Fizz was happy to find they were neighbors again.

It was Gurbachan, Rajinder's teenage son, who took Fizz's money at the checkout and it was obvious that he and both his parents were at loggerheads about something. Both Rajinder and his wife were uncharacteristically grim of face and brusque of movement and Gurbachan was keeping his head well down.

"See that big moron?" said Rajinder, in response to Fizz's quizzical smile. "Know what he did? Let the dog into the kitchen when the hamster was running about, that's all. Could you believe it? Nasira is going to go bananas when she gets home from the school and finds out what happened."

"It's dead?" Fizz said, unnecessarily.

"Nothing left but a wee bit of fur." Rajinder's accent after twelve years held little trace of his native Kalat. "If Nasira had been in at the time, there would have been hysterics. I don't know who's going to tell her."

"It wasn't my fault ..." Gurbachan started to say, but his mother silenced him with a thump on the shoulder.

"I suppose you've thought of buying another hamster?" Fizz suggested. "If you got a similar one, maybe Nasira wouldn't notice the difference."

Rajinder and his wife looked at each other with tentative hope, clearly wondering why this solution had not presented itself to them right away.

"I'll go!" Gurbachan jumped up, anticipating their decision, but his mother slapped him back down.

"You've caused enough trouble! I'll go."

Fizz left them to it but paused in the doorway to pull her hood up over her hair, and then she started to think: *just a minute, if that old trick could work with Nasira, why shouldn't it work with Frau Richter?*

She was amazed at the possibility. And it *was* a possibility. There was at least one other painting by Konrad Schlegel of the same beach. OK, it was a different part of the beach and it didn't show the cliff and the rocks, but Frau Richter would be made just as happy by that one as by the one she had never even seen. Well, happy enough to cough up the bonus, at any rate.

OK, OK. Think about it. A Konrad Schlegel would cost a lot of money—more than the promised bonus—but, on the other hand, if

217

Schlegel (wherever he was now) wanted the whole business hushed up before his cover was blown, he'd be only too happy to do a deal. Result: happy Schlegel, happy Frau Richter, happy Fizz.

Bingo!

"Something the matter, Fizz?" said Rajinder's voice behind her.

Fizz gave him a quick smile and shook her head. "What's the time?" she said. "I have to get out to Lamancha and back by five thirty."

"Lamancha? You'll be lucky if there's a bus there and back this afternoon. It's nearly two o'clock already."

"Damn." There was no point in asking Buchanan to taxi her, he was the last person in the world she wanted to know about this, so it would have to be the oleaginous Dennis. "Damn."

"I can run you over on my motorbike," said Gurbachan unexpectedly. "Can't I, Dad?"

"Aye, if you're careful." Rajinder's black eyebrows signaled a warning. "None of your speeding."

It seemed, to Fizz, as if the Fates were saying *Yes! Go for it!* So she did.

# Chapter Twenty-Two

Fizz loved motorbikes quite passionately, but only when she was actually on one. In anticipation and in retrospect, she thought that they were the work of the devil and that anyone who actually rode on one had to be in need of counseling. But with the wind rushing in your face, and the landscape rushing by in a blur, and the Tarmac coming up to meet you on a fast bend, all that went by the board.

When she got off the pillion at a discreet distance from the driveway of the Foundation, she felt as if she were still living too fast for her metabolism.

"This'll do," she told Gurbachan, as she gave him back her helmet and tried to tidy her hair. "I don't want to advertise my arrival 'cause I could be waylaid by the people in the cottages as I go in. I'll be about half an hour maximum."

"No sweat," her chauffeur replied. "I'll go for a tootle around and come back for you in half an hour. If you're out early, you can walk down and meet me."

He roared off along the country road and Fizz headed in the opposite direction, scooting as unobtrusively as she could past the cottages and giving the garden room a wide sweep so that she could approach the farmhouse without being observed by the other residents, one of which, she was quite certain, was Konrad Schlegel. She didn't know which, and she wasn't at all sure that she wanted to know, but, of course, it was almost certainly Bremner McGrath. He had been there since way back and he was obviously intent on keeping a low profile and, more to the point, none of the others really fitted the bill. In any case, she felt quite certain that, given the delicacy of her proposals, it might be better to deal with an intermediary like Teddy untrammeled by the presence of the principal.

There was orchestral music coming from the Samuels' cottage and she spotted a figure that was probably Marcia, surrounded by dogs and heading for the distant woods, but there was no sign of Bremner: he and the others were doubtless hard at work in their respective studios.

Teddy opened the door to her, wearing a pair of striped pajamas over his clothes, his hair covered by a black beret with a polythene shower cap on top of that.

"Been clearing out the cellar," he explained, leading the way into a long sunny lounge at the side of the house. "God knows when it was last touched, and the filth down there is unbelievable."

He gestured for Fizz to take one of the two armchairs and then stripped off his protective clothing and flung it behind the couch. "Marcia has just gone out with the dogs, but she won't be long."

"Actually, I was hoping to have a word with you in private anyway," Fizz said, watching him with some amusement as he dittered about, gathering up discarded newspapers and dog toys like a house-proud wife.

"Just with me, Fizz?" He looked at her over his spectacles. "Dear me. Why do I not like the sound of that? I do hope your search for the painting hasn't turned up anything upsetting."

For the first time, Fizz felt a little uncomfortable about what she intended to do. She felt sure that, whatever pressure had been put on Teddy and Marcia to cover up for Schlegel, they didn't deserve to be subjected to what was, basically, blackmail some twenty-odd years after the event. However, it was a bit late to be changing tack at this stage in the game, so she might as well get on with it.

"I'm really sorry to be saying this, Teddy, but I'm afraid that my investigation has led me into areas where, frankly, I don't want to follow." She didn't quite look him in the eye, but she was aware that he had come across the room and was lowering himself slowly into the chair opposite her. She had to force herself to be specific. "I have to tell you that I know Schlegel's suicide was a fake."

Teddy leaned his head against the high back of the chair and let his breath out slowly as if he had been holding it in anticipation of something like this. "How long have you known?" he said softly.

"Just a couple of days. I went across to the Isle of Arran and

220

checked out Camusfergus beach and, when you know what you're looking for, it's easy to see how it was done."

"And now? You are going to tell the police?"

Fizz looked at him and found he was smiling sadly at her. "No," she said, shaking her head. "I don't see what would be gained by that, really. If Konrad Schlegel felt it necessary to disappear like that twenty-odd years ago, it's no business of mine. I don't know what new identity he assumed, and I don't need to know."

Teddy stared at her in open amazement and seemed lost for words.

"Oh, I suspect he's living here at the Foundation," Fizz admitted, "or, if not, that you are still supporting him in some way, but I don't know who he is and it's really of only academic interest to me. I know that when he stole the painting from Herr Krefeld he probably saw it, in a way, as merely reclaiming his own property, and I quite see that he had to do it to protect his new identity. It's just a pity that it turned to tragedy when Herr Krefeld collapsed."

"My dear Fizz ..." Teddy took off his glasses and polished them on a fold of his sweatshirt. He sat, bent over, staring at them for a moment or two and then shook his head. "I'm astonished to hear you speak like this. Astonished. When you said you had uncovered Konrad's deception ... well, I thought ... being a lawyer ... you'd want to see everything ... regulated."

"I'm not a lawyer. I won't be a lawyer for years." Fizz's hand sketched a wide gesture that indicated a vast amount of time. "I've nothing to gain by dropping Schlegel in it."

"But, Mr. Buchanan? Surely he—"

"What Buchanan doesn't know won't hurt him," Fizz said firmly. "This was never his investigation."

"But, Fizz dear, Mr. Buchanan *is* a lawyer. I'm sure he'll insist on it all coming out—"

"He doesn't know what I've found out," Fizz claimed rashly, seeing her bonus in danger of slipping away. "All he did was to taxi me out here a couple of times and he has no part in any arrangement we may come to."

Teddy tucked his chin down and smiled at her over the top of his specs. With his thick white hair and rosy cheeks, he looked so like a cardboard Santa Claus she'd been given one Christmas long ago that she had a momentary suspicion that if she unscrewed his head she'd find Smarties inside.

"Any arrangement we may come to," he repeated. "If I didn't know you better, my dear, I'd think you were planning a little black-mail!"

Fizz had kept her conscience in virtually mint condition for twenty-seven years, but it was now in real jeopardy. "No. It's not like that, really," she said, looking at him earnestly. "It's just that … to tell you the truth, Teddy, I'm not getting paid for *looking* for Frau Richter's painting, I'm only getting paid if I *find* it and, frankly, I'm desperate for the money."

Teddy's smile faded. His eyes were huge behind the lenses of his specs. "And you think I should show my gratitude for your discre-tion by—"

"*No*," Fizz burst out, wincing with embarrassment. "That's not what I had in mind at all. I just thought … all Frau Richter wants is the picture that was her last gift from her brother and you have a picture in the collection that would be virtually indistinguishable from the one he bought, especially if you hadn't seen the original, and …"

"Ah!" Teddy's smile returned. He stretched a hand forward and patted her arm. "My dear Fizz. I owe you an apology. Of course! I see now where your thoughts are leading. As long as Frau Richter is satisfied, there need be no further inquiry and Konrad can continue to live in peace."

Fizz watched him fish out his pipe and stick it, unlit, between his teeth. He leaned back in his chair again and one hand rubbed gently at his temple as he thought the matter over. In the silence that followed, Fizz was annoyed to hear the approaching throb of a motorbike. Bugger Gurbachan. Why hadn't he waited for her at the end of the drive? Another few minutes and she'd have had the matter cut and dried.

"Your solution to the problem is certainly …" Teddy started to say, and then swung round to stare at the window as he heard what Fizz had heard.

"I'm sorry," Fizz said. "I'm afraid that's my transport. A friend gave me a lift because … well, you know what the buses are like. Always at the wrong time."

Teddy stood up and walked to the window, staring out and chewing thoughtfully at his pipe stem.

Finally Fizz had to say, "I really have to go now or I'll be late for my work."

Teddy slipped a hand through her arm as they walked to the door. "At first glance, Fizz, it looks to me that your idea is the perfect solution. I'm sure Konrad will agree. Can you give me a little time to speak to him about it?"

"Of course," Fizz beamed, awarding herself a Nobel Prize for lateral thinking and creativity. "I'll give you a ring, shall I?"

"Do that." He bent down and kissed her cheek, giving her arm a grateful squeeze. "All will be well, my dear."

Fizz smiled at him in full agreement. At that point, she rather thought it would.

The rain, which had been only intermittent all day, dried up before Buchanan left the office, so he dashed home, changed, and grabbed a quick nine holes before the light went. None of his cronies had thought it worthwhile to turn up, so he had a solitary snack in the clubhouse and was heading home by eight thirty.

In the absence of conversation, he had plenty of time to think about Schlegel's fake suicide and to ponder which of the Foundation residents he might have created as his new persona. Both Andrew and Bremner were in the right age group, but, when you thought about it, even Dodie could not be eliminated since he might well be older than he looked and, indeed, Konrad Schlegel might well be considerably younger than Teddy and Marcia. He had naturally assumed that, since they met at art college, they must be around the same age but, for all Buchanan knew, the Marriners could have been teachers and Schlegel a pupil. Or even vice versa.

All that was known about the artist was that he was German and, given that he had been at art school, as a teacher or as a student, more than twenty years ago, probably over forty-five. Maybe a good deal over forty-five. He could, in fact, be well into his seventies by now. If he was still alive, Bremner was, of course, the main suspect.

Had to be. One was virtually forced to view his taciturnity as nothing more than a cover for the dregs of a German accent of which, even after twenty-one years in the UK, there might still be a trace. Then again, Dodie's dense Glasgow accent was turbid enough to do the same job, and even Andrew's rigidly correct, old-fashioned diction could be suspect since it was precisely the pronunciation taught to foreigners.

Stopped at a traffic light in the High Street, Buchanan decided that, since Fizz had not yet phoned him, he would drop in on her and bring her up to speed regarding his new doubts about the post mortem findings. She might—he rather hoped she *would*—think it worthwhile to go back to the Foundation for another chat with the residents, to observe them with a new, less-gullible eye, and to ask the more pointed questions that had sprouted from the weekend's fresh information. Just what, for instance, was the illness or disability that necessitated Jean Samuel's regular visits to her doctor?

There was, however, no reply to his repeated assaults on Fizz's doorknocker and no sign of her in the vicinity, so his hopes were dashed. He had no idea where she might have gone, since her private life was a sealed book to everyone but herself, but he was quite confident that she was not at work. Mondays were her night off. Besides, she had promised, willingly enough, to phone the hotel and make sure that the unpleasantness had been cleared up before going back, and he knew that, as long as she was on full wages, she'd have no hesitation in keeping that promise.

He was sorely tempted to go back to the Foundation without her. The idea of a half-hour chat with Kat on her own had taken root in his mind and he was avid for the information he was sure she could provide. She had been there from the first year of the retreat's inception and she must know as much about the other long-term residents as anyone.

Fizz would be pipped if he stole a march on her but, hell, she couldn't have it both ways. Either he was a partner in this investigation, as she was never tired of insisting, or he wasn't, and if he didn't go now it might be days before he had another free evening.

It wouldn't altogether have surprised him if he had found Fizz there when he arrived, unlikely though he knew that to be, but there was no sign of her in the garden room when he drove slowly past. Only Dodie was in there, illuminated by the ghostly light of the television, the smoke from his roll-up curling out of his nostrils like ectoplasm.

Buchanan left the car in the car park and walked round the goat shed to the little detached chalet that was Kat's home and workshop. There were lights on behind the windows and the smell of cooking bacon drifted out on the still air. He tapped on the glass door and a moment later Kat's head appeared at a window to one side.

"Heavens, is that you, Tam? Hang on a minute till I wipe my hands."

She appeared at the door in a plastic apron, carrying a tea towel, and led him into a wood paneled kitchen. "I'm just making myself a bite to eat. I know, I know! It's a daft time to be stoking up but, to tell you the truth, Tam, the clock doesn't play a big part in my life these days. I eat when I'm hungry, I go to bed when I'm tired, and I get up when I wake. Which do you prefer, tea or coffee?"

Buchanan settled for coffee and was given a large pottery mugful with a roll and bacon. He knew what greasy food would do to his guts but, golf-club snacks being what they were, he was already hungry.

Rain rattled against the window as Kat drew the curtains across to shut out the night. "And where's your pretty little girlfriend this evening?"

"Fizz?" Buchanan smiled and shook his head. "Not my girlfriend, I'm afraid. Just a colleague, that's all. She's off on her own devices tonight, but I had a feeling you and I should talk."

Kat opened her eyes and sent him a look that, fifty years ago, might have been coquettish—though, even then, Buchanan suspected, there can't have been many in the queue to drink champagne out of her size nine slipper. She carried her own mug and plate to the table and sat herself down opposite him. "Well, that's nice. And what should we talk about?"

"I'm curious about the early days of the Foundation and how Teddy and Marcia came to set it up." Buchanan watched obliquely to see if she showed any discomfort at his choice of topic. She appeared surprised, but not uneasily so.

"My word, you do your work thoroughly, Tam, I'll say that for you. This is all to do with the missing painting, I assume?"

"Yes. We're still plodding away, but we haven't yet managed to establish the provenance of the painting. Whoever had it in their possession during the past twenty years is still a mystery. I wondered if Konrad Schlegel might have left it to someone in his will."

Kat folded two rashers of bacon into her buttered roll, topped it with a generous layer of tomato ketchup, and took an untidy bite. "Well, I can answer that question," she said, chewing vigorously. "Konrad never left anything to anybody except Teddy. Teddy was the sole beneficiary—I've heard him say so several times and he repeated it just last week when we were talking about your missing painting." She dabbed at her lips with a corner of the tea towel and added regretfully, "It begins to look as though we're dealing with a forgery, doesn't it?"

"That's possible," Buchanan admitted. In spite of the way things looked and the gut feeling both he and Fizz had experienced, there was still a possibility that they were both wrong. Schlegel's suicide could have been genuine and the picture, complete with rocks, could have been painted by someone else. Someone good enough to fool the experts.

He said, "Can I ask you something in confidence, Kat?"

She turned her head aside and looked at him out of the corner of her eyes. "You can ask, dear boy, but I won't promise to answer."

"I heard it was Schlegel's legacy that went to set up the Foundation."

Kat gave a snort of laughter. "Who told you that? What rubbish! It all came out of Teddy's pocket."

Buchanan nodded. "Yes. But Teddy made that money by investing Schlegel's legacy, didn't he?"

Amusement deepened the wrinkles around Kat's eyes and creased her leathery cheeks. "Tam, if you knew Teddy at all, you'd know that was utter balderdash. I don't know where you get your information, but I can assure you that Teddy wouldn't know how to go about making an investment. The darling man would scarcely know how to write a check; Marcia has to take care of all the money matters."

She got up and walked over to the work area to get the coffee pot while Buchanan assimilated this information. Somebody had to have it wrong, he was thinking. Either Teddy was a guy who'd once had enough business interests to employ a financial adviser in Cornwall or he was so unsophisticated in money matters that he left all that side of his affairs to his wife.

Kat appeared quite confident in her evidence, but so, too, had the estate agent, and it had to be highly improbable that Teddy would change his ways immediately after making a killing on the Stock Exchange. Not unless he had some obscure reason for doing so ... like ... like not *being* Teddy, for instance.

Buchanan became aware that Kat was speaking—had probably been doing so for God knew how long. Even now, he could hear her voice, but he couldn't concentrate on what she was saying. His thoughts were racing through his head so furiously he was deaf and blind to everything else.

Teddy? ... *Teddy?*

The facts went *click—click—click* into place like the suits piling neatly up on the kings at the end of a game of solitaire.

"Kat," he said, "I have to go ... Sorry, but I've just thought of something I must talk to Fizz about right away."

It seemed to take forever to extricate himself, apologizing on autopilot while the thoughts kept boiling up out of his subconscious. How could he have got it all so very wrong?

He wasn't sure where he was headed as he pulled out of the car park. Theoretically the police should be the first to hear what he had just worked out, but he didn't dare think about Fizz's response to that course of action. If only she had a telephone at home ...

The door of the farmhouse suddenly flew open as he passed by, and Marcia dashed out onto the steps, leaning forward to peer out into the darkness.

Buchanan slammed a foot on the brake in a reflex action and rolled down the window.

"Oh, it's you, Tam! I thought it was Teddy back."

She looked terrible. Wisps of graying hair straggled about her face and she had her arms wrapped tightly around her chest as though she was trying to control the shivering that even the dim light couldn't hide.

Alarm flared like a beacon in Buchanan's brain. This was not simply a case of Teddy's dinner getting cold: Marcia was jumping out of her skin. He said, "Is something wrong, Marcia? Is there anything I can do for you?"

"No, no." Her bright forced smile was horrific, stretching her mouth unnaturally wide but failing to convey anything but agonized dismay. She turned to hurry back indoors but paused as Buchanan called after her.

"Where's Teddy, Marcia?"

She took a shaky breath before she answered and to Buchanan it went on and on. There was something scary about this situation and, as usual, his first thought was of Fizz. He didn't know where she was and he didn't know where Teddy was and that thought, combined with the bacon sandwich, was turning his duodenum into a cement mixer.

"He went down to Lamancha for a pint," Marcia said. She was starting to get a grip of herself and her voice was noticeably steadier. "I do wish he wouldn't drink and drive. He knows how nervy it makes me and he should have been back by now."

It was good, but not nearly good enough. Buchanan knew she was lying. He got out of the car and went up the steps fast, pushing the door open and edging Marcia inside before she well knew what was happening.

"Let's talk, Marcia."

She stumbled over the threshold, staring at him with wild eyes. "What ... what are you doing, Tam? What ...?"

Buchanan looked over her shoulder and saw into a lamplit lounge littered with magazines and bits of discarded clothing. Blood pounded in his ears and his voice grated as he demanded, "Just tell me one thing, Marcia. Is Fizz in danger right now?"

She backed away from him fast. "What are you talking about? Have you gone mad?"

"Don't waste my time, Marcia." He grabbed her by the elbow

and hustled her into the lounge and pushed her down into a wicker armchair. He knew that the thing to do was to frighten her, maybe even to slap her face, but even in a situation like this he knew he wouldn't be able to do that.

"Listen!" he shouted as roughly as he could manage. "I know that Teddy is Konrad Schlegel. I know how you faked the suicide—"

"How dare you!" Her face was gray and haggard, but she just didn't know when to give up. "Konrad's suicide was no fake … You're quite mad!"

Buchanan abandoned his strong-arm tactics—they were failing to convince her that the game was up—and squatted down, gripping the arm of the chair on either side of her. "It's too late to lie. I've been to Arran and I know how you and Konrad did it. I know how you made the farmer believe Konrad was your husband and that Teddy was the depressed German artist. McFarlane never actually spoke to Teddy, did he? But, when he saw a figure dressed in that distinctive orange sweater throw himself off the rocks, he didn't doubt that it was the German he was watching. You and—so you claimed—your husband had just left, ostensibly for Brodick, but you were alone in the car, weren't you, Marcia? Teddy was, I assume, already dead and Konrad Schlegel was waiting in the cottage, ready to emerge in Teddy's sweater and stage the suicide. But you only drove as far as the next bay where Schlegel emerged from the water and became—for the next twenty-odd years—the man he had murdered."

Marcia was in pieces. Her trembling had now reached seismic proportions and her eyes were brimming with tears. She must have known that the ball was well and truly up on the slates, but she kept shaking her head and saying, "No … no … It's not true."

"For God's sake, Marcia!" Buchanan grabbed her by the arms. "Schlegel murdered your husband, he murdered Herr Krefeld—are you going to let him murder Fizz as well?"

She went limp under his hands and some of the fight went out of her. "It wasn't Konrad's fault, Teddy's death was an accident. They were fighting—Teddy found out that Konrad was the father of my baby. Konrad was only defending himself and—and the old man—Krefeld—he died of shock!"

229

"That's rubbish, Marcia, and you know it!" Buchanan's brain was racing. He knew now what had happened and he was stammering in his haste to rip the veil from Marcia's eyes and get her talking. "Krefeld wouldn't part with the giveaway picture, would he? I reckon that while he was trying to authenticate the painting he'd found out that Schlegel was supposed to have died twenty years ago—before the rock fall. That must have come as a shock to Konrad. Had he forgotten that the rocks were not there twenty years ago—or had he never actually visited that end of the beach before? Either way, he must have realized immediately that he had to destroy that painting and silence Krefeld. Konrad's a killer, Marcia! He has killed twice and he's going to kill again!"

Marcia pulled free of his grip and slid to the back of the chair, cringing away from him. "You can't prove that!"

"Dammit, Marcia!" Buchanan roared, "this place is going to be swarming with CID men before you can blink, and I've no doubt but they'll find a whole gallery of Konrad's recent work—all hidden behind trashy little garden scenes—all ready to be cleaned off and sold when the last of his 'pre-suicide' work has been converted into ready cash."

"But he didn't kill the old man—"

Buchanan set his teeth and shook her a little. "I don't give a damn if he wiped out half the population of Scotland, Marcia! I want you to tell me where he is. Is he with Fizz?"

"Fizz?" She screwed up her face till her swollen eyes were nearly closed. "Why would he be with Fizz? I don't know where he's gone."

"When did he go out?"

"Late this afternoon, I think." She slid her hands along the chair arms and took a tight grip of his sleeves. Now it was her holding on to him, Buchanan thought, disgusted at his ineptness as an inquisitor. "I went out with the dogs and ... when I got back ... he'd gone. He has never done that before."

"And none of the others saw him leave?"

Her eyes clung to his face as though he were the one sane thing in a world gone mad. It took her several seconds to respond. "Jean and Andrew did. He stopped by their cottage for a while. I don't know why. But he said nothing to them about going out. Oh, Tam, I don't know what's happening ... I don't know where he is ..." She started to sob.

Buchanan gave her his hankie and tried to think. What had Schlegel learned this afternoon that had set him off like a rocket? Was he running away or making a last-ditch attempt to cover up his crimes? And why pay Andrew and Jean a visit before he left?

"Marcia." The thought that had long been knocking at the door of his mind suddenly crossed the threshold. "Marcia ... what's wrong with Jean? Why does she see her doctor regularly?"

Marcia looked at him in amazement and seemed unable to gather her thoughts. "What?" she started to say, and then Buchanan's expression stopped her, "It's ... it's ... she's a diabetic."

Buchanan was storming through the hallway before he realized that he'd said nothing in reply. There was only one thought in his mind and it left no room for any other. Schlegel had stolen more insulin from Jean and was on his way to use it.

# Chapter Twenty-Three

Johnnyboy was in and out of the foyer like a piston from ten p.m. onwards. This was completely contrary to his usual practice, which—unless he had some social engagement—was to disappear up to his room as soon as dinners were over, and to remain closeted there until breakfast time. However, this mystery didn't tax Fizz's powers of deduction for long, since it was abundantly clear that the chef had his eye on one of the two minders who were orbiting the area.

"He used to be a soldier," he confided in Fizz's ear, leaning across the counter of the reception desk so that the object of his affections could get a good view of his designer jeans. "The Black Watch. I can just picture him in a kilt, can't you?"

Fizz could more easily have pictured the guy in a fleece since he was, to her mind, living proof that *Homo sapiens* could breed with sheep. The other one, Joe, was much hunkier, but there was never any telling who would turn Johnnyboy on.

"He comes into the kitchen for his tea-break on Friday night as cool as you please. Sits right down at my little side table—you know, sweetie?—and starts chatting away like he'd known me from school. Graham Murdoch. Nice name, isn't it?" Johnnyboy straightened and glanced across the foyer to where Graham was deep in the pages of a paperback. "I think I could form quite an attachment for him if he's here much longer."

Fizz remained unmoved by this. In her three months at the hotel, Johnnyboy had had more attachments than a Swiss army knife and none of them had lasted longer than a week. She said, "Gloria didn't sound too good when I spoke to her on the phone today."

"Sweetie, I could almost find it in my heart to be sorry for that woman. When Graham told me about her ex-husband and the way he's been making her life hell for years—well, honestly—I just felt so mean about the things I used to say about her." Johnnyboy looked soulful and preened the cravat that was meant to be concealing the venomous eruption on the back of his neck. "And Frazer! He's been curled up in a fetal position for two days and not a blind bit of good to anyone! According to Jason, he was taken suddenly drunk in the television room on Saturday afternoon and no one has seen a sign of him ever since. Poor Gloria has had to soldier on alone."

The sudden appearance of poor Gloria brought him rigidly to attention and put an abrupt end to his maudlin recital.

"What are you hanging around here for, John?" Gloria's eyes flicked, like a whip, over his off-duty finery and flashed with displeasure. "It's ten to twelve, for goodness' sake. If you've nothing better to do, you should get away up that stair to your bed instead of making the place look untidy."

Johnnyboy muttered something under his breath and sidled away, his lips moving in silent obscenity.

"Well, Fizz." Gloria straightened her square shoulders and essayed a weary smile. "Another evening gone by without incident. I wish to God something would happen to resolve this business. It's the constant waiting and waiting that's driving me up the wall."

"Cox is bound to turn up again soon," Fizz said, but not with any degree of confidence. She was beginning to swing round to the idea that Gloria's ex had sussed out the situation and gone to ground till he could see that the two-man protection team had been withdrawn, "What are you going to do tomorrow night? Do you want me to come in again?"

"I don't know, Fizz. I suppose I ought to talk to Mr. Buchanan again and see what he thinks we should do."

Fizz stifled a yawn and started piling her Law books and jotters into her shoulder bag. "OK. I'll give you a ring in the afternoon sometime."

Gloria nodded. "I don't need to tell you again how much I appreciate your support, Fizz. You take care on the way home now."

It was cold outside and, although the rain had stopped, the smell of wet grass rose to meet her as she ran down the steps. The moon had not yet risen, but there was just about enough light from the lamps in the porch and from the illuminated sign at the roadside to light her way down the driveway.

On each side, the rhododendron bushes grew in a solid, head-high bank and she was taken unawares when, about halfway to the road, a man stepped out of the shadows to block her way.

Buchanan had already eliminated the probable and was now starting work on the remotely possible. Fizz was not in her flat. Her neighbor, Mrs. Auld, who usually knew every time Fizz blew her nose, had not seen her since lunchtime. Her step-grandmother, Auntie Duff, whom Buchanan had phoned from a call box (ostensibly for a chat, for God's sake!) declined to mention, as she would surely have done had it been the case, that Fizz had gone home to Am Bealach for the day. There was no sign of her in the café beside the entrance to her flat and, although she was well known by all the staff in there, she had not been seen by any of them that evening.

That left the hotel.

Buchanan knew, even as he risked the loss of his license—not to mention his life—by scorching through the city center, that she wouldn't be there, but he had to do something while he thought of some other place to try.

Well sublimated at the back of his mind was the thought that the police would, by now, be looking for him. He had forced himself to halt, for less than three minutes, at Andrew's cottage, from where he had phoned the police and also warned the Samuels that Marcia was in need of succor. But his explanation had, of necessity, been condensed and only by dropping names had he been able to ensure an immediate response from Lothian and Borders Police. Right now, they'd be expecting him to help them with their inquiries and wondering where the hell he'd got to.

The car park at the Royal Park Hotel was behind the building, which meant that you had to drive right round the garden to get back out again, and Buchanan hadn't time for that. He jumped out of the car at the gateway and sprinted up the drive.

Had he been concentrating less on speed and more on looking where he was going, he would have been less surprised to find himself brought suddenly to a halt by the horrifying tableau of Konrad Schlegel pressing a pistol against Fizz's throat.

"Fizz!" he gasped. "Are you—"

The mouth of the pistol dug into the soft flesh beneath Fizz's jaw.

"Shut up!" Schlegel hissed. "One more word and she's dead, understand?"

Buchanan's whole body was screaming for action, his knees bending to leap, his fingers curling to grasp and gouge, his muscles bunching and twitching to wrestle Schlegel to the ground. And there was nothing he could do.

Schlegel, he now saw, had been in the act of binding Fizz's wrists with adhesive tape. She was standing with her back half turned to them both, but she twisted her neck a little and looked steadily at Buchanan, and in her look was a warning: "Don't do anything silly."

Buchanan was staggered by her bravery. He knew that he'd die before he let Schlegel harm her, but, while that gunpoint was where it was, Fizz's brain would be liquidized before he could lift a fist.

Schlegel was clearly thrown by Buchanan's sudden appearance and his eyes darted about as though he were in instant expectation of further interruption. Moving with jerky haste, he swung Fizz round to face him and, producing the roll of adhesive tape, started tearing at it with his teeth, his evident intention being to seal his prisoner's mouth.

Buchanan assumed that he might—if he was lucky—be next in line for this treatment, and knew that if he were going to jump Schlegel he had only seconds in which to do so. The gun was still pointed erratically at Fizz's throat, but Schlegel was partially distracted as he ripped free a strip of tape and prepared to slap it, one-handed, across her mouth.

As his hand reached out, however, Buchanan's eye caught a flicker of movement at the edge of his vision. He started to turn his head, but halted in shock as Fizz spoke in ringing tones.

"Oh, Mr. *Renton*," she said to Teddy in ringing tones. "This is the man who's been looking for you all week."

In the next half second, three things happened simultaneously. Schlegel, without pausing for thought, reared back and swung his gun sideways preparatory to crashing it into Fizz's face, Buchanan fired himself at Fizz in a rugby tackle that catapulted them both deep into the rhododendrons, and, with a scream like a diving Stuka, a leather-clad body erupted from the bushes, brandishing what looked like a rolled umbrella, and hit Schlegel amidships with a bang. Then the gun went off.

Blackness. Smell of wet earth. Leaves in his face. Behind him, out on the drive, the sound of running feet and people shouting. Somebody with a voice like a bullhorn roaring, "Stay where you are. Just stay where you fucking are, you motherfucker, or your balls are fucking pâté."

"You OK, Fizz?" Buchanan grunted, getting to his knees and turning her over on to her back. Fizz's face was a shadowy blur beneath him in the mud. She was frighteningly still. "Fizz? Oh, my God ..."

Fizz started to make wheezing noises, so he crawled out of the bushes on to the gravel and dragged her out after him. She was still trying to catch her breath, but her expression of bitter ingratitude was visible through a two-inch mudpack, making Buchanan deeply grateful that her hands were still taped together.

Joe and Graham, the two minders, were standing over the entwined bodies of Schlegel and his attacker and a stream of other people were running down the drive toward them, gaggling like geese. As Buchanan walked toward them, Graham yanked the smaller man to his feet. He was thickset and dressed in black leather. The man he'd seen leaving the hotel the night he had walked Fizz home from her work. Gloria's ex.

Schlegel didn't move. The pool of shiny liquid around his shoulder wasn't rainwater.

As Buchanan went back to Fizz and started pulling the tape off her wrists, Graham hurried past them, spreading his arms to halt the approaching guests and ordering them to go back inside and phone the police.

"What's happened?" Fizz said, peering down the drive. "Did someone get hit?"

"Teddy," Buchanan told her. "Schlegel, that is. Looks like he managed to put a bullet in his own shoulder somehow. Maybe he was trying to shoot himself in the head."

"Too bad he didn't make it," Fizz returned, trying to sound tough but making a poor job of it because her voice was all over the place and she had to draw a breath after every other word. Buchanan lifted an arm to put it around her shoulders, but she stepped a couple of paces aside to get a better view of the group around Schlegel and he let her go.

He could see her consciously taking deep breaths and straightening her shoulders and presently her head swung round toward him, her eyes shining whitely in the mud. "How long have you known Teddy was Schlegel?"

"Just since this evening," Buchanan told her placatingly. "I looked everywhere for you—except here. What in God's name were you doing at work, Fizz, when you promised me that—"

"Oh, gimme a break, will you? I've had enough for one day."

She found a tissue in her pocket and started to scrub ineffectively at her face. After a moment, Buchanan took it from her, cleaned a small square on one cheek, and planted a kiss in the middle of it. A small kiss. A light and brotherly kiss. It was the least he could do.

"I thought you were amazingly brave," he said, in mitigation. He thought he had never seen her so stunned.

"I was shitting bricks," she said after a minute, and walked briskly toward the foyer, Buchanan trailing at her heels.

The glass doors at the top of the steps were lined with curious guests squinting into the darkness and regarding Fizz's approach with speculation. Fizz stopped on the bottom step and swung round with her eyes on a level with Buchanan's own.

"Why were you running up the drive like that? Did you know Schlegel was after me?"

Buchanan tried to sidestep. "We'll talk about it later."

"We'll talk about it now, Buchanan," said Fizz, narrowing her eyes in the way he particularly disliked, "You were fossicking around out there at the Foundation behind my back, weren't you, you bastard? You bloody were! You found out I'd been talking to Teddy—to Schlegel—and you knew he'd come after me!"

"You were talking to Schlegel? You were out there on your own?" Buchanan actually took a step backward as though he'd been punched in the chest. "And he let you walk out of there alive?"

That shot hit its mark and made Fizz hesitate for a moment. Before she could speak again, there was a footfall on the gravel behind them and Graham appeared with a paper-wrapped parcel in his hand.

"Fizz, is this yours?" He held it out to her. "It was lying in the bushes and it has your name on it,"

"Yeah. I must have dropped it," she said laconically, tucked it under one arm, and added, "Thanks," as Graham retraced his steps.

Buchanan didn't flatter himself that he could always tell when she was bending the truth, but he could tell it now. He nodded at the parcel. "A pressie for someone?"

She looked at him mulishly and appeared to debate the pros and cons of telling him to mind his own business. Finally she decided to say, "It's a pressie for me. From Schlegel. He promised me a painting of Lake Schluchsee to replace the one he stole from Herr Krefeld, and this is it."

Buchanan's mind reeled. There had apparently been a lot going on that he was not privy to, but he doubted whether this was the right time to press Fizz for details. "You're going to keep it?" he said, pointing a finger at the parcel. "You think he really meant to give it to you? Surely he planned only to use it as some sort of decoy, if it became necessary? As bait in a trap?"

Fizz lifted her shoulders. "I don't care if he planned to use it as a suppository. Here it is. With my name on it, in his handwriting. I think we can assume that he intended to do the decent thing by Frau Richter, don't you? After all, nobody knows about it but you and I. I'm sure Marcia doesn't give a bugger."

"Well, but that's not the point, Fizz, is it?" Buchanan began, but she cut him short with a laugh.

"The point, my learned friend, is that possession is nine-tenths of the law. I've worked bloody hard to get my hands on that picture. It may have escaped your notice, but I'd have made a beaver look like a three-toed sloth, and I deserve every penny of the bonus I'll get when I deliver it to Frau Richter."

Buchanan, to his eternal shame, discovered that he was not about to argue with her.

She half turned, as though to resume her climb up the steps, but then changed her mind, "Once in a while," she said, pushing her button-cute face at him belligerently, "just once in a while it would be nice to get some reward for my labors. All I get from Gloria is an occasional kind word and what do I get from you for selling Greydykes to the Wainwrights? Not even a pat on the head!"

Whirling about, she swept into the lobby like a pop star, leaving Buchanan dazed.

Gray dykes? What were *they*, for God's sake? The words meant nothing to him. She seemed to be implying some connection with the office but, if so, it was some item of office work outwith his own area. The only connection he could make to the name Wainwright was an article in that morning's *Scotsman* about the takeover of some bottling plant and the consequent rocketing of Wainwright's share price.

He was well used to Fizz working herself into a temper over nothing on occasions like this. The only surprising thing was that she had let him off so lightly, this time, considering that he had just forgotten himself sufficiently to kiss her cheek.

The recollection made him feel light-headed.

He followed her up the steps, suddenly overcome by his own temerity and shaken by the realization that, had she not been temporarily operating at less than full power, he would at this moment be lying on his back on the gravel, coughing up his frontal incisors.

Even the small matter of a pistol in the throat would not normally have subdued her to any extent.

Maybe she was losing her touch.

Yeah, sure.

# Joyce Holms

One of Scotland's best selling crime writers and the author of nine Fizz and Buchanan mysteries, Joyce Holms launched her writing career in her twenties with short stories for women's magazines and the BBC. After a frustrating foray into the world of romance writing—where her editor complained, "this is not a romance, it's a romp!"—Joyce took her congenital inability to be serious for more than a paragraph at a time and turned to crime to find a literary home.

Joyce also teaches creative writing and gives workshops and classes to writing groups, readers' groups, schools and writers circles as well as humorous and entertaining talks to organisations such as Rotary, Probus, and Womens Guilds. Her other careers have included teaching window dressing, managing a hotel on the Island of Arran, and working for an Edinburgh detective agency. She is also an avid hillwalker and garden designer. She divides her time between Edinburgh and the South of France and is married with two grown children.

www.joyceholms.com

# Bloody Brits Press

PAYMENT DEFERRED
A Fizz & Buchanan Mystery

## Joyce Holms

When solicitor Tam Buchanan first encounters "Fizz" his heart sinks. The young woman with the guileless expression sitting outside his Legal Advice office looks too young to stand the pace as his assistant. But Fizz's innocent appearance belies the reality. Soon to be a mature student of Law, she's very bright, utterly single-minded, and has the rare talent for making people talk—people like Murray Kingston, who Tam, to his horror, finds ensconced in the office late one morning.

As far at Tam's concerned, his friendship with Murray ended the day Murray was convicted of molesting his daughter. But Murray's desperate plea of having been framed has persuaded Fizz, and somehow Tam finds himself digging into the past while Fizz undertakes to interview old witnesses. But soon Fizz begins to wonder if her confidence in Murray's innocence is entirely justified ...

Set against a backdrop of busy Edinburgh streets and Scottish Borders countryside, *Payment Deferred* is an irresistible and utterly satisfying novel, introducing two unlikely sparring partners whose conflicting approaches to sleuthing make sparks fly—but get results.

*Payment Deferred* is the first Fizz & Buchanan Mystery.

ISBN 978-1-932859-31-7 $13.95

Available at your local bookstore
or order online at www.bloodybritspress.com

# Bloody Brits Press

## FOREIGN BODY
### A Fizz & Buchanan Mystery

### Joyce Holms

"Fizz and Buchanan are ... a great double act and Holms's lively pithy writing is a joy to read" —*Crime Time*

Death in the Highlands usually comes in the shape of illness or accident, and few doubt that one or the other has taken the life of Bessie Anderson. They can't be sure, though—for eighty-two-year old Bessie has vanished without trace. But when the body of a hiker is found in the mountains, everyone knows it's murder.

When 'Fizz' Fitzgerald suggests a connection between the two cases, the police can barely conceal their amusement. Giving them her best Shirley Temple smile, Fizz takes matters into her own hands, enlisting the reluctant help of lawyer Tam Buchanan. Tam's supposed to be enjoying a convalescent break after surgery, but his plans for undiluted fishing and whisky-tippling are easily undermined by the single-minded Fizz.

Soon Tam is mingling with the locals, whose friendly banter conceals all manner of secrets. And it begins to look as though Bessie Anderson knew more than was good for her about one of her neighbors ...

*Foreign Body* is the second Fizz & Buchanan Mystery.

ISBN 978-1-932859-48-5  $13.95

# Bloody Brits Press

## THE SLEEPING AND THE DEAD

### Ann Cleeves

"Perceptive, convincing, and quietly compelling."
*—The Times (London)*

"Cleeves writes with an easy directness that brings alive the tensions in a place where everyone knows everyone else and nothing can be forgotten"
*—Times Literary Supplement (London)*

"A suspenseful crime story that puts Ms. Cleeves in the Rendell class" *—Peterborough Evening Telepraph*

Peter Porteous fled the pressures of big city crime to be a small town cop. But he soon finds out there's no getting away from murder. When water levels drop in a summer drought, Cranwell Lake reveals a thirty-year-old secret—a body stabbed in the back with an anchor tied around its waist. Detective Chief Inspector Porteous soon identifies the body as missing teenager Michael Grey. But that's only the start of the mystery.

Fifty miles away, prison librarian Hannah Morton is about to get the shock of her life. For Michael was her boyfriend, and she was with him the night he disappeared. The grisly discovery brings back dreaded and long-buried memories from her past and begins a deadly chain of events …

ISBN 978-1-932859-41-6   $13.95

Available at your local bookstore
or order online at www.bloodybritspress.com

# Bloody Brits Press

## LONELY HEARTS
### A Charlie Resnick Mystery

### John Harvey

"The characters in John Harvey's urban crime novels are so defiantly alive and unruly that they put these British police procedurals on a shelf by themselves."
—*The New York Times Book Review*

"Harvey's series about Charlie Resnick, the jazzloving, melancholy cop in provincial Nottingham, England, has long been one of the finest police procedural series around." —*Publishers Weekly*

Shirley Peters is dead. Sexually attacked and throttled in her own home. Just another sordid case of domestic violence. When the boyfriend she'd dumped is picked up on an express train to a distant destination, it looks as if the cops have an open and shut case.

But when a second victim meets the same fate, Detective Inspector Charlie Resnick can't avoid the conclusion that both women were murdered by the same sadistic killer—two lonely hearts broken by one maniac.

If Resnick can't find the killer soon, he knows there will be more victims on his conscience. And that's more than he can bear ...

*Lonely Hearts* is the first Charlie Resnick Mystery.

ISBN 978-1-932859-44-7   $13.95

Available at your local bookstore
or order online at www.bloodybritspress.com